Wither

Tracey Lee

Shooting Star Press

2nd Edition 2024

Shooting Star Press,
PO Box 6813
Charnwood ACT 2615

info@shootingstar.pub
www.shootingstar.pub

ABN 63 158 506 524

ISBN (pbk)

ISBN (ebook)

A catalogue record for this book is available from the National Library of Australia.

Cover and Art by
Wolfgang Bylsma
GESTALT GROUP
PO Box 1506 Applecross WA 6153
Australia

Contents

Chapter One

Night had become a battlefield. Dreams, turbulent and unbidden, disturbed my sleep and left me exhausted and bewildered. I had no idea why the invasion had begun; I had no idea what this nocturnal incursion meant; I had been so happy. Truly happy. Married to Phillip Swan for eighteen months and content that I had put the past behind me. Behind both of us. And yet, I remained sleepless.

I'd wakened, panicked and in a sweat. Phillip's arm reached out and flattened me gently back against the bed; he added something soothing and practised. 'Relax Lil, it's okay.' Or 'It's just a dream Lily, go back to sleep.' He'd been woken up by me now for weeks and at first was deeply concerned, now more complacent. He fell asleep again as soon as he had the words out. We had spoken about the constant disturbance to both our sleep needs but Phillip, in true Phillip style, remained seemingly unperturbed. If nothing else, he always had the belief that all would be well. It's hard not to love someone of such deeply ingrained faith that every problem had a solution; that nothing bad could last for ever, and if you waited long enough, the problem you were thrashing about eventually would solve itself.

In this matter I was nothing like Phillip. I was the hold-on-to-the-problem-until-it-consumed-you kind of person. Find-two-dozen-solutions-and-be-satisfied-with-none-of-them person. I continued to try and attain Phillip's level of contentment and live with the kind of Zen-like peace that he had mastered. And before this latest run of bad nights, I thought I might have learned to roll with the punches a little more.

Phillip breathed slowly, the deep inhalation and exhalation of sleep. His big body and long legs took up a considerable portion of the bed. I smiled as I thought about his logic in stretching diagonally across the mattress, his big feet resting freely at the bottom of my side of the bed. I wasn't using it apparently, being considerably shorter than him. He saw it as unused real estate that he was happy to lease from me. Two things that hadn't changed—his ridiculous sense of humour and his unfailing appetite. Margaret Swan, Phillip's mother, always said that I'd know when Phil had a problem—he'd stop eating and smiling. In these things he remained consistent. For the three years I'd known and loved him he remained untroubled by crises, calm in the face of difficulty and grateful for the small joys of everyday life.

As he slept, I let my mind wander back to the strained days of our first meeting and the painful events that brought us together. I remembered three things as clearly as if they had happened a day ago. The first was Phillip's steady conveyance of the bad news of whose bones had been found in the dried lake that once lapped close to my front door on Lake Road. The intensity of his measured delivery when he confirmed that those long-submerged figures were indeed my mother and brother made the truth of the matter undeniable. Even if I wanted to rant at the impossibility of such a travesty, there was no way could one introduce any form of violent denial in the face of Detective Sergeant Swan's calmness. I don't know if I fell in love with him then, but the combination of tenderness and self-assurance certainly drew me to him.

Secondly, I thought about the first big step in our relationship when he took me to his family home on the coast for a week at Christmas. His family—some of them—welcomed me with the same openness and warmth evident in their son. A few had been wary, and one sister acted with outright hostility. But even Sophie's rejection of me that Christmas couldn't dampen the growing connection between Phillip and me. If I had doubts about loving him, they were dispelled during that happy week. His brothers-in-law backed me when I joined their band and proved that I could play better than adequately and actually sing. Sophie's husband Max became my real champion in the family; much to his wife's irritation. It appeared that Max and I had a common bond—Phillip. Max and Phillip or as they were widely known—Fraze and Swanny—had been friends from the cradle and it was just good fortune that Max also became a member of the family. Max had a deep respect for his best mate; their bond as strong as any I'd seen.

They'd adventured as youngsters around the south coast beaches, making mild trouble for their families and getting quite a reputation among the locals. Even when Phillip left the coast for university in Canberra, the men remained in constant contact. Not even joining the police force rocked the boat despite Max's somewhat dubious behaviour. The family often joked, much to Sophie's horror, that Max only married her to be closer to Phillip. It was a joke of course but not one well received by Max's wife. And Max and I shared a secret. That same happy week, I nearly drowned. A misadventure circumvented by Max being in the vicinity when I went under. I didn't want him to tell Phillip as we'd had a rather rough start to our relationship. Much of the first year I'd been vulnerable and broken by discovering that my father had possibly killed my mother and brother. I wanted more than anything to show Phillip I'd recovered and could look after myself. Appearing to give in to a rolling wave that tipped me over and dragged me under was not an image I wanted Phillip having in his head.

Finally as my husband slept soundly, I let the most profound memory take shape in my mind. My last moments at Stone Orchard Farm. I'd sold the farm after the events of 2001. I had to let go of my Lake Road home and started a life free of the burden of the family property. But I'd failed to untie one significant cord that tied me to Lake George. One final severance that had been long overdue. I failed to make myself clear in a note to Phillip about my intention to spend a last night at the lake. I had said something about freeing myself of the ghosts of my past and he'd misread this as a suicide note.

He dragged our new friend Mick Flynn, a now-retired detective, out of bed to mount some kind of rescue mission. When they got to the farm I was nowhere in sight. Mick decided to scale the ridge behind the houses as I'd gone there in the past. Phillip, perhaps his sixth sense working, strode out across the dried lake bed and found me stretched out on the plot where the bones of Moya and Brannen O'Hara had been found. I had to make this final goodbye to my mother and brother. I had to leach the last of my grief, fear and anger into the earth where they had died. If I couldn't forgive her and lose the bitterness I held, I would never be free of Lake Road. When Phillip reached me, the night had darkened, the cold of a sub-zero night grew and the stars amassed in a snowy splendour above us. He did not chastise me, nor did he fuss about the impossibly dramatic manner in which I had decided to make my farewells. He just lay down beside me, pulled me close to him to keep me warm and waited silently until I was ready to leave it behind. If I didn't already know it, it was then that I knew I would love him without fail.

On that thought, my body gave into the need for sleep. Whatever was troubling me would have to be sorted another day, or I'd have another restless night of complicated dreams.

Phillip had showered by the time I woke. He had to get to work before eight so he could ensure we could get away to the coast by five that afternoon. I needed to get into the museum early myself. Both of us faced significant changes at work. Perhaps my uneasiness at facing these changes contributed to my inability to sleep soundly.

In typical fashion, Phillip had made himself a substantial breakfast. He ate healthily but he really enjoyed quantity. His cereal dish had the dimensions of a punch bowl and he filled it to the brim with Weetbix, two chopped bananas, a handful of walnuts and enough milk to drown a small mammal. He also had toast on the go and two coffees prepared. Luckily one of those had been made for me. He had generously also put a pot of my favourite yoghurt out on the table in the hope I'd consume something before we left for work. The anxiety of broken sleep and the residual exhaustion made the thought of food fairly unappealing, but to reassure Phillip, I made a few convincing attempts to swallow and retain the yoghurt.

In his typical fashion he joked that I'd get fat eating so much. He laughed at his own joke and patted his ever-toned stomach saying, 'If anyone has to worry about getting fat, it's this old boy!'

Phillip was nearly 37. He didn't look his age and looked as athletic as he'd ever been. His new job meant he had to be fit and strong. He had passed the physical without a single problem. The thought of him being overseas for the first three months of his appointment nearly had me hurling the contents of my stomach back into the yoghurt container. I had to walk away from the table, pretending his joke had been very amusing to cover the contortions of my face. I imagine he wasn't fooled for a moment. He knew I was inclined to introspective panic when things seemed to shift from their axis.

I also had decided to move into a new field of work and the preparation for it seemed to be enormous. The museum had given me twelve months sabbatical to complete my doctorate. I decided to collaborate on a tertiary textbook about curatorship and artefact preservation too. This meant ensuring that someone could step into my job and continue with the exhibition plans for at least the next twelve months. The job was going to Helena Howard, not only an excellent colleague but one of my dearest friends. So I didn't really need to have a day-by-day timetable to ensure things went smoothly but, as usual, I couldn't help but over-plan things. Also, Phillip and I had bought a house at the coast so I could live near his family while he worked overseas. Perhaps not sleeping well made some sense in light of the chaos that seemed to be pending.

Our trip to the coast would allow us to prepare Phillip's parents for all these changes. They would probably be pleased that we had made a tentative move to living in Broulee, where the entire Swan clan lived. They would, however, be apprehensive about their beloved son's decision to move into an area that would see him deployed overseas for months at a time. A new and frightening area for the uninitiated but exciting for Phillip. The world of cross jurisdictional police forces organised to combat organised crime and terrorism was not for the weak or foolish. But completely right for Phillip Swan. I would not stand in his way for a career making opportunity, but the thought of being without him left me feeling apprehensive. He assured me the job was academic—an office job really. His team would be dealing with data mainly and investigating the trafficking of drugs, people and weapons. He wouldn't be actually hunting down and confronting the perpetrators. Even with his most convincing charm, my mind and heart could not settle on the rightness of it. He'd be away, I'd be busy with research, his family would look after me. I'd be at the beach and miss the worst of Canberra's weather. What could be wrong with that scenario?

His absence. It would leave a gap in my life and it felt wrong.

Chapter Two

The day at work was not as busy as I thought it would be. I had one week left to ensure that Helena could take over the reins without feeling too overwhelmed by the responsibility. I knew there wouldn't be any angst on her part. Helena was one of the most intelligent and life-hardy people I knew. There was nothing that she couldn't overcome, little that she had not already faced and decidedly wouldn't be able to solve with good humour, courage and a chilled glass of champagne. It was her panacea for all the ills of the world. Laugh at it, face it down and swill icy bubbles of the best you could afford. A recipe for life's new and old players.

She would be ably assisted by another old friend, Brendan Holmes. Despite his own rickety life's path Brendan knew his job and had become an excellent researcher. He had married just before my own wedding and separated in what could only be described as a brief tenure. Mandi, fleetingly his wife, annoyed everyone. I worked hard to like her but could manage only short bursts. In all honesty I had little in common with her. She was sort of a prissy thing—hair and clothes seemed important to her. She had a limited line of conversation and most unsettlingly had flirted blithely with every man she met. Including Phillip. Her worst sin, her hatred of Helena who had in no uncertain terms recommended that Brendan did not marry *the prancing princess*. It could have caused a considerable rift in the friendship group, but we didn't have time for the problem to escalate. The wedding—excessive and dominated by pink frills and too much flouncing —a few months of wedded discord and then she left him. He was devastated. Helena was in full-scale "told you so" mode. I tried to be consoling and supportive. Our other dear friend, who we'd known since school, Jimmy, had flown in from the USA to act as best man at the wedding, flew back to fulfil best man/best friend duties in mopping up the mess.

Like an explosion it grumbled, it erupted, made a mess that had to be cleaned up. Normalcy eventually had been restored. Life went on.

Brendan would work happily with Helena. Despite being years older than him—and Jimmy and me—she was more than the matriarch of the team. She not only mothered us, she bossed us around, drank us under the table, revelled in our joys and yanked us out of any misery we thought we might wallow in. She could out-think, out-organise and out-talk anyone on the planet. The museum would not only survive my absence it would thrive under her supervision.

In yet another moment of contemplation I thought about my own wedding to Phillip. Helena and Mick Flynn acted in the stead of my parents. Mick gave me away in a rather traditional Catholic ceremony in the little church I'd been baptised in twenty-nine years before. St. Mary's Church in Bungendore had always been the O'Hara family parish. All of us had been baptised, married and dispatched from this little sacred place for the 170 years the family lived in the area. Who was I to interrupt the cycle—the last of my line. The last O'Hara of Lake Road to walk the few short steps from vestibule to altar. Phillip happily obliged. His family were lapsed Catholics—some baptised, some not. None of them church goers. I'd assumed Phillip had some faith in God—he spent a lot of time yelling "Jesus Christ"! On the occasions I took issue with his blaspheming, he denied he was doing so. 'Spontaneous praying, Lil! That's all it is.' I hoped the heavens wouldn't open up and strike him as he waited at the altar with Max. We had a lovely day.

Mick delivered me safely to Phillip and said quietly, 'Are you sure about this?'

Father Hart didn't seem to notice the joke and proceeded with the ceremony as if his life depended on it. We didn't put our friends through a nuptial mass. A simple rite of marriage ceremony in which Helena, Mick, Phillip's three sisters and Margaret Swan participated sufficed. We were consented, blessed, wedded and dismissed within thirty minutes. Father Hart galloped through the event as if he felt unsure that we'd stay till the end if he didn't hurry up. Our new rings were hardly on when we he gave us the nod to move on and ushered us outside for photos in the December sunshine.

Phillip had the rings made by the same silversmith who made the bracelet he gave me for our first Christmas together. In an attempt to pay homage to the Irish ancestors, the two rings had been made with a central platinum band. His featured a Celtic knot; mine, the traditional Claddagh. Two thin bands of gold bordered the silver. The symbolism of the knot and Claddagh were not lost on me. Eternity, loyalty, love and friendship. I wore the sapphire solitaire I'd found in my Aunt Billie's belongings when I packed up Lake Road as my engagement ring. We found other rings in my aunt's home and I could have chosen any of them. Billie had obviously been the custodian of the O'Hara jewels, such as they were, but this unworn and perfectly made blue stone had been my favourite. Neither of us worried that it wasn't modern or handmade like our wedding rings. It had been waiting for a happy day. The day Phillip and I decided we'd like to be married was that day.

We insisted that the photos be informal. I didn't want to be posing and fussing about the placement of veils and dresses. My dress had a simple design. I was too short for too much fluff and too many frills. It had a fitted, lace bodice and cap sleeves. I wore the highest heels I dared so I wasn't completely dwarfed by the family I was joining. The photos reflected the purpose of the day—the celebration and the joy.

A few old faces appeared at the end of the ceremony. I spent some time talking to Arlen Beltz, the old mechanic who had worked on the O'Hara cars, mainly about how happy I felt. Some of the photos of the two of us together were my favourites. He seemed more spry and yet considerably more ancient than the last time I'd seen him. He gave us a card written in perfect script and in German. *Mai Ihre Freuden so hell wie am Morgen. Deine Jahre des Glucks so zahlreich wie die Sterne des Himmels und deinen Arger, Fade in das Sonnenlicht der Liebe.* I had to ask for an interpretation. 'It's a German blessing for brides,' he explained. 'May your joys be as bright as the morning. Your years of happiness as numerous as the stars in the heavens and your anger fade in the sunlight of love.' Arlen put his hand on my shoulder, kissed the top of my head and moved back into the crowd. I wanted to tell him I'd see him again, but the hoopla of the day began to wind up and I become distracted by calls for my attention. When I looked for him again he was gone.

The reception, such as it was, meant we all had to hit the road and drive back to the coast. A party at the Swans was in full swing by four that afternoon. Music provided by every man and woman with an instrument; food by Margaret and Peter; frolicking by all our guests. I stayed in my wedding dress but ditched the shoes for thongs and covered the beautiful handmade ribbon lace on the bodice with an old hoodie Phillip had in his car. We had a happy, happy day. I drank too much champagne and really wanted to go to bed by nine but everyone made me stay up and sing. I carried on like a teenager who had been given too much attention.

I danced with Mick, who was well into his second bottle of red wine. He said wonderful things like he would be so proud if his own daughters had grown up to be like me. I also had a spin around the backyard dance floor with my father-in-law Peter and then with Max. Max was very drunk and had been severely chastised by his wife Sophie. She had gone home in a huff after Phillip told her to pull her head in. She thought I should have changed out of the wedding dress if I was going to wear thongs and ruin the look. She forgot to congratulate us and was too sour to even attempt to put on a happy face but made ugly comments about me keeping my maiden name. Sophie also hadn't forgiven me for having Carrie, Lisa and Robert's daughter, as my little bridesmaid and not Sophie's daughter Sarah. Even though logic dictated that at two and half, Sarah wasn't really up to the job, and Carrie had, over the last few years, become an ally in the family. She was musical and brooding and criticised by Sophie as being too self-absorbed. One might have drawn on the irony of such a comment if I'd really wanted to enter into combat with her. Max happily celebrated late into the night without her there.

Helena, later named dancing queen, spent much of the evening shoeless and perhaps legless as she and Brendan did some fairly dramatic twists and turns, seemingly in a world of their own, dancing to music that only they seemed to be hearing. Jimmy hadn't made it to the wedding but laughed hysterically on the other end of the phone when he saw the videos of the night some weeks later. Other friends and in-laws were in varying states of non-sobriety. By midnight a cool sea breeze blew in and calmed the revellers. Most had wandered off to the local caravan park and hotel that had been booked up for visitors from out of town. By one o'clock in the morning, Peter and

Margaret had gone to bed, Max had fallen asleep on the couch in the family room, and Phillip and his sisters, Lisa and Jessica, chatted about their weddings and the wild shenanigans of those nights. The two most sober brothers-in-law, Lachlan and Robert, helped me gather up glasses and load the dishwasher. A proper clean up took most of the next morning before further celebrations started up over a lunch-time barbeque. I was married to Phillip Swan and he to me, for better or worse.

I was interrupted from my reminiscing by some colleagues who had questions about the arrival of some international artefacts that were on loan to us. I had to shake myself out of my reverie and back in the real world of that day's jobs. In a week I'd be away from my much-loved collections and be preparing myself for the long slog to finish my degree. I was quite looking forward to being Dr. Lily O'Hara twelve months from now. But less enthused about the amount of research left to do before finishing my doctoral thesis.

The day ended with me creating my usual list of things to do in the coming week. I spoke to Helena and Brendan over a coffee before walking out to meet Phillip, who would be in the carpark at 5.05. He was so pathologically punctual. Occasionally, to ruffle him, I'd be deliberately late just to see if he could actually throw a tantrum. I was still waiting to see him lose his cool. Apart from his angry driving behaviour, where he shouted abuse at all other drivers for apparent sins against road rules—and the odd, 'Jesus Christ, Lily!'—I hadn't really seen him irrational. Today, however, was not a day to be late. The weekend's revelations would impact the whole family and their reactions might be either positive or negative. No doubt Sophie would have a strong opinion if she could be bothered to turn up for dinner tonight. Peter and Margaret, as I imagined all parents might, would be apprehensive. Phillip had made this decision, with me, to work in a law enforcement field that would be more dangerous than rounding up the criminal class in Canberra. Mick had put his two cents into the discussion over many nights before we made the final decision. It seemed that Mick had become an integral member of our little clan. He looked out for us, and we embraced his kindness and wise counsel.

I hoped the Swan clan would be as positive about the opportunities it would open up for Phillip and that they would be slightly happy to have me living nearby for at least the next three or four months. Mick had already decided that he would help us with setting up the house, some minor renovations and visiting on a regular basis. Phillip was happy with the arrangement. He hoped the brothers-in-law would also come to the rescue with some work on our little beach house. It was weather-proof, but somewhat rustic. It would need work but could be comfortably lived in while bathrooms, kitchen and painting happened.

The trip to the coast took the usual two hours. Not much traffic during the winter weekends. Cooler water temperatures and a tendency for coastal storms kept most people away during the middle of the year. In the warmer months, from November to April, the south coast became known as 'little Canberra'. The weekend and holiday exodus of city workers was well-known, sometimes frustrating but excellent for the local economy. In winter, the sleepy townships up and down the coast provided a much quieter and calmer lifestyle, unimpeded by extra traffic they developed a more isolated and wilder persona. I liked this time of the year but even with a steamer, a neck-to-ankle wetsuit, the water was too cold for me. Phillip and Max couldn't be held back. They'd spend some of this weekend on the water in one form or another. A surf, a bit of fishing, some diving for abalone or just putting about in a tinny for reconnaissance purposes would be acceptable to the two of them.

As we headed off I couldn't help but be a little nervous about the news we were about to spill. The lack of sleep and bad dreams hadn't done anything to offset the anxiety either. But speculating about how everyone would react simply wasted time. Phillip found worrying about other people's reactions a form of madness. His wisdom, as usual, couldn't be denied. 'We are not in control of how other people feel, Lil. Their reactions are their problem. Let it go.'

Not sublime advice but I certainly couldn't argue with its accuracy.

Chapter Three

As predicted we drove into the driveway at 7.05. Peter, Phillip's father, as usual came out to help bring in the oversupply of groceries I insisted we bring and our meagre little overnight bags that had a change or two of clothes. We left most of the things we needed for weekends in Phillip's boyhood bedroom. Warm clothes, coats, wetsuits, swimmers and even toothbrushes and toiletries remained in our room as if we lived here. It seemed to make Margaret happy to have the constant reminder that we would be regular visitors in her home.

We sat down to eat at 7:30 as Margaret had planned. As usual meals in the Swan household became big events. The family totalled fourteen when all the siblings, their partners and children attended. The sisters always brought additions to the meal. Tonight Lisa and Jessica both made desserts; and Sophie something to have with coffee. Margaret had produced a roast of epic proportions. I'd come to expect a laden table and knew that by the time Phillip and the other men had finished there would be few leftovers. The plates had barely begun filling when Robert—Bertie as he was known—asked us to get on with giving the big news. The general excited interest from most of the family had built up over the meal. The little boys were only interested in their dinner, but Carrie looked hopeful. Sophie remained hostile.

Phillip didn't interrupt the ladling of food onto his plate and started the announcement with, 'You know the old Harper place up on the hill at Mossy Point. well we bought it.'

This was met with general approval and perhaps a little disappointment on Margaret and Peter's part.

'Are you moving down?' Max asked with hope in his voice.

'Well Lily is, for a bit.'

This provided general bewilderment and everyone talking over each other. Only Sophie's comments could be heard over the general speculation. 'All over then is it?'

Phillip's hand came immediately to rest on the back of my neck. Either to calm me or prevent me leaping across the table with the roast in my hand to whack her senseless. 'If you'd all shut up I'll tell you why.' His voice stilled the clamour.

'I'm heading to Indonesia as part of team. It involves intelligence gathering and working with other international police forces to get more of a handle on these global criminal gangs. I'll be based in Jakarta but will travel about a bit.' There were questions about the dangers and if he would actually be safe.

'How long will you be gone?' Max asked.

'Three months to start. Maybe longer. A few more stints after that. It's not always clear until we get into a place and start the work. But the first will be a long one.' Phillip looked at me and nodded confirming all that we had discussed over the many weeks that led up to this conversation. 'Three months. It's not that long.' He repeated.

The explanation was not all that well received. Margaret and Peter were obviously a bit shocked, but the sisters and in-laws started the barrage of questions over the commencement of eating. Nothing could stand between Phillip and food, so he ate and answered in as much detail as he thought the family needed to know. He was emphatic about dispelling any sense that the job would be more dangerous than the one he did in Canberra. I lost track of who asked what but in the end it was Peter's question that touched me. 'And you'll be here with us Lily. Will be okay without him?'

I would of course be okay. But I would not be happy and part of me would be afraid for him. I assured Peter that I'd fare better now that I knew I'd be close to family while Phillip was away. It seemed to be a popular answer. I did confess to having really bad dreams and very little sleep since we made the decision. 'I've even been off my food for the last few weeks. But it looks like tonight's feast is going to cure me of that.' But it didn't. After all the talking and noise, I couldn't eat. I put food on my plate but the tumult in my head and stomach had me feeling nauseated. I could say the words and look convincing but the coming changes occasionally had me feeling terrified. Not that I couldn't be alone. I was practised at self-containment. And I felt so proud of Phillip, but I knew change always brought challenge, sometimes caused pain. It kept me awake at night and turned my stomach sour at the thought of food. Change.

My face must have been giving me away because Phillip's lips on my face brought me back to the next noisy discussion at the table. This time it was all about what the family could do to get the house ready for us. Phillip would be gone in two weeks. I'd finish work in seven days. The decision seemed to be that in the morning, after a surf, everyone would descend upon our new home and plans would be made to make it liveable and comfortable.

That night was more bereft of sleep than the previous ones. I tried meditation, warm milk, reading, and eventually got up and quietly walked upstairs and stood at the front windows and watched the moon and its reflection marking the minutes through the depth of the night. Eventually I tried sitting down to see if this would ease my mind. I sat in silence and stillness until finally my eyes closed and sleep came.

Phillip was strangely cross that I'd chosen to sleep curled up in his father's chair rather than beside him.

'I didn't want to keep you awake with my tossing and turning,' I said. 'I think I had heartburn.'

Before his parents woke, Phillip went out to meet Max and I went back to bed for an hour or so. This would be a fairly busy day with everyone coming to the new/old house and in typical Swan fashion, attempt to over-engineer the simple changes that I wanted to make. I would attempt some breakfast before having to referee the discussion between the family members.

Margaret worked busily making a hot breakfast. It was a weekend special. I thought a big breakfast consisted of bacon and eggs served with toast. But my mother-in-law set a new standard when it came to meal preparation. She had mushrooms, tomatoes, homemade hash browns, little chipolata sausages as well as the bacon frying in several pans on the stove top. The smell of oil and meat was a little too much for me. The offer of eggs in a several different modes added to the general queasiness. Phillip wanted scrambled eggs, Peter would have fried, Margaret poached. I offered to make myself an omelette but the minute I mentioned it somehow, she produced another pan and had the process underway. I didn't have the heart to stop her despite knowing I probably wouldn't get much of the meal down.

I'd become something of a master in disguising how little I was eating. I had ways and means of filling a plate, moving things around, chopping up bits and pieces and consuming only a few mouthfuls. I usually would enjoy this type of meal but whatever was happening in my head had put a road block up between my mouth and stomach. When I chewed I felt like I was eating cardboard. I wanted to cry with the effort of attempting to force food into my face.

While Phillip seemed to be a little worried, he knew me well enough to assume this probably reflected my adjustment to the changes ahead.

My mother-in-law on the other hand seemed to be regarding me with suspicion. She had always been worried about her son's rather insubstantial wife. Margaret liked me and always treated me lovingly, but I suspected she always thought that Phillip might have married a weakling. I felt a little offended by the thought but also knew that despite appearances, I was the right woman for her son. None-the-less I felt her watching me closely over the breakfast table. To offset any concern. I ate the omelette she'd produced and a few pieces of bacon. Within minutes of it settling in my stomach, I had to leave the table as the food had already worked out its exit strategy and was about to reappear.

I had hoped that I could mask the sound of vomiting with lots of toilet flushing and water running. When Phillip came down to the bathroom, he seemed none the wiser. Despite being a little flushed and clammy, I was ready for the rest of the morning's activities.

The entire family turned up at the house. Well, everyone but Sophie. Phillip had confided in me several months ago that his parents had to suffer the appalling jealous rage that she inflicted upon them when she discovered how much money I had after the Lake Road property had been sold. The money belonged to both of us as far as I was concerned. Decisions about the expenditure or investment had been made jointly. Sophie had said mean things about Phillip marrying me for the money. And worse things such as, I didn't deserve the money as my father was a murderer, despite evidence to the contrary. I felt somewhat bewildered and infuriated by her childish tantrum. But I didn't say anything to her about it. Phillip and I would never do anything to flaunt our good fortune and it wasn't as if we were rolling in millions. I remember Phillip telling me that, even as a child, Sophie had issues with envy. So now, because we had this house, she wouldn't even come and look at it. One advantage, I wouldn't have to endure her visiting me during the next few months as the place took shape.

But the rest of the clan responded with great enthusiasm. Jessica, Lisa and Margaret talked about the proximity to the family as a great thing. While the men talked about load bearing walls, and other technical sounding things, the women just planned my social calendar. There was yoga and golf, lunch dates, women's surfing groups, trips to Sydney for the theatre all being entered into iPhones before I'd agreed to anything. At one stage in the vigorous discussion, I laughed to myself seeing the five men in the family all standing in different parts of the main room with measuring tapes out. It seemed that I'd be living in a building site given my simple requirements of new kitchen and bathroom, painting and floor sanding had been circumvented by "man plans" for walls removed, windows turned into sliding doors, deck constructions, ceilings replaced and the possibility of an upstairs extension. Phillip must have read my expression quite efficiently as he invited me into the conversation about what I initially wanted, what could be accommodated while I was living in the house, and of course, what could be legally done without getting planning approval.

The general consensus was that the house was amazing. The view had to be capitalised on and that the next day they would demolish the existing kitchen and bathroom. They all made the promise that before I returned in two weeks, without Phillip, these two spaces would be done. Peter, Max, Robert and Lachlan plus an unspecified number of mates, would get it finished and then start on the other things. I could live with the in-laws while the painting and floors were done. Apparently, I could live in the house while the back wall, the side with view was ripped off and re-built. Someone had produced a piece of paper— I think the side of a box of beer—and some pretty impressive plans were rendered. Costings were loose at this point in the discussion. Phillip insisted that everyone would be paid. A little altercation over such a notion broke out, but the conversation rolled on for over an hour. The Swan family had everything sorted.

I loved the happy chaos, the insane enthusiasm, the family ties that bound each to the other. What I couldn't reconcile was Sophie's refusal to embrace the joys of this mad chatter, the great hopefulness that burst from being a part of a wonderful collective. I hadn't known this liaison in my childhood. I hadn't looked for it as I didn't even know it could exist. But this tribe had taught me, in the short time I'd been a part of it, that family was about connection. It was a jigsaw puzzle of strangely configured pieces, all individual, but somehow when fitted together revealed oneness, a unity, a single image. I felt sad for Sophie that she could not see this circle of men, women and children as something extraordinary. Something truly wonderful to belong to.

In spite of my nervous apprehension about Phillip's leaving, for the first time in weeks, I felt that the world had righted itself. All would be well.

Chapter Four

After the spirited discussion and planning at our new house, Phillip and I decided to walk back to his parents' home along the beach. We were relieved that the distraction of the house and my imminent move to the coast diminished the worry about him going overseas. I knew Phillip would want to spend time in quiet conversation with his parents and of course, with Max. A private talk mainly about me, but it would also be about alleviating their fears for his safety. I thought I could have some quiet time on the beach tomorrow morning so he could chat with his folks about the future. He'd go out fishing with Max in the afternoon before we had to leave for Canberra. I'd be happy for some time alone too.

The weather had cooled. The sun shone, the sky cloudless. We took off our shoes to stroll at the water's edge. Phillip rested his arm on my shoulders and we moved in rhythm and let the waves reach our bare feet. It was a happy silence broken only when Phillip asked, 'Do you think you might start feeling a bit more relaxed now the news is out Lil?'

I really wanted to allay his worries, but I had never been a very good liar. 'Probably not. I'm going to miss you.' The words that would have conveyed my fear for his safety remained unsaid.

'I promise to come back.' Words easily said, not always easy to fulfil. 'You'll make yourself really ill if you don't stop worrying.'

And as if on cue, a wave of nausea almost had me face planting into the sand.

Phillip stopped and looked at me with concern. 'It's just nerves, right?'

Of course it was my head playing havoc with my body. I spent too much time thinking about the consequences of things that hadn't been thought of. But as if orchestrated, on reaching the front yard of the house, I doubled over and vomited up the meagre contents of my stomach. What hadn't been thrown up after breakfast made its escape onto Phillip's bare feet and ankles.

He was mildly surprised and unusually angry. 'Lily! This is ridiculous. You have got to stop being so anxious and panicky about this work.' To punctuate his brief but emphatic logic, he grabbed the garden hose and began to spray his feet clean of the contents of my stomach. Before he finished, Margaret came into the yard with us.

'Are you two really this stupid?'

It was not really something I imagined Margaret thinking, let alone saying.

'Do you think for one minute that Lily's sleeplessness, nausea, vomiting and anxiety might be something else?' Margaret said. 'She's a very capable girl who will manage perfectly well without you for a few months Phillip. Have either of you considered another possibility?'

Like the two fools she'd accused us of being we stood mute and simply stared at her. What else could it be? What was she referring to? We looked at each other quite puzzled by her outburst.

'You're probably pregnant, Lily.'

The shock that trundled through me couldn't have been stronger if Margaret had slapped me.

Margaret continued, 'Well it is entirely possible, isn't it?'

Everything under the sun was possible but I was using contraception and surely I couldn't be in the one in a million where it failed.

As if slightly cross and entirely incredulous, Margaret went back inside and simply left the two of us standing in shocked silence.

'Lil? Is it possible?" Phillip sounded and looked like a teenager who had just learned he'd knocked up an equally gormless girlfriend.

For some strange reason it felt like we were in trouble. 'I don't think I'm pregnant, Phillip. You can stop worrying.' And then for an inexplicable reason I suddenly raised my voice. 'And even if I was you wouldn't need to do anything about it. You can just go off overseas and do whatever mad-arse thing you want to.' I attempted to stomp off but Phillip circumvented this by laughing and catching me around the waist impeding my exit.

'I would love it if you were. I would still go away because I know you can handle everything. I think we get nine months before I'd need to be around in a more consistent manner.'

I really had married a comedian. But an intrinsically happy one who was unable to conceal the excitement in his face at the thought of a little baby Swan. On the other hand, anxiety and nausea flooded me. I had no idea about being a mother. I had flawed parents who I never knew, and distant guardians, and I simply grew up despite those facts. Did I actually know what it meant to take on the responsibility of raising a tiny child? I'd only just recently allowed Phillip into my life and found my place within his family. Most of the time I was afraid of what loving someone meant; it meant you could lose them. It meant your heart could break. And a child would surely intensify that a thousand times.

I was lost in this internal world of panic when Phillip's hands cupped my face and turned my eyes to look at him. He did that thing he always did; just let his lips ever so slightly brush my cheek and brow.

'Come back Sherlock.' His ridiculous pet name for me. 'Everything will be fine.'

I loved my husband's optimism. It was almost contagious.

Back in the house we were met like two bad teens who had been up to no good. Margaret insisted we make some kind of effort to confirm her suspicions. We calmed her by the promise that on our return to the city, I would make a doctor's appointment or buy a pregnancy test kit from the pharmacy. We both asked her to keep her suspicions to herself for the time being as we felt a little overwhelmed by the attention our other plans were receiving. This bit of news would be too much. If it was not confirmed and everyone expected, hoped for baby news, then there would be too much discussion about when such an event might occur.

The weekend rolled on. Saturday ended with more food; this time consumed at the local club. It was a great to be in a busy and noisy place where no-one could tell that I wasn't consuming much or drinking. Phillip and Max continued discussions about the house and the friends from outside the family who had joined us talked about what they could contribute to the Swan project. It appeared as if we might be about to build the south coast's Taj Mahal! I asked a few questions that apparently confirmed my ignorance about building and after getting some vague confirmation that I would be able to live in the place come Sunday week, I decided to opt out of the conversation and concentrated on other things happening around the table.

About twenty people had been milling around the bar and then when the group decided it was time to eat, several tables were joined together to make one rowdy gathering. Some of the people had been at our wedding but I was meeting a few couples for the first time. They knew Phillip but primarily had remained friends with Max or someone else in the family. One couple, who looked our age, had a new baby with them. He was about eight weeks old and slept in his capsule despite the heaving noise of the club. I found myself more interested in the sleeping boy than I might have been at any other time. His mother Jean was a ruddy-cheeked young woman whose hair looked as wild as bracken. Not exactly curly, more like blonde frizz that probably hadn't had the benefit of a hairdresser for some time. But she was a delight and even though incredibly tired, spoke about her little one with such obvious joy that I couldn't help being drawn to the new family.

Jean lifted Isaiah from the floor between herself and his father, so I could have a better look at him. His smooth face and perfectly peaceful features made me suddenly interested in how they all coped with this agreeable little intruder. Jean confirmed that Issy, as they called him, was a disruption. Sleep was uncommon, but he fed well and tended to be a happy baby.

Isaiah's father was an intense looking man. He too had long blond hair restrained by leather tie into a full pony-tail, accompanied by equally impressive facial hair, and his blue/green eyes were almost obscured. Benedict Jepp was a friend of Max's. And of course his mates didn't call him Benedict, or even Ben. For some reason that I wasn't privy to at that point, the baby's father was called Kitty. For the first time in the conversation Kitty spoke and had an incredibly soft voice. He added to the conversation that I was having with his partner, Jean Parrish. He impressed me with the gentleness with which he spoke about how precious the little boy was to them both. To further his point about how lucky they were to have him, Kitty lifted the sleeping wonder out of his container and lay the tiny boy on his chest. 'No better feeling in the world than this.' Kitty Jepp seemed to be the perfect father.

I continued to speak to Jean as her partner seemed lost in the pleasure of holding his sleeping son. She was a local girl who had grown up here. A story similar to Max and the Swans. She and Kitty had a place at Congo. She started working in her parent's café after she left school and would return to work there as soon as she found a childcare place for Isaiah. We made polite talk until it was time for everyone to head home.

As I drove Phillip and an assortment of family home, I thought about the possibility of bringing a son or daughter into the world. I certainly wouldn't be going biblical in the naming of our child. A Gaelic name like my father or brother would be nice. Cillian or Brannen but I doubt I would choose my mother's name if we had a girl. There would not be a Moya but perhaps I could call her Billie after my aunt.

I was brought brutally out of my contemplation by a sudden movement which caught my peripheral vision. A slamming on of the brakes shook everyone in the car out of their boozy sleepiness. But unfortunately did nothing to stop a big grey kangaroo thundering into the front wheel of Phillip's car. As someone who learned to drive in the country, I did the usual thing. I pulled over to the side of the road to check firstly that the car hadn't sustained any damage and secondly to ensure that the wild animal was actually dead and not dragging itself about on the road where it could potentially cause other accidents. But the impact had broken the kangaroo's neck. She lay about four metres from where I hit her. Max went out onto the road to drag her lifeless body to the shoulder where we used the police-issued torch in the glove box to ensure the mother didn't have a joey in her pouch. It was standard practice to check all marsupial kills for an empty pouch. Sometimes the joeys survived the impact of the accidents and could be rescued and hand-reared and then released. The thought of an unwitting baby kangaroo starving to death in the growing cold of its mother's pouch was a much too poignant image.

Phillip and Max were a bit inebriated, but the shock and the cool night air made them more useful in the minor procedure that followed. Someone else held the torch so I could look at the pouch and despite the blood from the mother's injuries, a joey was alive inside. The mother's belly heaved from the movements of a shocked baby who had probably felt the impact of the car and the mother's fall. I sent Phillip back to get a towel out of the boot; there was always some item of clothing there.

I wrapped the joey quickly and attempted to assess whether he or she had been terminally injured. If it was, then the little joey would be joining the mother as one of us euthanised it. But this little girl, as it turned out, was not hurt but deeply shocked. Sometimes the offspring died from the shock even after they had been rescued. Getting her out and wrapped up and quickly to a ranger or wildlife rescue volunteer would be her best chance.

She looked about the three or four months old. She was just developing her fur and would die in the cold quickly. Getting her back to the house would be the first step in her survival. Getting her specialised care would give her the best chance to live beyond a day or two. I dropped my passengers off on the way, but Max insisted on coming to the Swan place to sort out Lizzy-Loo. Yes, the little macropod had a name and had been jokingly baptised Elizabeth-Louise before we got her into the car. As per the coastal way, she became Lizzy-Loo before I got back on the road. Phillip held the little animal firmly in his arms, cocooning his hoodie around her to create a pouch-like warmth and spoke softly to her as if she were a baby needing soothing. Disregarding the distress of killing Lizzy-Loo's mother, I couldn't help by smile at the gentleness of the two big softies who had become completely enamoured by the frail joey.

Max had a friend who volunteered with WIRE, the wildlife rescue service. She would be able to pick up the joey first thing on Sunday morning. She gave us some advice about keeping Lizzy-Loo alive for the next ten hours but also warned that many joeys died soon after their mothers were killed.

For some unknown reason the three of us seemed to be committed to keeping LL—she had been further abbreviated—alive while in our care. We spent the night with one of us awake and holding her while the other two slept taking turns of keeping her warm. At around 5am the sun was just beginning to lighten the morning sky when Lizzy-Loo gave into the shock of the accident. As I held her, and Phillip and Max were deeply asleep, the little one fell into a stillness that could only have been a sign of her death. Her heart had stopped. It was so foolish to feel the depth of grief for the joey's death but perhaps sleeplessness and my own potential impending motherhood had fractured common sense. I held her little fuzzy lifeless form closer still and wept not for Elizabeth-Louise, but for her mother, who could not protect her from the violence of a human world. The thought of mothers and the terrible, tremendous responsibility of that job was incomprehensible.

When dawn broke fully I informed Phillip and Max that the woman from WIRE would not be needed. Phillip took the joey and buried her somewhere in the scrub in front of the house. Max made coffee and discussed how he would explain his overnight absence from Sophie. 'Don't tell her you spent it with Lily and Lizzy-Loo,' was my best advice.

Before Phillip returned from his sombre duties, Max pulled me into his arms and hugged me. 'I think you're going to be my best friend, Lil.'

'Maybe. We'll see.'

We finished with a laugh when Phillip arrived in the kitchen saying, 'Max, get away from my wife. How many times do I have to warn you?' This accompanied by him hugging both of us. We failed rescuers of wildlife; we contented few had a life stretching out ahead of us with things unknown and bewildering to come. Only one thing seemed certain—we would face it together.

Chapter Five

S unday unfolded as I had expected. Phillip and Max went out surfing soon after dawn. I went to bed for a few hours of sleep. Margaret and Peter made the considerable breakfast banquet that could have fed the neighbourhood and, despite the amount of food, nothing was left at the end of the feeding. I knew Phillip had talked to Max about looking out for me while he was away. It was probably unnecessary.

Sometime during the morning Phillip would want time with his parents to continue assuring them of his safety while he worked overseas and simply talking about the possibilities of the future. He was very close to his parents. Their natural affection and respect for each other was so touching. It was a relationship that I happily wanted to continue. I'd heard colleagues at work complaining about their in-laws, whining about the husband who refused to cut the apron strings, but I had quite a different point-of-view. A man who respected and appreciated his parents and family seemed to have the skills and heart to cherish those who loved him. I thought staying connected to his clan meant he valued everything about family. Surely this had to be a good thing.

While the Swans had their quiet chat, I went over to the beach. The days were cool and the water cold but the sun's weak rays created a warm haven in the sheltered curve of the beach that led to Broulee Island. The small bank of sand that separated the northern part of the beach from Shark Bay impeded the wind from the south. I had a thick towel and one of the padded beach mats we had bought at the local markets during the previous summer to wrap myself if I felt chilly. I had kept a bit of breakfast down and thought I might risk taking a thermos of tea and some dry toast with me to have as a snack. So with comfort, sustenance and a book, I set off for a few hours of isolation. Phillip duly informed of my intentions and whereabouts was the last part of the organisation.

The day looked as if it might be as near to perfect as winter gets. The temperature would be 18 degrees, light wind, no chance of rain. And no-one else within a kilometre or two. This was a great place for contemplation. I could see our house perched on the hill over Candlagan Creek to the far left of my cosy spot. It would be wonderful to spend the rest of winter and the beginning of spring sitting out on the deck that was part of the refurbishment plan. I couldn't help but feel so lucky to have been able to buy in such a brilliant location. I'd always liked a water view. Growing up on Lake Road, even in the drought, there was something about the proximity of water. The complexities of all it brought to the senses were brought forth from now distant memories. The Lake had its smells, its sounds and idiosyncrasies. Even in the dry years when the lake becomes merely a paddock there was always a waft of some dampness, something muddy and organic waiting for the first sign that the rain would come. Here on the coast the noises, movement and smells were different and in equal measure calming and threatening. The incessant thrust and withdrawal of the waves became mesmerising. The sweeping towards and away from the high tide mark lulled me into a state of relaxation and further introspection.

I wondered what life in the town would really be like. What it would be like with Phillip away and then when we lived here together? If we were really expecting a baby, would this be the right place to raise him or her? As usual I got ahead of myself. The habit of trying to control the world had not been entirely eradicated. While Phillip's calm and unflustered manner had done a great deal to unknot my more disconcerted world view, I had not fully acquiesced to the "let it be" lifestyle. I let my eyes close and lay down, pulling the towel over me to further the warming power of the sun. I didn't sleep but let my mind rove about the images of my life, the past fears and loneliness, the joys and friendships. What in this strange life has prepared me for motherhood? Raised by well-meaning but constrained relatives, abandoned by the dual suicides of my parents, and the self-imposed isolation that came from keeping the world out of my past for the first twenty-six years of my life were not qualities that immediately sprang to mind when considering what an ideal mother would be like. Not exactly a suitable platform to inform my own foray into parenting. And, of course, ever lurking in the darkest part of my mind the greatest fear of all…the terrible possibility that maybe I would become ill like my mother.

The thought of her last month's being full of angst and anger troubled me. A bewildered and broken young mother who thought death was preferable to staying with her little family. Drowning herself in the same lake that framed my childhood seemed impossibly cruel. Taking my older brother with her, intolerably cruel. I tried not to dwell on these discoveries because they did little to enhance my happiness or bring me the peace that uncovering the truth should have. Moya O'Hara was mentally ill, dangerously so. My father, Cillian, ill-equipped to undo the damage she caused, took his own life too. I had worked hard to forgive them and had learned to be grateful for the life that emerged from these tragedies. But obviously the anxiety of change and perhaps the hormonal surge of pregnancy were bringing the past to the surface. The unremitting waves of memory matched the persistent movement of the tide. It bore down on me and momentarily relented only to reach out and lap ever closer to my tenuous hold on my emotions.

Before a metaphorical drowning in sorrow, Phillip dropped down beside me and rolled me from my back onto his chest. 'Hello Mummy.' Accompanied by his usual happy laugh at his own little joke.

'Don't get ahead of yourself there. This may just be your mother's wishful thinking.' I didn't add, *and yours*. But it was completely obvious that Phillip was utterly hopeful that our first venture into parenthood may be underway. I couldn't take that away from him with my barely contained paranoia about inheriting my parents' less-than-committed nurturing skills. I didn't want him going away knowing I was afraid to be a mother. Not that I wasn't just a little bit excited about the possibility.

'Where are you now?' Phillip's ever intuitive questioning brought me back to this happy moment we were sharing. 'You are not your mother,' he added.

I hated how he seemed to read me like an open book. Could everything in my head be so patently obvious on my face? I was able, at least, to reassure him that I knew that.

He rolled us back onto the beach mat, this time him on top. 'I'm going to miss you, Mrs. Swan. I almost don't want to go.'

For the first time Phillip sounded anything but totally self-assured about his choice. The best I could do was to let him know that I was confident about surviving the next few months without him. I told him that with his family and Mick, who wouldn't be kept out of things, I would not feel alone. Helena and Brendan would visit, or I would catch up with them on regular trips to Canberra and they would ensure there was never a dull moment.

'And Max will be a constant companion,' Phillip added.

'You have problems with that, Husband?'

His laughter let me know he didn't. Phillip trusted Max more than anyone. It was likely that he felt concerned that I'd end up trying to sort out the problems between Max and Sophie and be distracted by that mess than doing the work I was supposed to.

When he sat up, he told me that his parents had real concerns about Sophie's marriage. Margaret and Peter looked after their grand-daughter Sarah almost daily and saw more of Max than they did of Sophie. Phillip explained, 'She is angry and critical of me and our sisters. And you too. Mum and Dad don't know what to do.'

I added, 'She really seems to hate me.' Phillip didn't deny this. He had real concerns that Sophie would leave Max and that despite his friend's laissez faire attitude, a marriage break- up would hurt him badly. Max was the extreme version of Phillip. He believed the world was essentially good, bad things would be overcome by waiting quietly and simply doing what you loved was the recipe for a great life. These were the small joys of being.

I loved the fact that Phillip cared so deeply for his friend and despite loving his sister, Max would need us most when the crash came.

'You'll look after him won't you Lil?' It was a question that needed no answer. Max would look out for me and I'd be there if he needed a friend in the looming marital catastrophe.

We spent the rest of the day on the beach and walking back to our new/old house to wander about the empty rooms trying to visualise what it would begin to look like once the renovations began. True to his word, before we left for the city, Max and an assortment of capable men invaded the house with demolition on their minds. Phillip and

I couldn't stay to see the first sledgehammer blow, but we were to be kept up to date with photos and videos of the procedure.

Margaret made sure she reminded me about getting confirmation of my "condition" before we left them. I was sure Peter was in on the secret because for the first time he hugged me longer than he hugged Phillip when we finally left. We would be back in week. I would be finished work and Phillip would have five days before his departure. I had a terrible habit of measuring time in this way. But it kept me focused and allowed me not only to count down to the sadness of goodbye but count forward to the days when he would be home.

Chapter Six

The week was busy, work responsibilities distracted both Phillip and I. Strangely, I was sleeping and eating better than I had been, and my mother-in-law's deduction seemed utterly incorrect. Phillip was particularly busy with sorting out his packing for overseas and tidying up any financial issues that might come up over the next few months. I don't know why he felt so responsible for such things as electricity and gas bills, but I thought if it made him happy why not let him manage this aspect of our lives. It wasn't as if I was incapable of paying accounts and counting our pennies but I had no interest in keeping such a close eye on things. I had a greater faith in the bureaucratic process.

In this demanding time, we just got on with the things that each one of us felt compelled to do. I had boxes of things such as bedding and kitchen utensils on my mind. Pregnancy tests were not on the radar despite Margaret's calls to remind us to prioritise this. At the end of the week when a moment opened itself up I thought I would simply buy a test from the pharmacy, do the peeing thing and then ring her to let her know that there was no baby Swan on the way. I felt so much better and Phillip was more than pleased that the sleepless nights and nervous vomiting seemed to be behind me.

The few days I had left at work were demanding and full of social activities such as morning teas and drinks after work and a farewell dinner on the Thursday night. Phillip was too busy to attend, and it was really just my colleagues and best friends from the museum who came along. While Phillip loved their company he just couldn't fit in a wild night with Helena and Brendan. As designated driver for the evening I was not drinking alcohol, despite it being my farewell. I felt that my pals needed to party a little harder than I needed to. And the evening unfolded as expected.

We had a lovely shared meal at one of my favourite Asian restaurants in the city. Wine flowed, clubbing was suggested but I vetoed such activities, so we retired to Helena's apartment and the dancing and singing ensued. I made it home about midnight after leaving the revellers at Helena's. I imagined that my last day, Friday, would be a slow workday for those still kicking up their heels when I left. Phillip was asleep and woke briefly to ask about the night's activities and promptly fell back to snoring after I described an abridged version of events. I slept as deeply as him and woke very early.

Last day of work. One week of Phillip.

In pre-dawn coolness, I took the pregnancy test out of my work bag and sat on the toilet reading the directions. Once I had released the plastic stick from the packaging, I set to following the instructions exactly. I showered and waited the requisite ten minutes for the test to complete its figuring.

By the time I'd dried off and pulled on some clean track pants and a hoodie, I thought I'd check the stick and toss it away because it would obviously be negative. A blue cross had appeared in the little window. I had to retrieve the packaging from the bin to check if I'd misread the directions because if the data was to be believed, I was pregnant.. *Surely, a cross meant no, not pregnant.* But the instructions adamantly confirmed that a blue sign meant yes, and a red minus sign meant no.

I could not have been more shocked. I felt elated, confused, terrified and bewildered. All I could think of was that Phillip would make sense of it.

He had just woken when I jumped back into bed with him and held the little stick up in front of his face. He thought I held a thermometer and that I was going to take his temperature for some bizarre reason. 'In my ear or under my tongue?' His question left me more confused than the result of the test.

'Neither you fool. It's a pregnancy test.'

'You were going to put that in my mouth!' His laughter was accompanied by a clumsy wrestling move that nearly had me bouncing off the bed. 'So what's the result?' I could tell he didn't think for one moment that we were going to be parents as he crushed me into the bed and buried his head into my chest.

'Positive.' What else could I add.

Phillip was beyond delighted. He held my face in his hands and kissed my lips, my neck, breasts, and belly. He kissed me again. 'This is amazing Lil. I'm so happy.'

He strode about our house like a man who had invented procreation. His happiness offset all doubt.

'It's just a home test Phil. Take it easy on the strutting. I'll need to see the doctor just to get confirmation.' But I could not diminish his total belief that his child was already growing inside me. I'm sure that before we finished breakfast Phillip had planned the little one's life from birth onwards. I was surprised that we hadn't already started discussing which university the baby would attend. In a moment of calm and clarity I suggested that we keep this to ourselves for a little while. That meant lying to his mother that we hadn't done the test and that we would if the symptoms returned.

I didn't want to keep Margaret out of the wonderful news. I just needed to be certain and have had time to digest the great and frightening reality of what we were embarking on. Phillip wanted to tell his mother before he left for his posting. He thought Max should know which meant the known world would be told as I'm sure this secret was one he couldn't keep. Mick would need to be told at the same time as family, as would Helena. She wouldn't keep the excitement to herself and Brendan and Jimmy would know within minutes of her being told. Helena didn't believe that joy should be contained.

I had to get through the last day of work without adding to the chaos. I would, however, make sure I had a doctor's appointment so that before Phillip left in a few days' time there would be confirmation and a chance for him to spread the good news. At least to his mother, perhaps.

As it turned out, the day at work was quiet. Many hangovers and slowly moving co-workers made any perceptible changes in my demeanour undetectable. I was a little vague and a touch jittery, but it was entirely legitimate to explain this as last day nerves. Even Helena, usually so observant, had been hindered by the previous evening's antics. The day concluded; the last week ended. And whatever was beyond this day had entered the construction phase and had already become in some way beyond my control. This train had left the station.

Chapter Seven

The days before Phillip left were a blur. Things moved so quickly I didn't seem to have time to lay down any memory of them. The only request I had was that perhaps we could keep the pregnancy a secret between us and we would leave revelation until Phillip came home after his three months overseas. According to the doctor and ultrasound, I was only about ten weeks pregnant and any obvious bump was months away. And even if some abdominal explosion occurred over the coming weeks I could easily keep it hidden under baggy jumpers. Despite his bursting joy at the news, Phillip had enough sensitivity to realise why I felt the need to keep the news between us. If I had to deal with Margaret's excitement, Sophie's jealousy and Max's over-protection by myself, I might just run away.

There was enough emotion to cope with on the day of farewell. A truckload of possessions and new furniture had already been delivered and installed into the nearly liveable renovations of our new home. It was lovely and would be even more beautiful when finished. The view over the creek and down the long expanse of beach to the island as breath-taking as always. We were so lucky. But the agony of our goodbye had left me too raw to appreciate my good fortune.

Phillip simply held me close, kissed me and told me not to miss him too much. Sometimes there weren't enough words or strong enough ones to tell a person how much you love them. So I just cried and waved goodbye. I refused to do the farewell at the airport. The thought of breaking down in public seemed too much. Mick told me he would deliver Phillip to the plane and promise Phillip he would be keeping an eye on me.

I locked myself in, lay down and prayed for Phillip's safety. I hadn't said a prayer since school ended but my faith seemed to emerge like a submarine breaching the surface when I was afraid. 'God, please let him come home.'

I wanted to sulk alone for a few days but the incessant phone ringing made that an impossible choice. Margaret rang the most. She now lived a kilometre away but was inherently worried about my aloneness. We had lied to her about the pregnancy, but she seemed doubtful. Phillip and I were not natural liars but she was an amazing mother who seemed to sense that other things were in play. She asked if she could bring me food, have me around for meals and take me to lunches with her throng of friends. Phillip's sisters Lisa and Jessica called frequently, playing their part of checking on the newcomer. I relented a few times in the first week but had to knuckle down to work and limit the socialising and eating if I was to establish a routine. Sophie remained conspicuous by her absence. Max didn't bother with the phone; he simply turned up. If I happened to be out he would do some finishing touches on the projects about the house. When I was home he would sit with me and talk about Phillip, his problems at home and the happiness his little girl brought him.

He thought there would be more babies but their trouble con-ceiving Sarah had put that hope away. Instead he would be happy with his one and the brood of nieces and nephews that followed him about like fans. 'Maybe you and Swanny will contribute to the clan,' he said. 'If you can keep him in the country that is.'

We talked a lot about Phillip's work. Max admired his friend's achievements. There was never a hit of envy or disinterest when he spoke about Phillip. He was pleased that we had returned to the beach and seemed to think that this would become our permanent home. An unlikely prospect with both of us still with jobs in Canberra. But if I'd learned anything in life, I know that nothing is utterly knowable. Things change and we mere humans must change with them.

This thought that came to mind ten days later when I'd seemed to be settled into the house and established my writing routine. The house had a new shower and toilet, but the bath had not been in-stalled. The kitchen cupboards had been reclaimed from a building project that had gone belly-up and were now nicely installed in our house, but we had no benchtops yet. The new oven and range-hood would arrive in a few days. It felt a bit like living on a building site but tolerable.

The opening chapters of my thesis started taking shape and I had my workspace organised for maximum efficiency. I missed Phillip but refused to pine for him. We spoke every day, so frequently in fact, that I wondered how much work he was really doing. They were wonderful conversations full of our anticipated reunion and the promise of our lovely little baby. He would be out of contact for at least a week, maybe longer. His team had to head out to a place he wasn't allowed to reveal to me. It sounded like part of some covert operation classified beyond his wife's security level. He was, however, so matter-of-fact about it I thought my concern for his safety was probably unwarranted. Then change, as it does, arrived.

This time it took the form of Max. I had arrived home from the local markets early on Saturday morning. I'd taken the chance to get in early and have first pick of the local fruit and vegetables. I arrived home by 8am laden with fresh food. All I could think of was scrambling two free range eggs and serving them with handfuls of the fresh spinach that had been picked by the grower only hours before. But one look at Max slumped on the front steps told me breakfast would be delayed.

Normally he would let himself in and have coffee on the go and be pottering around with some task. He looked dishevelled, gaunt and possibly drunk. The closer I got to him the more I could smell the cloying stink of whisky and sweat. This was not a Max I'd ever seen. Drunk and happy Max, sad and reflective, even angry Max. But this incarnation was not familiar.

When I spoke his name he barely lifted his head. He simply said, 'Sorry, Lil.' And then fell to silent weeping with his arms wrapped around his knees.

'Is itPhillip? What's happened.' It was hard to keep the near hysteria out of my voice. My imagination had taken over in the seconds after his two-word conversation.

'Not Phil', he slurred. Relief flooded me that Max wasn't delivering some terrible news about Phillip. It was obvious that something else quite awful had happened thought. I might be small in stature but I'm strong. Even with hessian bags full of produce I could still haul Max to his feet and steer his ungainly frame through the front door. The last thing I really needed was my new neighbours and passing tourists to invade this terrible and private catastrophe happening to my friend.

Phillip told me to look after Max and I had obviously not done a very good job.

I dropped the bags at the door, imagining that the eggs would be a sticky emanation over all the fruit, as I directed Max to the nearest chair. When I had him seated that I realised the smell was not just souring alcohol. What I though looked like mud or grime caked into his feet and legs was something else. It was dried and organic. Blood. Lots of blood. Max remained incomprehensible, inebriated and crying. I felt panicked that he had injured himself and became more so when I came to realise that the blood did not come from his body.

'Oh God, Max what have you done? What's happened?' My imagination again took me to places I didn't want to go. His relationship with Sophie was rocky but surely it couldn't have come to violence. Max was the most gentle and sweet-natured man I knew. He wouldn't hurt anyone, let alone the mother of his child. But Max could not tell me what catastrophic event had brought him to this condition. In a final shudder of abject wretchedness, he fell into a sleep so deep that I had to risk a further assault on my senses by getting close to ensure he was still breathing.

I needed help, but being afraid that he had committed a terrible crime I felt I shouldn't yet involve anyone who knew Max. I can't explain why I thought I could delay what was ahead by keeping quiet. I knew only one person, in the absence of Phillip, who would come when I needed him. Mick Flynn. My call was brief and inconclusive, but Mick came.

Within two hours he arrived at the door with news. He still had contacts with a number of New South Wales detectives and plenty of sway. Apparently there had been a death near us. A suicide but he didn't have a name. My gut reacted. My heart and then my head. The brutality and tragedy of suicide leaves a mess. Not just the kind that Max dragged into my house but the sort that leaves loved ones wondering why. I thought I'd vomit at the smell of blood but it was the realisation that someone, known or not, had opted out of their life.

Mick roused Max and put questions to him in a practised and rather abrupt manner. Max confirmed in his stupor that he'd been with a friend who had killed himself. He had tried to help him. He'd held his friend and tried to stop the bleeding. He had called an ambulance, but the rest was mutterings and further fits of crying. Mick got him to his feet and into the shower. Cleaned and dressed in some of Phillip's underwear and a t-shirt, he went back into a deep sleep in my bed. I made sure he wouldn't choke if he vomited, and I joined Mick in my nearly finished kitchen and heard him on the phone with a local officer who filled in the gaps.

Apparently, a man in his thirties was found dead in a place called Bingie, a rocky outcrop between Congo and Tuross Heads. The body had been recovered from the rocks after emergencies services had been contacted by the deceased's friend. That was Max.

'According to witnesses who knew the family of the dead man, Max had been called to help find the fellow who had been missing since last night. They want to talk to Max this morning.'

But Max was unlikely to be useful for at least four or five more hours. 'Could it have been an accident? A fall off the rocks if he had been fishing?' Rather naive questions I realised after Mick described the means used by the man to take his own life. The still unknown friend had cut deep wounds into both forearms and over a period of less than an hour, he exsanguinated. According to the first responders the man had probably been dead only an hour when Max found him in the early hours of the morning. About 4:40am the call for emergency services came. Max had tried to bind the wounds with his own clothes, but his efforts were completely redundant as brain death and heart failure would have started when the victim had lost about two litres of blood. It must have been at this point that Max's legs and arms became covered in blood. The details provided a form of detachment. A way of seeing without feeling. It seemed that people who had to deal with the awfulness of human frailty spoke about death in this manner as if it helped them cope. It didn't help me. The process of death did not make me immune from the consequences of loss. Someone had to have been told that a man was dead. That he had chosen death over life.

Poor Max. I wondered which of his friends had been so desperate that dying a lonely and painful death seemed to be a solution to whatever his problem. I wouldn't know more until Max had slept off the whisky and the shock. In the waiting period, Mick and I talked about the new house, my research and Phillip's absence over coffee and a belated breakfast using the eggs that hadn't been broken when I dropped the bags at the front door. And we waited for Max.

Max awoke around noon. Sick and bewildered, but compos mentis enough to tell the story and answer the questions put to him when the police arrived.

At first, I couldn't believe what Max was telling us. 'Kitty hadn't said anything, to anyone. We thought he was so happy with the baby. With Jean.' It simply didn't fit with the image I had of the man and his family. Although only having met them once, I thought Benedict, aka Kitty, his wife Jean and their baby Isaiah seemed the quintessential "Happy family". All I could think of was Kitty's son, now fatherless and having to grow up with the knowledge that death by his own hand was the preferred option. 'I'm sorry Lil. I didn't mean to mess up your place. I just didn't know what to do.'

'I'm sorry too Max. Sorry for you and Jean and baby.'

I knew from experience that learning about suicide so close to home was hard to process and terrible to discover the truth after many years. Hopefully no-one will lie and conceal the awfulness of the truth from Isaiah as he grows up. Because being exempt from the knowing makes for a very lonely road particularly when everyone else knows the truth. But I had to remember that this wasn't my story; it was now Jean's and her little boy's. It was Max's story too. He not only had to grieve for a lost friend; he had to come to terms with the fact that he could not save him.

Chapter Eight

Max sobered up somewhat and Mick took him home that afternoon. Sophie was furious at his unexplained absence and only when Mick intervened and told her what had happened that she quietened down. Not surprisingly she was not comforted by the fact that Max and come to me before seeking out his wife. Her less than sympathetic response to Kitty's suicide and his family's grief was typical of Sophie. Even after knowing the circumstances, Max's disappearance and its impact on her was all she could talk about.

'Do you know how worried I was?' It was a reasonable question, but it wasn't followed by any forgiveness when she was made aware of the facts. 'I called everyone and they all said you were out looking for one of your fishing mates. But you didn't call as usual. I was on my own and of course you ended up at Lily's!'

Max had no response to this. He was in pain and filled with loss; and still feeling the effects of too much alcohol. It was likely he had been seeking solace in a home that would attempt to understand that sorrow. If he had turned up at his home in that state, likely Sophie would have refused to let him in the house. She had little compassion for anyone. Perhaps she had no empathy at all because she focused on what she considered the shortcomings in her own life.

An autopsy had been conducted and despite no official report everyone knew Benedict Kitt Jepp's death was a suicide. The locals had decided that there were no suspicious circumstances, just a whole lot of unanswered questions. 'Why?' The most predominant and unanswerable question of all. Why would Kitty Jepp take his own life? He had everything to live for, including a family who loved him.

The funeral had to be planned and conducted. Jean was too shocked and overwhelmed to make many decisions but with the help of her parents and Max a fitting ceremony was organised. Kitty had been raised a Catholic by his mother, whose fundamental belief in church doctrine outweighed her belief in family. Jean was emphatic that there would be no religious service to farewell her husband. She wanted something that Kitty would have loved. Something with music, the sea and colour. A sombre congregation in black with a morose dirge intoning in the background was not in keeping with his love of life and peaceful nature. So of course Max thought I could help.

How could I refuse Max, or in fact Jean? If she thought I could help, despite being an outsider, I was willing to do so. My role would of course be around music. Two days after the awful discovery, Max drove me out to Kitty and Jean's home in Congo. The little township that sat on the edge of the New South Wales coast between Moruya and Tuross. Max couldn't tell me why the village had been called Congo. The region had a long history with indigenous people who fished and lived in the area centuries before surfers and fishermen found refuge in the tangled coastal forest. And among the coachwood and scribbly gums the Jepps had made a home.

When Max picked me up in his ute. It was no cleaner than the first time I climbed into the front seat. I had to negotiate the fishing rods, tool boxes and beach towels that littered the passenger's seat. Luckily, I was able to squeeze in without having to do too much rearranging. It would take fewer that thirty minutes to get to Jean's house. The turn off to Congo belied the strange forest that lay beyond the highway. As we drove further off the main road the ordered paddocks gave way to what seemed to be a track etched through the bush. The landscape seemed to change quite dramatically. The trees embraced the road and created something fitting of Tolkien's imagination. It had an other-worldliness about it that seemed to separate the houses from the real world. The ute had to negotiate potholes and poorly graded gravel patches as the plants and trees seemed to be attempting to reclaim the space. The greenery provided a canopy that allowed only shards of sunlight through. I wondered where Max was taking me and why Jean and Kitty had chosen to live out here.

On arriving at the house I had my answer. The location was beautiful. The simply constructed timber home was rustic but had been built on the beach side of Point Parade. Nothing stood between the house and the drop to the beach. Kitty had apparently built a shed on the block fifteen years ago. He had lived there alone for ten years or more but when Jean agreed to be his partner, a house seemed more appropriate. With Jean's father and a few friends the first part of the house went up in five months. The additions and little luxuries, like indoor plumbing, came as the couple saved enough to afford them. The arrival of Isaiah had predicated the need for flyscreens on windows and doors, a little insulation and better heating.

Jean didn't come out to see who had noisily arrived on her patch of paradise. We found her on the back deck sitting quietly in a swinging chair with her sleepy son latched onto her breast. The first time I met her, her hair was wild, but now it looked positively dishevelled. I wasn't judging but recognised this as the descent into despair that followed loss. In the agony of anguish there never space or time for self-care. Jean looked as wild as the snarled wonga wonga vine we had seen binding the trees together on the road out here. She was pasty under her tan; her face looked like a deflating balloon that lay withered on the floor after a party. She looked airless and tattered. I wondered how she would come back from this state to mother the little baby who sucked at her breast. He was blithely unaware of the great disservice his father had done him. Only in the future would Kitty's choices bring Isaiah pain. The same ache that gripped my gut when I heard of Kitty's suicide hit me again. It took several deep breaths to calm myself. And several more to stop myself from thinking about Isaiah's future.

When Max spoke, Jean seemed to come back to consciousness. 'Hi Jean. Do you remember Lily Swan?' She greeted us graciously and asked if we would like tea. I think Max and I both said no but she struggled out of her nest and plucked the baby's barely sucking lips off her nipple to go to the kitchen. Absently she handed me the drowsy boy to hold as she went robotically about making her guests welcome. The baby was in that extraordinary state between aware and asleep. So full of milk and contented enough to be held by a stranger. I didn't think I'd have many instincts for this role, but I immediately found myself rocking from foot to foot in a swaying motion that Isaiah found pleasing enough. His eyes closed, and the long fan of ginger lashes washed over his milky skin. The perfection of his tiny face overwhelmed me. The father, who had only a few weeks before had protested his love for this child had now deliberately absented himself from this joy. He had made the choice to never again look upon the innocence and flawlessness of his son. A little bubble of milk formed on Isaiah's pouty lips and I marvelled more at his loveliness.

My contemplation was interrupted by a woman's voice. I looked up to see an older version of Jean. She asked me about tea. 'Would you like green or black tea? If you like it white, I can only offer you rice milk.' Before I could answer she formally introduced herself. 'I'm Barbie Parrish. Jean's mother.'

I would have put my hand out to shake hers, but I was too afraid of trying to wrangle the sleeping baby into a one-armed embrace. But I was able at least to say my name and offer my sympathy for the loss of her son-in-law. Barbie did not seem to be a sentimental woman. She thanked me for my kind thoughts and moved straight on to why Max had brought me out to Jean's place. 'How do you know Jean and Kitty?'

'I think Max has asked Jean if she would like me to provide some musical component to the ceremony.' I sounded ridiculously formal, but I didn't know these people or their preferences for funerals. Jean came out and asked me to put Issy in his cot inside since he was asleep. She seemed to be under the impression that I would know where in the house that might be and that I would have some competence in putting him into said bed. I could see she was not able to answer any kind of question, so I walked into the house and was surprised to find the building consisted of two rooms separated by an intricate timber panel. One side of the house was a living space and kitchen. The other side a bedroom.. At the end of the unmade bed stood a brightly coloured cot. Isaiah didn't stir as I laid him down and extracted my arms from under him. Obviously the Jepp family stayed in close proximity. The two rooms, although substantial, offered little in the way of privacy. The timber screen had been made of several panels. Some of them were solid; others carved with swirling cut-outs that gave a glimpse into the rooms they separated. More interestingly, each panel was made of a different timber. Some panels designed to be static; secured on the floor and ceiling. Others constructed as retractable doors that had been fitted into runners so that the space could be opened up even more. It was a unique idea.

'It's all Kitty's work.' Max filled in the gap. 'He wasn't a carpenter, but he was really talented in furniture and cabinet making. More an artist than a builder.' Max looked around the room pointing out the bits of construction he had helped with until Barbie called us back out to the deck.

She had poured tea and Jean was back in her swinging chair sipping from a Wedgewood cup. The delicacy of the china looked a little out of place. I'd expected hand thrown pottery or enamel mugs but here we were drinking from Tea Garden cups patterned with typical Wedgewood mint greens and yellows. Barbie must have sensed my appreciation of the crockery explaining that the set had been her mother's and that Jean had been given the tea set as a wedding gift. 'Of course we thought she'd be living somewhere a little less rustic, but tea always tastes better in nice china.'

'And we didn't have a wedding as such, Mama. Don't forget to add that.' Jean didn't sound bitter or cross with her mother's comment about rustic living. It was the first time she had spoken as if she was engaged in the conversation. 'We had a commitment ceremony and a naming day for Issy. We don't do conventional events.' Which brought us to the next event in Jean's life, the funeral for her husband.

It wasn't to be called a funeral. Jean wanted to call it a farewelling. 'A farewell ceremony seems to be more appropriate.' I wasn't sure changing the name of the occasion would make the process any easier, but I was only there to contribute music and song. I'm sure Barbie and her husband Nick had made enquiries about the legal and practical components of a farewelling ceremony. By the end of the afternoon the key moments had been worked out. Jean wanted few formal elements apart from a welcome and eulogy by Max and a few tributes from friends. It seemed that two other musicians and I would play some of Kitty's favourite songs as people entered the crematorium. 'There has to be songs. Kitty loved music.' Jean asked if I would sing her favourite song at the committal. I felt I couldn't refuse her anything, but I worried about her choice of song. I said nothing but internally worried about my ability to sing without wailing and ruining the day. Kitty's ashes would be committed to the water not far from where he ended his life.

Three cups of tea and two hours of planning were enough. Through most of it, Jean cried silent tears wrapped up in her swing that undulated with each deep inhalation of breath. In that time Jean's father and sister arrived to help with meals and the baby. Isaiah obligingly slept the whole time allowing his mother to concentrate on the task at hand. I admired her general composure under the circumstances. Despite the tears she remained calm and quiet. If I'd been planning to "farewell" my husband, I wouldn't be able to contain my grief. The thought of it made me shudder and tear up. It was a change in mood not missed by Max. I wondered if Jean had been given some sedatives to ease the terrible transition to widow. It seemed reasonable to think so. Max later informed me that her passiveness was primarily due to her considerable usage of marijuana. While I had genuine misgivings about breast-feeding mothers smoking dope, I couldn't really blame her for wanting to deaden the pain. Who was I to judge?

On the way out of the town Max let me in on other secret. Kitty had left him a letter. He hadn't left one for Jean or anyone else. Just Max. It had been posted the day of Kitty's suicide. By the time Max had received the letter, his friend had ended his life and all that was left to do was work out why. Max couldn't make any sense of the letter and I knew he would ask me to read it. To help him understand Kitty's last thoughts. I felt inadequate to the task, but I knew if Phillip was home Max would ask him. I had to be the stand-in friend who would do as a replacement given the circumstances.

Leaving Congo and its claustrophobic forest and house of grief made me feel like I could breathe again. The disorder of the tangled plants made me grateful for the orderliness of the highway. The day was ending and there were things to be done, including songs to be practised. I had four days before the funeral, the farewell ceremony. And in that time I knew I'd come to know more about Benedict Kitt Jepp by reading his message to Max. I had learned a great deal about my own father when I read his farewell letter to his sister Billie. He made it clear why living had become impossible. I hoped Kitty's letter would be equally illuminating.

Chapter Nine

The day was nearly at its end when we arrived home. 'Could you look at the letter tonight, Lil?' Every part of me wanted to say no—take the letter and burn it—but there was something so vulnerable in his voice that I could never refuse him. Out of the chaos of the glovebox, he handed me Kitty's letter. It was strangely pristine, as if Max had opened it reverentially, afraid to treat something so precious with rough treatment. He couldn't stay. Sophie would be already furious that he'd spent most of the day with me. She would make her usual complaints about her needs not being met and how Max only ever thought about himself. The accusations seemed more than ironic, in fact downright laughable. If anyone thought only about herself and ensuring her needs were met it was my sister-in-law.

So alone I sat in front of my new windows and took in the view. The light had faded, and the pink tinged clouds of twilight cast a gloomy shadow all the way along the beach from the creek to the island. I checked my phone and emails just in case Phillip had been able to reach me. In the absence of any distractions, I opened the page that contained the last thoughts of Benedict Kitt Jepp.

It started so casually I could hardly believe that this man would end his life on the day he wrote it. He talked about how he loved the sea and living on the south coast. *"The water cleanses us, Maxie."* I thought the wording sounded odd. It had some ritualistic or religious overtones but according to Jean her husband had no affection for his Catholic upbringing. He went on, *"But some things just can't be washed away."* The letter was sounding like a confession. A burden of guilt? Had Kitty done something terrible and felt he couldn't atone for his actions? The letter included several things he was grateful for: his wife, friends and most of all Isaiah. *"But I can't stay and watch him because I know I can't protect him."* From what? What couldn't this loving father protect his son from? I could see why Max felt confused. Kitty had left vague clues but provide no answers.

The letter concluded with the most cryptic thing of all: *"Ned Kelly and Elvis always knew the truth would kill us."* I wondered if this was reference to a song or a philosophical insight shared by a bushranger and a singer. Kitty's letter offered no clear rationale for his suicide.

I tried to imagine what his state of mind when he penned this jumble of ideas. I thought about the hours after he posted the letter. From some of the fragments gleaned from the police it seemed that Kitty had told Jean that he was going fishing. He left the house at noon. He hadn't said where he was going but he didn't take the boat, so it could easily be assumed he would fish off the beach at Pedro's Point, or the rocks at Bingie. Perhaps he would go further afield but usually he would tell Jean his location if it wasn't local. Kitty was the kind of man who could let time get away from him but his non-appearance at home when the sun went down caused a few waves of concern.

Jean called Max when the dark set it. By the time he got to Congo and talked to Jean, it was nearly midnight. Things looked a bit grim so as a precaution, Max had called a few mates to alert them to the possibility that Kitty might have taken a tumble somewhere and that he would go to look for him. Armed with a torch and a pack with some emergency gear, Max set off first to Pedro's then walked a bit of the beach before heading to Bingie.

The night was clear, but hours had ticked by before Max had walked the track out to the rocks that formed a clear division between two long sweeping beaches. The outcrop had dozens of drop-offs and nooks where a man might bunker down if he'd decided he wanted a night out under the stars. Max looked not only in the snug spots between rocks but in the gullies between land and the surging tide. If Kitty had fallen into the water, then Max was too late; but he looked anyway. From low on the slippery platform, Max shone his torch up the striped face of the point. The stripes were caused 380 million years ago when magma spewed up through the basalt face and created a pink aplite band. Dangling over the black and pink rock he was bare feet. The owner remained non-responsive to Max's shouts and torch-waving from below. His climb was met with the miserable scene of Kitty's bloody, lifeless body cocooned by stone. He had obviously found the perfect spot. He could watch his beloved sea roll in and out and be washed by plumes of mist as the bigger waves hit with force. The blood from his self-inflicted wounds pooled under his body and with the spray from the sea and the assistance of gravity the redness inched down the rock face and into the water.

Kitty's eyes were open, according to Max. But the life had gone from them. Max tried to wrap the deep channels Kitty had carved into his arms and attempted to lift him out of his stony cradle. But the blood, water and dark night made the task impossible for one man.

The thought of Max having to walk alone back up the track to get a phone signal so he could call emergency services, made me ache with sorrow. Poor gentle Max. And poor Kitty. What terrible secret had made this lonely death preferable to life? How could he let go of a life with his son? It filled me with something greater than sorrow. It was rage and disbelief. Perhaps feelings I had no right to feel. I realised, I projected my own lonely childhood on to the life Isaiah might have. At some point the little cherub I'd held that afternoon would have to know the awful truth of his father's decision. Issy would be shaped, for better or worse, by this. If he could come to understand the reasons for the death, logical or not, maybe he would be able to forgive his father.

I had, in time, come to forgive both my mother and father for their sins. But it was only when I had delved deep into their lives that I'd been able to understand. It is the story before death that one must know if the question is to be answered. "Why?" Why had Kitty taken his life?

And this was what Max was hoping I would do. Find the answer and gift the story to Isaiah.

Chapter Ten

Phillip had finally been able to make contact on the night before the funeral. We talked about the death and how Max was holding up. Phillip gave the usual warnings about me not getting involved despite my obvious curiosity and desire to help. We talked more about how I felt and what, if any, symptoms were evident. I think Phillip had thought I might have swollen to epic proportions in his absence. I hadn't but for the first time in weeks my appetite was rampant, and for the first time since Phillip left I ate really well. I told him about his family members and who was doing what including Sophie's ongoing sullenness. When the call ended I realised how much I missed him. I hoped to God I'd never have to say goodbye in the way Jean now had to face farewelling her husband.

I had rehearsed with Andy and Flash for a couple of hours the day after I went out to see Jean. Andy and Flash were good friends of the Jepps and the Swan clan. They were locals who ran the surf school and played music when the waves disappeared. Flash, whose real name was Fenton, was also related to Barbie Parrish. I didn't quite understand the connection, but they were family. We had organised to play at the front of the chapel at the crematorium as family and friends arrived. Jean wanted favourite songs, and it seemed that all her choices had something appropriate to say on such a day. We all had guitars and I'd also have my mandolin for the solo I would perform at the committal. I decided I would look straight out over the heads of the mourners and not watch the coffin make its silent and eerie descent into the bowels of the building.

As the chapel filled, on cue the three of us started our confirmed play list, starting with *Yesterday* by The Beatles. We sang softly just to take the edge of the quiet chatting voices and awkward silence. It was followed by Eric Clapton's *Tears in Heaven* and as the last of the people arrived, we sang a gentle of version of *Have I Told You Lately That I Love You* by Van Morrison. I made the terrible mistake of meeting Max's glassy eyes midway through the song and choked a little leading to some fading on the lyrics. But I was fairly well-practised in performance. I had a technique for bringing myself back into focus and, with a sharp heel pressure on my own foot, I took my gaze elsewhere in the chapel. Looking at unknown and hopefully impassive faces would help. Helena had a technique of her own she had taught me. "Just relax and let the tears flow Lily." She believed the struggle to stop the emotion led to explosive sobbing and strangulated voices.

On the last few words of the final song I found myself absorbed by the myriad of faces and the vast gathering that had spilled out onto the paved areas outside. As per Jean's request, there was little that appeared sombre about the gathering. The congregation looked like a rainbow. The coffin had been painted orange and laced with flowers that had been interlinked to form a daisy-chain. Its beauty made me smile even in the midst of such sadness. The kaleidoscopic effect of bright fabric and flowers made the one woman dressed entirely in black a stark and mesmerising contrast. As Andy, Flash and I moved our little ensemble further to the side wall, I watched the impassive and pinched face of the woman, whom I could only imagine was Kitty's mother. She seemed wildly out of place, awkward and stiff in the flow and ebb of colour. Her son's life must have been a mystery to her. The people around seemed free of the yoke of tradition and structure. Yet here she was—here to bury her son.

An unlikely fellow had been asked to officiate the proceedings. His name was Pastor Stan, a local indigenous minister attached to a Christian church that I hadn't heard of before. I wasn't listening carefully enough to catch its exact name. He did make it clear that he wouldn't be performing any official religious duties he was just stage-managing the events. He asked Nick Parrish to speak first. Jean's father dressed splendidly in fluorescent tie-dye and teal jeans spoke quietly and with a bit of discomfort at talking in public. He, however, welcomed the guests warmly. He especially looked at and spoke to Teresa Jepp and said that he, Barbie and Jean felt the great loss of her son. 'He was a grand boy, our Kitty.'

Teresa Jepp seemed to bristle at the use of her son's nickname. I suspected she should get used to it as no-one was likely to be calling him Benedict.

Nick then asked Max to come and speak about his friend. Max was not a natural speechmaker, but he was an instinctive storyteller. As he began to talk about how he and Kitty had become friends, I felt little hands on my knees. Sarah, Max and Sophie's daughter, had escaped her grandparents grasp and made her way to me. She called out to Max who stopped and acknowledged his little girl, much to the amusement of the crowd. I told her she had to be quiet now so that her daddy could concentrate and while I happily held the wriggling pre-schooler, I also really wanted to hear Max talk about Kitty. He talked about how as a seventeen-year-old Kitty arrived in the area and set about making his mark as a fisherman. He worked out on the Kennett's boat and also on the Sharman's oyster lease. Details of why a boy of that age had left his home in Gipsy Point in Victoria were not shared but stirred my interest. More details about how this kid from the south managed to save enough for his Congo land and build a shed. Max made us laugh about the impressive styling of Kitty's shed. It seemed that some of the panels in the house he built once adorned the corrugated iron walls of his first home. Kitty had a hammock for hot summer nights and Balinese-inspired sleeping platform for winter when he needed to be ensconced in pillows and mats to keep him safe from southerly winds that frequently nearly blew the shed down. There were tender comments about the civilising effects Jean had on Kitty's life. He spoke emotionally about Kitty's love for Isaiah and courageously talked about the elephant in the room. Kitty had died by his own hand. His mental illness had remained undiscovered by his many friends and loved ones. 'It shouldn't happen. But our promise to Kitty is that we'll not let it happen to anyone else.' Max's words were so sincere and spoken with such steadfastness that in that moment I believed it to be true.

Jean sobbed audibly. Barbie embraced her with all her strength, as if she could stave off the awfulness of her daughter's grief. There had obviously some tension between mother and daughter over life choices, however, her child was in agony and everything past and future meant nothing. Barbie would hold her child till the pain eased.

Nick held his grandson close to his chest to protect him from the worst of the grief. And all the while Teresa sat seemingly unaffected. She appeared indifferent to the sadness around her. Stoical in her black mourning dress, she looked neither at Jean nor her grandson. Her eyes merely rested on the cascade of colour that bore the body of her son.

Pastor Stan embraced Max and briefly followed up on the issue of looking out for each other. He called forth other speakers who lay tributes at the coffin and spoke briefly. These were not great speakers, but each set of words was heartfelt. At the end pictures and a kayak paddle, fishing rods and a surfboard adorned the altar. These elements reflected Kitty's life. They marked his years from seventeen to thirty-four. What happened before was not evident in the objects laid at his feet. His mother and the people who walked with him in those early days when he was Benedict Jepp did not pay homage at his death. He was farewelled by these glorious, caring men and women who knew him as Kitty—partner of Jean, father of Isaiah and man of the sea.

The final words before the committal instructed the mourners that Kitty's ashes would be spread at sea on Sunday. There would be a blessing of sorts, a song and everyone who could was invited to come by boat or surfboard to see Kitty returned to the water. The pastor invited me to come further forward to sing the final song that would end the service, but I was not keen to move into the direct line of sight of Mrs. Jepp. I had to separate myself from Sarah who didn't want to leave me. Max scooped her up off my knee and leant down and kissed the top of my head. It was his way of reassuring me. Unfortunately, a move not missed by his wife. I could feel the heat from her gaze despite her actual distance from me. But I couldn't be distracted as I had a job to do.

Jean had asked me to sing the Dylan classic *Forever Young*. It was a song that worked well when accompanied by some simple strumming and slow chord change on the mandolin. As I started, singing I realised that while I sang it for Kitty in that he would be forever young, this song was really for those of us left behind, particularly Isaiah. Life mattered and what we did with it mattered. To my delight into the second verse most of Kitty's friends joined in and filled the room with a resonant call to life. Teresa Jepp remained unmoved.

The proceedings ended, and the coffin ceremoniously lowered from our view. The mourners had to make the awkward move from grieving to greeting. Cups of tea had to be made, beers and other drinks to be released from icy bins all accompanied by sandwiches and cakes. Everything at the wake had been provided by Kitty's friends so Jean and her family had to bear none of the costs. This generous community took care of its sons and daughters. Wakes in general signified that the end of life had to be inevitably accompanied by the beginning of another journey. While Kitty's body would soon be ashes and spread over the pulsing waves at his favourite beach, we the living, had to get on with things.

The general sense of relief the end of the service brought out the talking and reminiscences. It made a noisy cover for me to watch the crowd as they milled about. Many of the faces I knew in one capacity or another, somehow linked to my new family. The people who looked most out of place were obviously not locals. Mrs. Jepp was the obvious outsider, but she had deemed it appropriate to take a cup from Barbie and to stand with Jean forming some sort of united front. The topic clearly focused on baby Issy. While his grandmothers looked at him simultaneously it was easy to see that Barbie connected with the little boy. Teresa on the other hand showed little emotion when she cast her eyes in his direction. But other strangers also caught my eye.

I intended to make a beeline to them and simply introduce myself and ask questions about their connection to Kitty. Before I could extricate myself from Margaret and Peter, I was confronted by a red-faced Sophie. 'You and Max are making quite a team, Lily.' There would be no response that would in any way appease my sister-in-law.

'It's just to help Jean.' I thought it would suffice as an excuse for the time I'd spent with Max. I wanted to say, just to hurt her, that her husband spent time with me because she was cold and self-centred and did nothing to ease his pain. But common sense prevailed, and I simply shrugged my shoulders and moved away.

Peter moved close to his daughter and spoke sternly. 'Pull your head in, Sophie. This is not the time or place for you to be carrying on.' It was so unlike Peter to be cross and raise his voice, but I knew that her behaviour had been driving them mad over the past few months. Her father's displeasure sent Sophie off in a huff, leaving both Max and Sarah with no way to get home.

The little commotion gave me the opportunity to wander over to the strangers. Two men in particular were standing together refilling their plates with food. 'Hi, can I get you two a drink?' It was a simple enough invitation to further discussion. I pressed on with introducing myself. They said polite things about my singing and that they thought the songs really suited Bennie. So these two knew him as Bennie, not Kitty nor Benedict.

'How are you connected to Kitty?' I hoped that in the short time I'd have to speak that I would glean something about the first part of the dead man's life. They introduced themselves as Archie and Henry. They had grown up with Benedict in Victoria.

'Gipsy Point?' I'd remembered that this is the place Max had mentioned in the eulogy.

'Near enough.' Archie laughed. 'Between the lake and Mallacoota. We went to school together. Eleven years of it.'

I readied myself to ask what kind of boy Kitty had been but was interrupted when Mrs. Jepp joined us. The two men, although in their thirties, greeted the woman as if they were schoolboys. She had a severity in her manner more about austerity than grief. Again I introduced myself.

'O'Hara. You must be Irish and Catholic.' But before I could answer she firmly chastised me. 'I thought as a Catholic you might know better than to sing ditties at a man's funeral.'

She gave me no chance to respond. She simply left me standing, quite bewildered.

The silence finally broken by the new acquaintances. They dared to laugh, only after she was out of earshot. 'Still an old bitch, then.' Archie's comment, hardly profound but I couldn't argue with his precision. It broke the ice.

'I'm assuming she's always been stern.'

The men laughed a bit louder.

In the ten minutes we had before the next interruption I learned that Kitty had been raised by his mother; no father on the scene and they had presumed he had died. The three boys went to St. Finbar's College from the age of four to sixteen. They seemed to have been very close in those early years but had hardly seen Bennie aka Kitty since he moved north.

'He was always going to live by the beach. It was always the place he escaped to,' Henry said.

I wanted to about to ask what sorts of things Kitty had to escape from but couldn't when Max joined us. He carried Sarah who immediately wanted to come to me and clambered out of her father's arms and into mine. I briefly introduced everyone but before I could steer the conversation back to the Mallacoota days the men started talking about fishing and the weather. I did squeeze in a question about whether they would be staying for the ashes ceremony on Sunday. I was glad that they would be there. I would make an effort to find out more about his life and attempt to make some connection between those days and the choice he'd made to end it. Their information might help Max understand Kitty's suicide. Might help us all understand why a man with everything to live for decided on a lonely, self-inflicted death. The two men were not at ease. Henry in particular looked well-worn. I noticed his hands shook as he took a beer from Pastor Stan, who had moved from the role of master of ceremonies to waiter.

The wake finished soon after. Peter took Max and Sarah home. Margaret would stay and help the Parrish family clean up and I simply wanted to pack up my instruments and have a quiet night at home. Hopefully one that would include some kind of contact with my husband where he would reassure me of his safety. I could describe the funeral and give him an update on how Max had coped with the day.

Chapter Eleven

Sophie barged into the house without any formal announcement such as knocking on the door. She was livid, her face flushed and sweaty. *Deranged* came to mind. *Dangerous* when she started waving her arms about.

'Who the hell do you think you are?' she screamed.

Silence once again seemed to be the sensible response.

'You evil midget!'

Unfortunately this slur made me smile. And that was flawed thinking.

Sophie lost complete control and rushed at me, knocking me off my feet landing on top of me in what could only be described as a classic rugby tackle. I was winded and frightened. Frightened because it seemed that Sophie hadn't finished her attack and all I could think of was protecting my body that housed my growing baby.

She made her first mistake by attempting to stand up, I imagined so she could start kicking or punching. In the moment she was unbalanced and with her face in range, I lashed out with my bare foot and caught her across the nose. Her shock gave me time to get up. I had no idea what my next line of defence would be but thankfully Max and Peter arrived negating the need for me to recall any kind of self-defence moves.

Sophie screamed and cried wildly. I cried, more from shock and fright. Peter and Max wrestled Sophie to the kitchen table and held her arms and stemmed the nose bleed I'd caused with a tea towel. The noise must have been heard throughout the neighbourhood. Her sister Jessica and husband Lachlan turned up and dragged the sobbing mad woman out of the house. Peter went with them. Only Max stayed.

'Are you hurt, Lil?'

His gentleness was my undoing. And without wanting to I spilled the beans, I said,

'I'm pregnant Max. What if this has hurt the baby?'

His response was automatic. He held me close and said soothing things that made me less fearful. 'Better check with the doc though. I'll take you to the hospital. Who knows about the baby?' Max was surprised that Phillip and I had kept this to ourselves.

I tried to explain that it wasn't planned, and we wanted to be together when we told his parents. That we had decided not to tell anyone, and I honestly couldn't stand for Sophie to know. I apologised because she was his wife and I knew that he must have been horrified by her behaviour.

'I think we both know that it's over. Sophie wants a different life to the one she has with me and Sarah. She's leaving me and going to Sydney. There's some friend up there who's got something arranged.' Max sounded heart-broken. 'Phil doesn't know yet.'

'There's quite a few secrets being kept in this town.'

Before I could say more, Peter came back in to check everything was okay and to apologise for his daughter's attack. Max walked outside to watch Sophie being driven away. Peter wanted to know if I needed any medical treatment, but I assured him I felt fine. Apart from a really sore spot on the back of my head and a mighty big bruise forming on my backside and worrying about the baby, I was fine. I felt sad that whatever drove Sophie's ill-temper now manifested itself in violence and breaking her parents' hearts. I couldn't begin to imagine how this was affecting Max. His wife was leaving not only him, but their daughter too. The life without her child must have been incredibly appealing. 'I think I should run her up to the hospital just in case.' Max's suggestion had Peter's approval. But I knew it was overkill and just adding to the melodrama of the day.

I needed that quiet evening more than ever. I persuaded both men to leave me to rest. I texted Max the minute the door closed telling him that he had to keep yet another secret. He responded with a simple, 'Of course.'

Perhaps I should have told my in-laws not to say anything to Phillip until I'd had time to tell him, but my luck didn't hold out. Somehow Margaret and Peter had got a hold of their son and told him what had happened. In his panic he blurted out that I was pregnant and that they had to check on me. By the time Phillip had managed to make a phone call to me, the grandparents-to-be where knocking my door down. Phillip had to make a quick confession that he'd betrayed the secret. I thought about telling him that I'd done the same thing with Max but didn't. The phone call became a four-person fracas which was only calmed when I agreed to go to the hospital for a check-up. I promised to ring or email or both as soon as a doctor examined me. It was an unnecessary and hysterical part of an already overwhelming day.

As predicted I was fine. Bruised but fine. The ultrasound confirmed that baby Swan was also fine. His or her little heartbeat strongly and steadily. The images showed a tiny shape rocking comfortably, suspended in impact-absorbing fluid. I might struggle to be comfortable with my bruising and any pain could be managed with paracetamol. All was well.

I insisted that Peter and Margaret went home. It was nearly 11 by the time we got back from the hospital. I just wanted to go to bed. They were reluctant to leave but my insistence eventually got them to go.

Sleep, not surprisingly, eluded me. I thought about the service for Kitty and his old friends. I wondered what they thought about his death. I thought about his mother's strange reaction and her aloof manner. Her blank face and cold eyes stayed with me. The ashes would be spread on Sunday and we would hopefully meet again. Perhaps she would be less impassive then as the realisation hit that this marked the very end of her son's life. Or she could be equally disparaging of the song that would be sung before the ritual. Ditties as she'd called them.

At some point I must have stopped thinking about the woman who had come to farewell her son and was claimed by sleep because the next thought came when the sun woke me at dawn. I had all of Saturday to myself. I had hoped that everyone would leave me alone and that the crisis with Sophie could be sorted without me. I had a short rehearsal with a local choir at five to practise the song. But the day was mine, if my well-meaning friends and family left alone.

I spent the morning emailing back and forward with Phillip. Mainly about Sophie and choices she had made. Phillip was not at all concerned about Sophie's jealousy of my relationship with Max. My husband had a deep trust in his friendship with Max and obviously did not contemplate that his sister's behaviour had any justification. In fact I think he was happy that we had formed a liaison, a mutually protective closeness that would help both of us survive Phillip's absence. He apologised for telling the secret but I had no leg to stand on given I'd also blurted out the truth. It seems that Phillip and I are more alike than even we knew; neither can keep a secret when afraid. Neither of us would be good candidates for torture.

The Swan family left me alone. A couple of texts checking on me came from Margaret and Max. I was surprised but pleased. I imagined that everyone might have been trying to sort out the Sophie crisis and I only wanted to hear about it when the final solution had been reached. I ate homemade vegetable soup and rosemary pizza crust made from scratch. I listened to music and sat on my deck and watched the tide move the sea in its incessant rhythm. The heartbeat of the world is measured in the movement of the oceans. And the predictability of the ebb and flow acted as a mantra that brought a strange calm to my internal monologue. Death, grief, madness and violence seemed to diminish in importance when one watches the enormity of nature. We are such tiny things in comparison.

I wrote a little; read some journal articles and went to my rehearsal with the Deep Creek Choir.

We would sing *If I Should Fall Behind* acapella style. The simple arrangement simply had me singing the lyrics and the choir providing a deep reverberating hum and a hand clapping beat. It was a gentle love song about the journey of lovers who lives take different paths. The choir consisted of women who had a love of singing and lived locally. Most of them knew either Kitty or Jean or the Swans. The community was small enough not to necessitate six degrees of separation; two at the most. Everyone knew someone who was connected to the person at the heart of every conversation. The coastal people reminded me of my childhood on Lake George. We were inextricably linked through experience or bloodline to those who lived near us and shared the best and worst of life. Each person a piece of the puzzle.

So it was in this community. The talk turned after the rehearsal to two topics. Firstly the women spoke about Jean. Some had been to school with her; others knew her through the Parrish's café and some because their partners had been associated with Kitty. There was no intentional unkindness but some brutal honesty. The general conversation focused on the strange house the couple lived in. The older women in the group talked about the laissez-faire lifestyle that included a fairly permissive approach to drug use. This became the theme of the gossip. Concern for Jean and bewilderment at Kitty's suicide ran a close second in the conversation. Insight, hearsay and matter-of-fact declarative statements peppered the chatter. It finished with one of the local matriarchs stating that Kitty Jepp had to be depressed. 'The truth of his mental state will come out,' she said. 'We just have to ask the right questions of the right people.' And I couldn't help but agree.

The same woman, who even though in her sixties, still worked as a nurse at the local hospital then shifted the conversation to a less comfortable topic with the question, 'Lily, what's happening with Max and Sophie Fraser?'

I felt the heat rush to my face as the group's collective attention swung my way.

'She's leaving him, isn't she?'

'I'm probably not the right person to answer this question. I don't know what Sophie has decided to do.' It really wasn't my place to be revealing my family's private pain but in the absence of my information the locals built the picture. Carole Kent had been to school with the Swans. She led the conversation with a character assassination of Sophie based on her behaviour as a teenager. 'She was the biggest bitch in school. If Phillip Swan hadn't been her brother, she wouldn't have had a single friend.' There was some eyebrow raising and nodding from others who had gone to Moruya High. 'She went out with just about everyone in Phil's year and snared poor old Maxie.'

The women's general consensus was that Max was the one hard done by in the relationship. 'Too gentle for his own good. Didn't know what he was getting into with Princess Sophie!'

Other comments suggested that Sophie had created a lot of bad blood and that her friendship group had always been rather slender. A rather terrifying-looking woman spoke quietly but commanded the attention of the group. She had tattoos on much of the skin that showed; her neck, arms and legs provided a stunning pictorial account of her interests and important people. Surprisingly her voice was melodic and tender. 'Sophie is simply craving a life that doesn't exist outside the pages of fiction. She wants a perfect partner, affluence without toil and to be adored without earning respect. She's just bought the lie that the rest of us rejected.'

There was a lot of nodding and murmuring about the truth of such unobtainable things. It made me think of Sophie's actions more sympathetically. Phillip had said she had been a difficult child, always desperately jealous and dissatisfied with wonderful life her parents had provided for her. Her sisters and brother were grateful for the simplicity of their childhoods and the love their parents had obviously shown them. But not Sophie. I wondered if it stemmed from her being the youngest of the three girls and then had been usurped by Phillip's birth; the obviously much longed for son. Had she felt lost because she was just one of Phillip's sisters? Or are some people just born with a grudge? The group seemed to know that she had decided to leave town and head to Sydney with an outsider. The greatest tut-tutting for the fact that she would be leaving her child behind. No-one knew who this person was but there was plenty of speculation. I just hoped the rumours didn't filter through to Max.

The conversation ended with a comment from the tattooed woman who I learned later was called Martha. 'Sarah has her father and her grandparents to love her in the absence of her mother. And her Aunt Lily. She won't be lonely or unloved.'

I warmed to Martha and her wisdom. She was right too. A mother's love was not something that always had to be given by the woman who carried the child. A mother's love could be given by a grandparent or aunt. That had been my experience. The woman who stepped into role and was prepared to put a child first above her own desires was surely more a mother than the one who had the title simply through a biological event. Of course I thought of my own mother and not Sophie. In my kinder moments I imagined that Sophie did love Sarah but that somewhere in her own crazy thinking she had lost sight of the wonderful life she had. Phillip and I would look after both Max and Sarah if Sophie decided to stay away. The whole family would. It seemed inevitable that the community of friends would too.

As I drove back home I kept thinking about mothers. I wondered about Teresa Jepp and whether she had loved her son unconditionally and unfailingly. What was her relationship with Kitty like? Was his mother at the heart of Benedict Jepp's problem?

I called in at Peter and Margaret's on my way. I just wanted to let them know I was okay and that our relationship was not strained because of Sophie's attack. There were no other cars in the drive so I thought I'd be safe to enter the house without causing any kind of problem. I knocked gently on the door and called out. Peter arrived in the hallway first and scooped me up in a bear hug. Margaret joined us. They had both been crying. In all my thinking I'd forgotten the pain that Sophie had obviously caused her parents. They loved their daughter. Her behaviour and their love were inextricable. Unlike other relationships where one party injures another and you can pack up your toys and call it quits, a parent doesn't get to do that. Even the worst human in their worst moment is probably still loved by a parent. There is no divorce procedure for that kind of commitment.

I stayed for dinner. We talked about Phillip and of course the newest Swan-to-be. Margaret seemed to have no resentment that we lied to her about being pregnant. I assured them that I didn't feel anything regarding the fall and reiterated my forgiveness of Sophie. They confirmed their concern for her mental health but couldn't stop her leaving for Sydney. She hadn't said anything to them but her car and belongings had gone this morning. The little girl had stayed with her grandparents and Max slept in his car. By the time he had got back to house she was gone. Max cleaned up the wreckage she had left in the wake of her packing. Sarah hadn't asked for her mother. They would, it seemed, survive even the most painful changes.

Chapter Twelve

The Sunday ceremony was scheduled for a two o'clock start. The family and friends gathered on the beach and Pastor Stan described the day's events as our final farewell to Kitty. Archie and Henry who had travelled from Victoria dressed casually and were going out in one of the smaller row boats and I intended to talk to them at the end of the proceedings. Jean was going out in one of the surf boats carrying the locally made urn that encased Kitty's ashes. Other family, just as Max and I were, would paddle out in our kayaks. There were other means of conveying the grieving to the dropping point, surfboards and stand-up boards, surf rescue craft and a range of inflatables. We looked like, under any other circumstances, an amusing flotilla. The skilled rowers helped the less confident in finding space to make our ceremonial procession look more dignified than a strange race. Jean's hair billowed out in the light breeze that would blow against our backs as we went with the waning tide.

Before we took to our crafts, we sang beautifully. The depth and power of the women's voices created a sense of the spiritual enormity of the moment. The song was not a ditty but a powerful reminder of the importance of love and the pain of goodbye. I felt that my voice sounded strong enough for the lyrics to make sense to the listeners. 'The simple message of the song repeated several times and seemed to resonate with us all. There were tears but generally acceptance.

The rowing was easy as we were not going against the tide. The day stayed calm and with the words of an Irish blessing Jean placed the unglazed urn in the water, watched it bob on the surface and then gently sink several metres to the sea floor. She leaned over the side of the boat and watched the container rock to and fro in rhythm with the tide. Kitty's urn had been especially made for such farewells.

Unglazed, the lightly dried pot would take on water and fill, and then sink allowing the tiny vessel to burrow into the soft sand below. At some point in the distant future the clay would dissolve, and the ashes would filter out. The cycle would be complete.

The silence was accompanied by the sound of the water slapping against the sides of our small crafts and in that quiet I looked towards the beach. One car held an occupant who stared out at the strange sight. She didn't walk down to the beach to hear the song, to participate in the ritual, to feel the palpable loss. Teresa Jepp had turned up to view the ritual as an anomaly; as an event one might describe as implausible to those who did not see it. I wanted to get back to the beach to ask her one more question if she'd let me. My kayak, in my silent musing, bumped gently into the boat in which Henry and Archie sat. I saw the raw sadness on both their faces. Each man placed a white rose over the side of the boat. Both appeared to be praying. Archie finishing with the sign of the cross but not with a traditional amen but with the Latin words *noli timere.* My Latin was rudimentary but I'd studied the poetry of Seamus Heaney and I knew it to mean *don't be afraid.* It seemed both odd and yet beautifully poetic. It would be another question I would want answers for when we got to shore.

We rowed away from Kitty's resting place and there was a flurry of activity as people secured boats and retrieved trailers and trolleys to move the fleet off the beach. It gave me the opportunity to speak to the two men. They appeared more relaxed and a little more open to talking. 'Why did your prayer end with *noli timere?* Was it something you learned at school?' Knowing full well it wasn't a Catholic prayer.

'We went to Catholic school, picking up a bit of Latin was unavoidable,' Archie offered as an explanation.

'Did every prayer end in *don't be afraid?* Were you afraid?' My question remained only partially answered. Henry laughed it off by saying it he usually said at the saying of grace because the food his mother's cooking was so bad. I laughed with them but wanted to pursue a more informative conversation. I wanted to know what Kitty was like as a boy and what in his past had been so difficult that he felt he couldn't be cleansed. 'Kitty left a letter. He sent it to Max. I want to talk to you about the contents of it.'

'Does he say why he killed himself?' A blunt question from Archie followed by what I thought was relief when I confirmed that the letter was cryptic. I asked if I could talk to them later in the day. 'Sorry Lily but we are leaving straight after the service because we don't want to be driving most of the way in the dark.' They both had work in the morning. But Archie gave me his email address and I had to commit it to memory before getting back to the car where I wrote it down.

It was an abrupt goodbye as the two went to speak to Jean before making their way back to their car. I knew I could follow up with them by email but my other "informant" probably wouldn't want to prolong the friendship. As I walked towards her I noticed an older man on the hill, staring at the men as they made their way to the carpark. He lifted his hand and as if he wanted to wave but then seemed to think better of it. I wondered if he found himself there by accident and stopped to watch the sad parade.

Teresa Jepp hadn't moved. She stared out to sea and despite me walking directly towards her, she jumped in surprised to see me at the driver's side window.

'Mrs. Jepp. I was wondering if I could speak to you.' Her face was unreadable. I thought she looked as if she might have been crying but the pinched lips and flaring nostrils made her seem angry, rather than grief-stricken.

'What would we have to talk about?' Teresa Jepp's question was terse and succinct. A sarcastic remark rose in me but a more polite response might bring her around. I thought launching in to ask her about why Kitty took his life might engender more of a response but she beat me to it. 'Why are you so interested in my son, Miss O'Hara? He is dead by his own hand. He has committed a mortal sin in doing so.'

I felt bewildered by her cold demeanour. I could not understand how she could distance herself from her child, who had obviously been in terrible pain for some reason. She was not the sort of woman who would appreciate sentiment or my hedging around the topic, so I commenced with the most important element. I told her about the letter Benedict had sent to Max. Initially she simply regarded me with her pale blue eyes, her brow slightly furrowed.

'It can't bring him back.' Her conversation came when she looked back to sea.

It was a redundant statement but made clearer when she continued in her deadpan voice. 'Nothing good can come from digging up the past.'

My point-of-view was the opposite. Everything good can come from finding an explanation for the behaviour of those who leave us in this way. Understanding Benedict's pain would have an impact on his family and friends; it had the potential to bring them out of the dark and have a better bearing on the future. 'Kitty's past and death are part of the story that will shape Isaiah.' I hoped that appealing to the image of her grandson would bring her back to the discussion. But the woman simply started her car.

'There's no more story here. The last chapter is now being dragged about in a pagan urn on the bottom of the ocean.' She put her car into reverse and started to move backwards almost taking me with her. I stayed close to the driver's window, walking back in an attempt to get a last bit of information out of her.

'Why would Kitty think that Elvis and Ned Kelly had some of the answers?' Momentarily Teresa Jepp stopped reversing.

'You should have asked them.' And before I could ask how that might be possible, she must have read the incomprehension on my face. 'Archie King and Henry Kelly are Elvis and Ned. Ridiculous nicknames. I never could stand it.' She moved her car forward kicking sand and dust up around me. She stopped only momentarily to look once more at the group of dwindling mourners on the beach and beyond to where the waves were mounting a campaign to turn the tide.

I almost had the answer in my grasp but too late today as the men had already left the beach and driven away. They had a piece of this puzzle whether they knew it or not. And sooner rather than later they would have to face the message Kitty left behind. Max would come with me, Mick too. Despite what Kitty's mother thought, the past is never forgotten and when you least expect it, it comes roaring back into life.

Max was down on the beach, almost alone. He had upended the kayaks to drain the water out and to put the wheels on to make them easier to drag through the sand. He cut a lonely figure down by the sea, a man obviously burdened by his collective losses. His shoulders were hunched and he kept rubbing his eyes as if to eliminate the tears that betrayed his sensitivity. Max was very much a physical man driven by his love of action and the outdoors. His work and pastimes all revolved around him doing things and engaging in the labours of building, fishing, surfing and being in the company of men. He was, however, a gentle man with deep feelings for his child and friends. I knew little about his actual family and his life other than that as "friend of Phillip Swan". The incessant banter of the collective Swans and his marriage to Sophie completed the limited knowledge I had. And it wasn't good enough to simply have Phillip as the common thread in our friendship.

When I reached Max I gave him an awkward hug and took my kayak from him to wheel it the last twenty metres to the ute. When we positioned the boats to lift onto the trailer I said, rather cryptically, 'I know something.' Max seemed unmoved but when I revealed that I knew that Elvis and Ned were actually Archie and Henry, he made a move as if to suggest that we abandon the kayaks and chase the two men all the way to the border if necessary. I, however, wanted a more planned approached.

I explained to Max that we would be going on a road trip. We would head south to Eden and then across the border to Mallacoota. Our informants all lived within the area and over a couple of days we would visit the three players we already knew had pieces of the puzzle. Mick Flynn would come with us. His skills as a detective had provided me with exceptional outcomes in the past. He simply seemed to know where to look and who else would be worth talking to. He heard things in conversations that we mere mortals ignored. We needed a clearer picture of the life Benedict Jepp lived before he became Kitty. I felt the more we pushed, particularly on their territory, the closer we would come to unlocking the truth. Kitty's cryptic letter could be deciphered and one day Isaiah would have his story.

Chapter Thirteen

I didn't want Phillip to know that I had ignored his advice and keeping out of other people's business. I knew that recruiting Mick would eventually mean the secret would get out, but Phillip was in one of his uncontactable phases so with any luck I would be able to get away and get back with answers before the information had made its way to Indonesia. Mick was thrilled that Phillip and I were having a baby. He was restrained in his congratulations but even more vigilant in his protection. When he found out about Sophie's attack on me, I became more concerned for her safety than my own. Mick was furious and pushing for the police to be involved. But with Sarah and Max the ones likely to be hurt even more, I encouraged him to drop the notion. None-the-less I did find him checking locks on doors and putting the local police number on speed dial. I wondered if this was what fathers did; blustered, panicked a bit, made things safe and then hovered. I kept smiling at the thought of Phillip emulating this paternal routine in the years to come if any fool thought they could push over our child and get away with it.

I thought of Sophie, and not unkindly. Surely, she missed her little girl. I understood in some way her bid for freedom, but not when everyone else had to pay the price. Peter and Margaret were paying too. Sophie had simply ignored them since her dramatic flight. They were embarrassed and frightened for her mental well-being. She hadn't told them where she was staying or who she was with. I asked Mick if he could find out so that if Sophie needed anything her parents could get to her.

'Now I know your history. You're not going after her are you?' Mick at his hilarious best. He remembered my trip to Sydney to confront a lawyer called Roland Devine, who had in the past done my Aunt Billie a great wrong.

I confirmed that as with Mr. Devine, I would not be committing any acts of violence against my enemies and that the contact was for my in-laws. With that out of the way, the three of us discussed the story and the letter several times. Mick read the letter and made notes on a copy that I'd given him. Knowing what we were looking for was as important as who we were looking for.

'No point in conducting an interview if you haven't got an agenda,' Mick said.

We planned to drive down and stay overnight. This would give us two days in the region and allow us time to see both Archie and Henry on separate occasions. Mick insisted it was always best to talk to witnesses alone so that their version of events was not clouded by something another might say. No two experiences were ever viewed in the same way and it is the specific lens through which one sees something that can often provide a version of the truth. He also liked the surprise tactic—no time for the villains to get together and start concocting a sanitised version of events. Sometimes Mick's forensic mind and his tendency to divide the community into "them" and "us" worried me. I tried to remind him that no-one was a criminal here; we just want to know about Kitty's past. But he was already "on the job".

In my email to Archie King, I didn't confirm that my posse would arrive sooner than later but did ask where it would be best to meet him if I came down to Mallacoota. Luckily, he replied stating he could always be found in the pub. Not drinking—he managed the place. I thought during the conversation he would then be able to tell me where Henry lived. Jean Parrish had provided the details of her mother-in-law's address.

I also intended to surprise Teresa Jepp. She had moved apparently from Gipsy Point to Eden—not the biblical paradise but a fishing town on the far south coast of New South Wales. For some reason, she thought moving fifty kilometres north would be better for her disposition.

The trip should render results. Or at least a more detailed picture of the people Kitty had spent the first part of his life with.

I had booked us three rooms at a lake lodge called Karbeethong. It sat on the shore of the bottom lake just minutes from Mallacoota. The grand house had an amazing history and had shared facilities such as a kitchen and sitting room. I imagined the three of us sitting in front of the fire watching the sun set over the lake, discussing the information we gathered from the two men. We would leave the visit to Teresa Jepp for the trip back. My optimism about the ease with which we would extract Kitty's story was probably misplaced. But my expectation of the region's beauty was not.

I didn't want to travel in Max's ute as the thought of sitting on top of the tool boxes, fishing gear and flotsam and jetsam of his life for four hours did not appeal to me. Taking my car seemed to be a wise choice because the driving could be easily shared with Mick or Max if I felt too tired to cover the 300 kilometres in one stretch. But I needn't have worried about getting tired as it seemed that Max assumed he would take the driving duties, Mick was riding shot gun, and I was ushered into the back seat to be chauffeured south. Despite my immediate desire to argue the outcome I actually relented easily. The thought of sitting back and watching the world go by seemed a pleasant enough way of travelling. The quiet would give me time to think about the questions I wanted to ask Archie and Henry.

I didn't just want to know the wrongs of Kitty's life, I wanted to know the good too. If I was going to be able to construct a proper picture of this lost man, I needed the whole story. Thirty-three years of details was the only way to really know what brought Kitty to his final choice. And "Ned" and "Elvis" obviously held the clues.

Chapter Fourteen

The journey south unfolded uneventfully. The stop for morning coffee and cake at Pambula gave everyone time to stretch and have a quick look at the local shops. I found myself searching for a public toilet. Apparently the bladder gives up even early in pregnancy. I refused the sticky cakes that Mick had bought and sipped on black tea and ate a bite of the impossibly large raisin cookie that Max had chosen. The general queasiness of being pregnant had left me, but the thought of sugary food really turned my stomach. As had my appetite for coffee and dairy products. Apparently, cravings were not real but none-the-less I had a strange hankering for Asian food, particularly Thai noodles with handfuls of coriander and basil. Hardly on the menu in any bakery on the south coast.

Back on the road it became clear that the landscape was changing. The highway lay between the Howe Range that kept the view of the sea hidden, and the lower mountains of the Kosciuszko National Park. As the border between the two states got nearer the thickening density of the cool temperate rainforest became apparent. The trees formed a wall of green on both sides of the road and what lay beyond was uncertain. The Croajingolong National Park, through which the road meandered, was home to thousands of unique species of trees and plants. The area's traditional owners, the Gunaikurnai people, had words for the place that meant belonging to the east.

The area was ruggedly beautiful and yet it felt as if danger threatened if one should wander away from the bitumen road. The forest went all the way to the coast, punctuated by dark lakes and barely moving tributaries. Mallacoota and Gipsy Point, our destinations, lay east of the highway. The towns were built at the end of roads and possible to miss if you simply kept to the highway. One road in and the same road out.

I must have dozed off as the turn onto Mallacoota Road woke me with a bit of a jolt. The town was only twenty minutes away. Max pointed out the road on the left which would later take us out to Gipsy Point. The local cemetery had been built right on the corner, an interesting place for the dead to watch the holiday makers coming and going. The road wound its way through a more rural landscape and finished at the town that perched above the sea's entrance to the lake. The village itself was self-contained and quiet time of the year. The size of the caravan park and camping ground spoke of its popularity in the summer months. The combination of beach and lakes brought all water sport fanatics, fishing folks and boat enthusiasts here in droves from Christmas to the end of the school holidays. Warm and early Easter breaks no doubt saw the hordes of holiday-makers return for the last sunny weeks of the year.

Despite the substantial morning tea, Mick and Max were ready for lunch. Lucy's Noodles our first stop. Surprisingly I could satisfy my cravings with a Thai beef salad before we ambushed Archie King at the Mallacoota Hotel, just across the road from the little restaurant. On the short walk Mick suggested that our discussion should start with general questions about the town. He had this notion that people said more if they weren't on the back foot from the outset of a conversation. And most people like to talk about the places they lived in.

The public bar was fairly quiet, a few locals and one or two older tourists. The lounge and bistro were empty, but the tables had been laid for the evening trade. Our appearance seemed to warrant a little attention and a friendly barmaid asked us what we wanted. Two beers, a sad sparkling mineral water and a question— 'Is your boss about?'

Archie arrived at the same time as the drinks. He'd been in the kitchen with the chef checking the orders, his surprise evident, his apprehension more so. 'Well when you said you might come down, I didn't think you meant immediately.' His attempt to be light-hearted did not reflect in his eyes. However, Archie graciously invited us into the unoccupied lounge where the fire had just been lit. The leather sofas arranged in front of the enormous fireplace seemed an appropriate place to grill the man for information. Initially he stood facing the fire, prodding it a little, adjusting the weighty log that had been added to the red-hot kindling.

Mick started the conversation. 'Have you always lived here Archie? It's a beautiful place.'

It seems the minute you ask an easy question the information flows. The Kings had lived in the area for at least four generations. They had a small farm further south but kept a holiday shack on the lake since his great-grandfather's time. While they were cattle farmers, they were also fishermen. Archie's father, Kevin King, sold the farm after his wife died. 'I went to university in Melbourne and my sister moved to London with her husband. Neither me or Amanda wanted to run a farm, and Dad had lost the will to do so.' He died a few years later and Archie for some reason returned from Melbourne, renovated the shack and took on running the pub. 'I'm an accountant but hated the work. Managing the pub came easily as I have a good head for business and don't mind the odd beer or two.'

'And school?' I asked.

'Well it was school, does anybody love it?' Archie tried to laugh but again the spirit of his words failed to take the sadness out of his face. 'St. Finbar's is closed now. There were only a few classes after us who made it to Year 10.' He sat down, giving the impression of being more resolved to fill in some details. The school only ran classes from Years 1-10. To complete the final years of high school, all students had to go to the local public school or to boarding colleges in or close to Melbourne. Archie and Henry went to the local school; Kitty went to Bairnsdale and stayed with an aunt, so he could continue in a Catholic school. Apparently, Teresa wouldn't have her son tainted by rubbing shoulders with the heathens in public education. As Archie said this, I could actually see Kitty's mother saying those words. It must have made her wildly popular in the town.

Max went to the bar for more beer and a lemon squash. Archie joined the post lunch drinkers with a bourbon and dry. He directed the staff not to charge Max for the drinks. He was either warming to us or keen to get our questions answered and to get us moving. He continued his story about the friendship between the three boys. St. Finbar's was apparently run by lay staff. The days of religious orders having enough brothers and priests or nuns to run schools were long gone. Even in the 1970s when the boys were at school. The local priest ran the parish but not the school. Archie wasn't Catholic; the staff tended to treat him with contempt because he was not baptised. Generally the teachers were seemingly brutal to all the kids not just him. 'But some of them were total nutters. They didn't mind using the cane on boys like us. They thought we were all sinners with minds that would be diverted from dirty thoughts by violence.'

But Henry and Kitty had been altar boys, along with another young fellow in the year below them. 'We thought they would be treated a little better than the rest of us.' Apparently, Kitty was the brightest of them. Kitty excelled at Maths but loved reading and writing too. He won competitions and actually won an academic bursary to study in Melbourne. But his mother didn't let him go.' Apparently, he could sing and act and had the lead in the school plays that were held every year. Every girl in town loved BKJ. Benedict Kitt Jepp. He was the star of the town and everyone expected great things of him. 'But it doesn't always work out that way.' Benedict Kitt Jepp. Kitty. It all made some sense now why his mates called him that.

Archie made us all laugh with tales of the boys making off with the altar wine so that they could make the school chickens drink it. Their English teacher caught them. She had been less concerned about their theft of sacred wine and more outraged by their animal cruelty. She was the only female on staff and didn't believe in the thrashings meted out by her male colleagues, so she kept their transgression a secret. They hadn't even thought about being cruel, they were experimenting to see if they could get wine flavoured red eggs. He told stories about the fishing and camping expeditions, the hours of swimming, cycling, surfing and bushwalking. Sundays were sacrosanct, and the two boys had to be in church, home for lunch and indoors for studying. But every Saturday and holiday was time for Ned Kelly, Elvis and Bennie to engage in what seemed like a boy's own adventure story.

'So what happened? Why did Kitty, sorry Bennie, disappear from your lives?' Another of my questions that took the glee from Archie's face.

'What always happens. You have to grow up.'

When the school shut up shop and the boys had to move on, it was clear that Kitty would move to Bairnsdale. 'It was strange, because in the end he didn't even fight it. It was like he wanted to go.' And it did seem strange that a boy who had great friends and a life full of outdoor activity would acquiesce and move to an unfamiliar life.

'So who did the beatings at St. Finbar's?' Mick got us back on track and following a line of thought not lost on us.

Archie's answer fuelled the notion that life was not all boyish escapades and tearaway fun. He took a long drink and drained his glass. Momentarily he closed his eyes, sighed and drew forth information he had all but forgotten. Hitting boys seemed to be the only disciplinary strategy employed. 'We got caned for poor work, no homework, running too fast, moving too slow, eye-rolling, fighting, rudeness. Sometimes for irreverent behaviour. Most of the time for blasphemy. You know shouting Jesus Christ couldn't always be passed off as spontaneous prayer.' Archie smiled and we obligingly laughed. Kitty and Henry, however, apparently copped the worst of it along with a younger boy called Miles. It seemed that Archie's indiscretions were expected, and despite being told that he wasn't worth saving still got the strap regularly.

Finally Archie answered Mick's question. 'The Rottweiler was a complete bastard.' Mick's usual technique of waiting and expecting more information was rewarded by a chilling description of a teacher more suited to a Dicken's novel than a rural Australian school. The Rottweiler, an obviously suitable nickname for the discipline master. His real name was Roger Wheeler; the alias came not only because of his vicious character but a clever play on his name. Nominative determinism if ever I'd heard it. The name reflected his job and his nature. Mr. Wheeler allegedly strode the playground seeking the indiscrete child who might be engaging in some level of poor behaviour. He pulled boys by their ears off the playground to stand with their toes and noses touching the wall outside his classroom. Frequently used the public address system to call reprobates to his office where he would make them wait for an hour or more before punishing them for offences never fully explained. The cane, as a discipline method, was abolished in most schools by the late 1980s. But Kitty and his mates attended St. Finbar's from about 1974 to 1984 and corporal punishment was still being practised, particularly in private schools. Most teachers realised that it was barbaric and unsuitable as a means to modify behaviour but some sadists like the power and inciting the fear. Roger Wheeler no doubt the latter kind.

'He used to cane the hands and legs. But I'd seen Henry and Bennie's bodies after a session with him. He had a bad aim, apparently, because the two of them often had welts on their bums and backs.' Archie rubbed his eyes wearily. 'We all wanted him to die.'

I couldn't help but prod Archie's memory. 'What did the teachers do about him? And did Teresa Jepp just let this happen? And Henry's parents, didn't they say something?'

It seemed that no-one complained, not the families anyway. Apparently a few teachers made it known that they disapproved of the discipline master's methods. Their English teacher, Connie Harlow, always attempted to circumvent sending boys to him. The drunken chicken incident was just the tip of the iceberg. Miss Harlow wouldn't write up any of the boys for classroom infractions. She became particularly protective of Bennie and Henry. And the younger boy Miles. Archie's face softened when he spoke of Miss Harlow. It appeared that she provided some sort of haven for the victims of The Rottweiler. 'We all had a mad crush on Miss Harlow. Her class became an oasis. She was the calm when everywhere else was cruel.'

I toyed with asking why Bennie/Kitty was a special victim of the discipline fanatic given the academic and creative gifts he displayed.

'The altar boys got the worst of it. Wheeler was an acolyte in the church and he was responsible for the training of the servers and preparation for Masses.' I thought Archie had read my mind. 'He spent a lot of time with the three of them.' Archie also mentioned the parish priest. 'He was a gentle man but not even he had control of The Rottweiler.'

Silence. The four of us momentarily lost in the unspoken impressions of Archie's words. A violent man left alone with frightened children did not conjure a story of hope. And where were the adults who through their own inaction seemed to condone his methodology in beating boys into contrite and penitent believers. Archie had not finished though. He had another thing to say and he made us wait. He adjusted the log on the fire, straightened up a table that did not need straightening, and then stood with his back to us. 'Something happened. I don't know what.' He was now wound and coiled, his face red, and angry tears appeared in his eyes.

I held my breath, as did Max and Mick.

Archie repeated, 'I don't know what happened. But someone burned The Rottweiler's house down in the middle of the night.'

It was tempting to think that this might have been a crime committed by angry little boys whose bodies had been bruised by an unreasonable and erratic despot. It may have been the truth Kitty alluded to in his letter. I wondered if the boys had actually killed Wheeler.

'He lived. Wasn't home when the blaze went up.'

Chapter Fifteen

Archie was spent. He had to work and left us at the fire. He'd reserved a table for us if we wanted to come back for dinner. The meal would be his shout. 'The least I can do for Bennie's friends.'

Of course Max had only known Benedict Jepp for the last seventeen years of the man's life. Not the piece that Archie had given us. Not the names that Mick had been furiously writing down on his notepad. Two names at least to follow up. Roger Wheeler and Connie Harlow. Both might be dead of course, but probably unlikely given Archie's vague description of their ages at the time they worked at the school. There would be some searching to find their whereabouts, but no-one can really disappear anymore. Everyone leaves a trail and if someone wants to find you, then you will be found. Particularly, if they're not hiding.

The drive and the heavy conversation left me weary. We drove out to Karbeethong Lodge and I was thrilled to find that it looked even better than it did on the website. Its deep sweeping lawn drew the eye to lake's shore and across the water to the Howe Range. The long and low building had a veranda that stretched across its length. The proprietor was friendly and happy to see visitors and asked lots of questions about why the three of us were in town. We said we had come to see some people we knew. Nothing else was forthcoming so he explained how the lodge worked. The kitchen and lounge were shared spaces and no-one else was here, so he'd light the fire for us at about 5 o'clock and then we could keep it going until we went to bed. He'd put us in the three rooms closest to the main area. Each had a bathroom, double bed, and heater. And a view of the lake. Despite the dropping temperature, sitting on the veranda and watching the sun set seemed to be the best way to unwind. Max made us coffee and tea and the three of us sat in relative quiet as the winter sun made its descent into the lake. The moon rose early and replaced the warm sunlight with cold beams that glowed on the still water. Karbeethong—it meant light shining on the water. It could not have been more precise in its description.

We had a quick dinner at the pub. Archie was nowhere to be seen but true to his word, we did not have to pay for dinner. I drove back to the lodge via the bottle shop; it was apparently a red wine night. I didn't mind not drinking—it wasn't something I did often enough to really miss and I was more than happy to get my friends safely back to the warm fire that had been burning for a couple of hours before we got there.

The lounge was warm and comfortable right beside the fire. The bay windows couldn't be closed to the night as the lack of curtains let in a certain chill that you felt if you moved away from the radiant heat of the flames. I had tea while the men opened the first bottle of red. I knew the conversation would be a dissection of the afternoon's encounter, but I was happy to simply take in the surroundings while we all settled.

Mick started with a question. 'What are you thinking about this Roger Wheeler then?'

'Total bastard!' Max's response hardly incorrect, but I felt that there was something more sinister than just him simply being mean. After all I'd been taught by some insensitive, sarcastic and uncaring individuals but I never felt afraid of them. Never thought that their cruel words indicated a darker purpose. But a man who regularly beat children had to have been a special kind of bastard.

'Someone hated him enough to burn his house down.' Mick would be following this up in the morning. The local paper, police and library that might offer up a few details about the fire. It appeared from Archie's version that it was definitely arson and that Wheeler had survived. I wondered if he had intentionally or accidently linked the two boys' treatment at the hands of the discipline master and the fire. It certainly seemed a possible cause and effect. I thought further about Kitty's letter to Max. 'Max do you think that the fire was the *truth* in Kitty's letter?' In answer to my question Max just shrugged his shoulders.

'Maybe if it was about to become public', he added.' But no one died so it wasn't such a big deal would it?'

'Would a teenager's act of revenge be enough for a man to take his own life? Arson is a serious crime. But he was just a kid when it happened' Mick said. The discussion took the men into the second bottle of wine. They were getting off topic when Max started listing whose house he'd burn down if he could.

While I knew we were together to unravel the mystery of Kitty's suicide, Max had led me to my other agenda. To get to know the backstory of both Max and Mick. I had snippets and had put together a half story, but I really wanted more. 'Max what were you like as a kid?' A safe enough question.

'I was a bit wild. Hated school.' Max was a little drunk—beer at lunch, wine with dinner, and a bottle by the fire had him loose and unguarded. 'But had Swannie!' My husband had always been Max's best friend. And Max's home life? He was raised by his mother after they had escaped an abusive drunken father. 'Mum was nearly as bad.' And so Max's story began to unfold. The father apparently left to work on the north coast and never returned. 'He broke Mum's nose that Saturday night, kicked me so hard he cracked my ribs.' Max's tone as he recalled the violence of his father remained calm. 'While we were bawling our eyes out, he packed his bag and left.' Max finished off the wine in his glass. 'It was a relief in one way, no more beatings, but there was also no more money.'

Karen, his mother, lay in bed for weeks according to Max until Margaret Swan turned up and brought food. She cleaned the place, got Karen out of bed and down to social security to apply for the dole. Max hadn't been to school while Karen refused to leave her bed, so Margaret cleaned him up, put him in one of Phillip's uniforms, cut his hair, bought him shoes and drove him to school. For weeks Margaret held them together until Karen realised that she was on her own and that Max needed at least one functioning parent. But the realisation was long in coming. Max's mother had a history of mental illness and despite everything her friends tried to do for her, Karen had to be hospitalised for a period of time. In the absence of a parent, the Swans took Max in and even fought off an attempt by community services to put him in foster care. 'I loved Swannie's mum. Still do'

Despite the sadness of his mother's illness and his father's callous abandonment, the six months he spent living with Phillip and the Swans was the happiest time of his childhood. 'It's amazing what a predictable routine does for kid. I knew that I'd get fed at six and be up at seven. That I'd have clean clothes and expected to do my homework. No-one shouted much except for the girls, and Phil was always there.' So something steady and unswerving was the key to child rearing. I'd try to remember that.

Max's face had become rosy from the fire and the wine but it also finally relaxed. He had been through quite an ordeal in the last few weeks. His marriage was over, and he'd lost a friend. He had a complicated past, and the future looked difficult as he was setting out to be a single parent to Sarah. I'm sure his own childhood experiences weighed heavily on him. He had been cast aside by a selfish parent and now his wife was doing the same to his little girl. Ironically the Swan family came to the rescue again. Max and Sarah would have stability and unfailing love from all of us. The tribe would rally. And Margaret would make sure no one went hungry.

'The curse of the absent father. Sounds like an Agatha Christie novel.' Mick's voice brought me out of my projections for the Swan clan.

Of course Mick had been that absent father. I'd forgotten about the first time I met him and how he'd mentioned his failed marriage and disconnection with his girls. The fire and the wine had combined to overheat him, and he had moved over to the cooler side of the room. He looked clammy and flushed and I worried that we upset him with the talk about fathers.

He closed his eyes for a moment and said, 'I never stop missing my daughters.' With the wine on board, Mick talked about his early life as a young cop. He graciously skirted around my father's case which had Mick about to charge him with murdering my mother and brother back in 1975. My father absented himself from the role by taking his own life. Until I met Mick and some of my parents' friends, I didn't understand that the O'Hara deaths had such a deep impact on others.

For Mick it was an immersion in this case, and others that had distanced him from his wife and daughters. 'The drinking and nights I didn't come home didn't help.' In those days he had been working homicide for a few years. He was ambitious and in his own words, thoughtless. His daughters were about nine and seven when his marriage fell apart. I knew that one of his girls had died. The other had disappeared. His wife Angela had barely spoken to him in the twenty-nine years since they separated. They came together to bury Belinda, their youngest, in 1986 after she had accidently—or deliberately—overdosed in some ratty apartment in north Canberra. She had been hard to manage from the time she turned twelve and had been in and out of school until about fifteen when she dropped out completely. Petty theft, affray and drug related charges saw her have a stint in Quamby Youth Detention Centre to assist with rehabilitating her. But the six months in the institution just gave her access to a more dangerous type of criminal. If she'd lived a little beyond her eighteenth birthday, she would have faced real prison time. It would have been a terrible situation for a police officer trying to move up the ranks.

Belinda Flynn's life was a brief and tempestuous one. She apparently had expected that her father, a detective, would be able to help her when she got into trouble. To his obvious regret, he did not. Mick had thought that the shock of incarceration would wake her up and frighten her into getting back to school and making something of her life. He had not seen his little girl for about three years until he had to identify her body at the Kingston Morgue. She was ruined by the drugs; thin, translucent, barely recognisable. But his child none-the-less.

'Angela didn't come to help me identify her. She waited at home for me to confirm that Belinda was actually dead. Our oldest daughter, Sandra, waited with Ange' It must have been a journey Mick would have given anything to avoid. When he arrived at his ex-wife's home in Belconnen 'I couldn't go in for about twenty minutes. I sat in the car crying for the pain I knew I had to deliver. To her and my twenty-year-old daughter I barely knew. I loved them.' Mick said that he felt a hundred years old as he dragged himself towards that front door. 'A mother doesn't ever need the words—she just knew that Belinda was dead. She threw herself into my arms and screamed.' But his oldest daughter wouldn't come near him. Sandra stood in the hallway and witnessed her parents' grief-stricken reunion. 'She was the same at the funeral. Distant and emotionless. I'd tried to talk to her and explain what had happened to me, to us.' He had to stop there. He had desperately wanted to make Sandra understand that he was sorry for staying away. 'I blamed myself for Belinda's death. Told her I knew I was weak but Sandra remained impassive, totally unmoved. The only words she said were, 'I'm leaving. Don't try to find me. I'll never forgive you and I don't love you.' The angry words of a bewildered young woman, barely out of her teens, punished the people she held responsible for her pain. It was understandable then but it didn't really explain why she chose to continue hurting them.

And soon after the funeral, Sandra left Canberra and broke off ties with both her mother and father. Allegedly unheard of since.

'Mick, it's not like you not to be able to track down someone's whereabouts.' I suspected I knew the answer before he spoke again.

'I didn't say I didn't know where she lived.'

Of course, he knew where she was. Sandra had moved to Queensland. She had at first lived in a group house with some other young people. She started studying nursing at twenty-one and moved in with a man she eventually married a few years later and divorced soon after. Sandra still lived in North Tambourine Mountain with her second husband and two boys. So Mick was a grandfather. I wondered if Sandra had ever told them about her parents or her sister. She would be nearly forty, if I had the maths right. 'Surely it's time to make peace Mick. He looked at the bottom of glass. It made me wonder what Angela had done to make Sandra so angry with her. How could it all be put back together before it was too late?

These questions had to go unanswered for a time. We had been listening and talking for hours, the fire had died down and the room started to get cold. It was just after midnight and the next day would be long. And at least two of us would be head-achy for a good part of it. I needed water and in the few minutes I was in the kitchen Mick wandered off to his room. Max had fallen asleep in his chair and lightly snored. I sat opposite him and noticed that when he was not full of angst, Max had a handsome face. His fringe fell over his closed eyes and mouth had relaxed into a natural pout. Recently he had been so strained that he looked older than thirty-six. But in his boozy slump he looked like a boy.

I reached out to push his fringe out of his eyes and to wake him so that he could make his way to bed. As I touched his face, his eyes opened. 'You fell asleep Max. Time for bed.'

He let me help him up and, with his arm around my shoulders, we walked out into the cold night to make the short walk to our rooms. I shivered as the night breeze contrasted heavily with the fire-warmed lounge. Max hugged me closer. 'If you're cold I could sleep with you.'

I was taken aback by what seemed to be the most inappropriate suggestion. And a little guilty that I'd been thinking about what a handsome man he was.

'I'm just lonely, Lil. I miss the thought of having someone beside me.' He really was a needy child.

'Well it's not going to be me, Max. Try explaining it to Phillip that we shared a bed because I was cold, and you were lonely. Not happening.'

Max staggered to the next room. He struggled with his key, blew me a kiss and noisily bumped his way around in the darkness of his room. I imagined that he didn't brush his teeth or struggle out of his clothes. I smiled at his offer. I wondered if Phillip might find it funny. Perhaps it was another little secret between Max and me. Despite the cold and my tiredness I wasn't ready for bed. The night had become clear and starry. The moon that had made its appearance early in the evening developed into a bold disc of light that illuminated a path across the lake. I walked down the steps to the gravel pathway and over to the lawn. At the edge of the garden was a drop to the road below. A steep, but negotiable track led to the jetty that formed a dog-legged platform out into the water.

The day had been full of stories. None of them happy. Mick's loss of his family, Max's abandonment, and the growing picture of something horrible in Kitty's past. I was almost afraid of what else might be revealed in the coming day. Henry Kelly possessed a puzzle piece that would make clear what happened at that school. Archie remained the only a witness to the effects it had on the three little boys who seemed to be singled out for The Rottweiler's attacks. And who was Miles? What happened to him? The teacher and the priest were also players in the unfolding of Kitty's story. Not to mention his mother. I felt some anxiety about seeing her tomorrow. Anxious that she would slam the door in my face and that I wouldn't get to talk about Roger Wheeler or the fire.

The temperature over the water dropped a few degrees lower but the sounds of the night enticed me to walk on. The moored boats barely bobbed as the lake was so still. But each hull made the occasional plop as the water rippled around them. Sleeping pelicans propped on pylons beside the walkway. They were impossibly balanced on the tall wooden posts that seemed to have little purpose except to host the large billed birds through the night. The trees made no sound. Tiny rustlings erupted intermittently as nocturnal wildlife made its way under the brush. It seemed that in the dark our other senses heightened; our sixth sense too. Somewhere along the dark shore I felt a pair of eyes trained on me. Scouring the boardwalk that ran south to the township, I could make out the shape of a person who stood, not moving at all. A lone female figure standing on the jetty after midnight might have caught the attention of a resident returning home or a late-night dog walker. Despite the brightness of the moon, I could not make out the shape as a man or woman. But my peering in his or her direction made the figure step back into the shadow of the trees. It unnerved me even though the person's actions were most likely as innocent as my own. Someone just enjoying the crisp late-night air, sleepless because the day had been too full. But then he shouted, 'Go home!' And it seemed more personal.

Regardless of his motive, I felt vulnerable trapped at the end of the jetty with just the pelicans for company, so took off at a pace across the worn planks. Knowing my less-than-agile running style I feared that in my haste, I might fall into the water and drown. I sensed the figure, that I knew was male from the voice, slowly headed my way in the shadows and that he might cut me off before I got back to the path that led to the lodge's front lawn. So I headed north to the access road that went past the houses and eventually led to the front gate of Karbeethong. I'm not a runner at the best of times but in the dark, a little pregnant and totally disorientated, I became breathless within a minute. Fear, however, was my ally. The adrenalin pumped and within a few minutes I made it to the grounds and within seconds got to the veranda. It was at that point that my non-athleticism reappeared, I tripped on the first step and landed heavily making a strange squealing noise in the process. My shin was on fire from the impact and my breathing laboured from the effort of the run. The noise could have woken the dead.

It didn't but it did rouse Max from his stupor. He appeared at his door, as I'd predicted fully clothed and bewildered. 'What are doing Lily? Jesus; are you okay?'

As the explanation tumbled out, even I felt I'd over-reacted. It was, as Max pointed out, someone who thought I might be up to no good with the fishing boats. 'Someone could have thought you were a kid doing something he shouldn't.' In the dark it might have been possible to mistake me for a teenager. I wore jeans and a hoodie. I felt foolish for being so frightened and couldn't quite let go of the fact that the unknown figure was more threatening than a local worried about graffiti. Max had taken my key and pushed me into my room. He said he'd wait until I'd settle down. I thought a shower might relax me and at least rinse off the sweat I'd broken into during my midnight sprint. When I'd finished with washing, teeth cleaning and the whole face routine I'd recently adopted, I was definitely ready for sleep. Max's vigil had come to end by him falling asleep on top of the bed. At least he only lay on one side and completely clothed. I had no intention of waking him and making him go back to his room. I covered him with the spare blanket and squeezed under the duvet into the space he'd left. With the lights off, Max's deep breathing and the quietness of the night returned, I slept. Max's suggestion had, by default, come about.

By six o'clock I woke. Max had gone and the sun was threatening to appear. Breakfast provided by the lodge could be served from seven. I needed a hot drink and a cold pack for my banged-up shin. I showered and dressed and made my way into the main building. The world was silent. With the tea made, I sat in the dining room, watched the light return to the lake and wondered about my overreaction last night.

My phone went off. Max's text— "You snore and fart in your sleep!" I couldn't help but laugh. My hero was so juvenile and it required an equally immature response. "How could you hear my noises over your own? You farted so loud it almost broke my hip."

I heard him laugh from the veranda. Mick followed asking 'What's so funny?' Last night's escapades would remain unexplained. My shin, however, was evidence of my stupidity and despite the pain, I'd keep it to myself. As we ate, we further refined the plan. 'We will drop you in town Mick, so you can follow up on the fire and make enquiries about the three people we learned about from Archie. The two of us will drive out to Gipsy Point to see Henry Kelly.' With these two things done we would drive back across the border to Eden, so I could see Teresa Jepp, we could lunch at the wharf and then drive home and be back in time for dinner. There would be other people to talk to and we might just find that we would be back in Mallacoota if our other witnesses were still in this district. But for now, we had two important stories to try and elicit from possibly reluctant players.

Henry Kelly, aka Ned, knew some truth that Kitty referred to in his final letter. From my two meetings with him, he seemed to be a fragile kind of man. He had been nervous and a little furtive at the funeral. Of course it could simply have been grief and being around strangers, but Henry had a damaged look. He seemed to be a man who might have lived his life looking back over his shoulder. Perhaps I'd start my questioning with the line, *"noli timere"*. Don't be afraid.

Chapter Sixteen

We dropped Mick at the pub. Not that it was open, or that he needed a drink, but it was a central spot from which he could walk to each of his proposed destinations. I drove us out the main road back to Gipsy Point. The turnoff was fourteen kilometres from Mallacoota. The bleak cemetery marked the intersection. I had thought that on the way back we might stop and look. I've always been drawn to these isolated graveyards in small towns, after all, my family occupied a considerable swathe of the one in Bungendore. A place I must get back to in the coming weeks.

Max was a bundle of nervous energy, a little hung-over, shy about discussing us sharing my bed the night before. He also seemed eager to talk to Henry Kelly. I reminded him of Mick's methodology to leave questions hanging and not to be too quick to prompt. The silence between a question being asked and the answer that was given was sometimes as profound as that answer. It was a time of neural storming when the witness tried to work out the right answer when they don't always want the truth to come out. The problem would be keeping Max quiet.

Deep thickets of pristine forest lined the Gipsy Point Road and rang incessantly with the trill of bellbirds calling back and forth creating a wall of sound. It was a strange experience to be engulfed in so much high-pitched noise, in a place that one might expect to be hushed. The three kilometres from the cemetery to the river appeared almost to be a portal to another place, another realm. A short distance but a world cut off from the rest of the country. Beautiful, serene, and surreal. The bird noise could have been a welcoming or a warning.

This again, was a one road in and out hamlet. Several homes nestled among the trees and at the road's end a small resort and the boat ramp had been built. Moored at the jetty was a small riverboat that took wilderness tours and could be hired for fishing expeditions. The boat, "The Ned Kelly" had to be Henry's boat.

I parked the car right beside the river. Max and I had hoped that by asking for the boat's owner at the hotel, we would easily be able to find Henry. But the bush telegraph had been working overtime and Archie had obviously told him to expect us. Henry sat at the picnic table in front of the jetty, pouring himself a drink, possibly coffee, from a very large thermos. As we approached, he poured two more and motioned to us to come over.

He greeted us by thanking us for our part in Benedict's funeral. He thought it a fitting send off. 'I loved your singing. Bennie loved music.' He looked tired. I've never seen someone look so tired. His skin was grey and the bags under his eyes were blue and padded. Henry looked like a man under duress and I realised that a gentle approach might be needed. Max obviously intuited my feelings as he put his hand on the man's shoulder and patted him softly. 'It's a tough time losing a mate.' Of course Max was also grieving for Kitty and all that had been lost.

'You mentioned a letter. What did he say?' Henry slurred his words; from tiredness or emotion, I couldn't tell. But I had deep suspicions that it might have been alcohol and lots of it that had contributed to Henry's condition.

So Henry led with a question of his own. There was no use hedging the issue so I simply passed a copy to him. He read in silence for a few minutes and then put his head down on the table. He seemed to have fallen into a deep sleep. If it wasn't for the slight shuddering of his shoulders that indicated the weighty emotional battle going on inside him, Henry Kelly might simply have died right there on the spot. So we waited in the throng of bird calls, the slap of the Wallagaraugh River on the side of his boat until he recovered enough to talk.

'*Noli timere*, Henry. Don't be afraid. Whatever you can tell us to help make sense of all this might help you too.' I hoped my voice would encourage him to relax. 'We know from Archie that the discipline master at St. Finbar's had been a brutal man. Can you tell us about him?'

It was a question he didn't immediately answer but I wasn't going to interrupt Henry once he started talking. He talked about the house Benedict and Mrs. Jepp lived in when they were here in the district.

'Up there. That's where they move to.' He pointed to the hill above the boat ramp where a simple timber home stood. The view of the river and hills would have been spectacular from the back windows. 'No-one's lived there permanently since she sold the house about ten years ago' By *she* I assumed he meant Teresa Jepp. It seemed to be a waste of the natural spectacle of the area. 'You know the Jepps didn't always live out here at Gipsy Point. Benedict's life started in the town. Rumour had it that Teresa had moved them out to the Gippsland area to get away from a drunken husband.' Henry had another long pause. Apparently according to the same rumour mill, she had been living somewhere on the Mornington Peninsula, possibly Crib Point. 'Bennie never mentioned his old man but once said he thought the man was dead. No one confirmed one way or the other and we certainly weren't going to ask the old bag.'

The three friends had met at kindergarten and went at school together until the college shut up shop when the boys all finished Year 10. They were 15. When Teresa moved into the house at Gipsy Point, she drove Benedict to school each day and he came back on the bus and walked the three kilometres home. If it rained, his mother met him at the cemetery. When he was older, he rode his bike to and from school. On the weekends, she let him take his little tinnie and wend his way down the river, through the narrows and tie up at Stingray Point. 'We would then spend the days together putting around Rabbit or Horse Island, or up to Cemetery Bight and walk up to the Spotted Dog Mine. Once we had tried panning for gold. The long summers were times for planning'. It had been their plan to get out of town as rich men and never look back.

'So you wanted to get out of Mallacoota?' Max's question led Henry closer to our real purpose.

'Get out of *Coota*? Man we couldn't wait.' The place had held little joy for the boys according to Henry. Yet much of what both he and Archie described, the outdoor life seemed Tom Sawyer-like. A life on the lake, adventure, goldmines, fishing and freedom. But of course all young people want to escape the confines of the fishbowls they grow up in. Small towns can hardly offer the young much more than the jobs their old man did and most go away to study and are called to the cities where the action is.

'Did you get out, Henry? Archie went to Melbourne. Kitty further north.'

Henry turned to look out at the river.

The water was so still and the day so bright that it was hard to tell where the land ended and the reflection began. It took ages for him to start talking again.

'I couldn't leave.'

Apparently, Henry's parents ran a fishing boat and it they expected Henry and his two older brothers to take over the business. But one brother joined the army and the other married a musician and decided a life on the road was better than 4am starts and a life of smelling like fish. Henry was obliged to stay particularly after his father's accident that saw him lose his hand. A one-armed fisherman was something of a business liability. While the others got out of *Coota*, Henry had to stay. He said all of this without bitterness, just matter-of-factly. 'Someone had to help my old man or the business would go under and we would have lost everything.'

Things changed too. He met Tilly Harper when she worked at the caravan park one summer holiday. They fell in love and married the following summer. 'We have a daughter, Jasmine. She's beautiful like her mum.' Things, however, did not go well. The wife left him for a real estate agent and moved with the child to Wollongong. He barely saw Jasmine and hadn't for a year. She would turn ten in December and didn't remember him particularly well. He said this without any particular regret. It seemed that Henry was almost relieved that they were out of his life. It was if he expected it to be a disaster. 'It's less complicated not being married.'

I couldn't help but notice the hurt in Max's face. It might be less complicated for the adults but not so much for the child. And not so much when it was new. Max probably shouldn't have come south to do this but, as usual, my realisation came way too late. I also knew that trying to leave him behind would have caused a ruckus. It was a bit of no-win situation.

I needed to steer Henry back to events alluded to in Kitty's letter. I wondered if the mention of Roger Wheeler might redirect him.

'Did you have a lot to do with Roger Wheeler when you were at school? Did he beat you too?' A blunt reminder of the information we were after. Henry turned around and stared at me. His red eyes sat deep in his fatigued, flushed face. I was now quite sure Henry was drinking heavily, He had that worn-down, aged look of someone who lived too close to the bottle.

'Did the Rottweiler beat me? That bastard beat everyone. He couldn't keep his hands off us.' Henry went down to the boat and climbed on board. He rattled around in the cabin for several minutes and came out with a bottle of vodka.

My suspicions confirmed. Few people crack open the heavy stuff before 10 in the morning.

As if trying to disgust us into leaving, Henry took a long a deliberate swig straight from the bottle. 'If I have to talk about him, I'll need to be numb.' And then he added almost to himself, 'I hate that bastard.'

In an attempt to reconnect with pre-vodka Henry, we climbed over the rail and sat under the cover in the back of his boat. I wanted him to realise that we weren't going to be driven away so easily. I tried again when the belligerence waned. 'What happened, Henry?'

To further steel himself, he took a huge mouthful straight from the bottle. The thought of the alcohol burning its way down his throat made me almost gag. It took practice to be able to drink like that. I had assumed by his actions that Henry was addicted. Being an alcoholic would not only explain the vodka, but also the look of him. He was ruined.

I wasn't so naive to not have been making my own connections between Archie's information, Kitty's death and the violence of Roger Wheeler. These little boys had been terrorised by a man who might have had other inclinations. The fact that the welts had been on their legs and bottoms might suggest some sexual overtones. But was there more than just the thrashings? There had been allegations made for years about abuse occurring in religious and non-religious institutions. A call for a Royal Commission in Australia had started in the 1990s to follow along the lines of the Irish government commission into child abuse. This dark and terrible injustice against children and vulnerable people had become a public conversation but nowhere near resolved. What might have happened to the altar boys at St. Finbar's might just be a part of that revelation. I was unsure of my own preparedness to cope with the information.

Henry started talking after another long drink of the vodka. The thought of it turned my stomach again but I wasn't going to flinch and distract him. His recollections were vague at first and came to him as if he recalled something he heard about or had experienced in a dream. The bellbirds continued their noise, almost reaching a crescendo as the puzzle pieces fell into place.

The three altar boys, Benedict, Henry and a boy called Miles started going to the school residence to be trained as servers when they turned ten. Miles, although a year below them at school, was the same age. He had repeated a year at some point because everyone thought he didn't have the skills to progress. Mr. Wheeler had been installed in the house that had been built for the priest when the school had been run exclusively by the church and the parish had a fulltime father. With the move to lay staff and itinerant priests, the house became available for the most senior member of staff. It should have been the principal, but he lived with his wife and kids just out of town. Principals didn't last long. St. Finbar's had become a stepping stone to more desirable positions closer to Melbourne. But the deputy principal's job, the discipline master, was filled by Mr. Wheeler for the eleven years the boys were enrolled and probably the ten before that. He was an institution, a stalwart of the community, deeply religious and unfaltering in his commitment to educational principles that had proven to be at the least inappropriate, and at their worst criminal. He embodied the persona of the "spare the rod and spoil the child" educator. Bad boys had to be beaten into submission and reverence. And no-one questioned such a good man who had no wife and trained boys in his own home. The alarm bells in my head rang loud.

With this background, Henry began to shade the obvious gaps. Training included learning to drink the altar wine. Lots of it apparently. He spoke of the three boys becoming intoxicated in The Rottweiler's house. Henry liked the feeling even then of being numb. The three boys would get giggly, then sleepy and eventually sick. Benedict learned quickly how to appear to drink as much as the other boys by becoming the apprentice barman. He found he could feign the sniggering and staggering quite easily. 'He eventually taught me how to fake the amount I drank too. Bennie just appeared to be filling our glasses and we spilled some and tipped it into plants and other places.' Roger Wheeler drank along with the boys but Miles didn't get the tip-off that the boys just pretended to drink.

'Why did he want to fill you up on wine?' My question seemed naive and asinine. Anyone with a sense of appropriate adult behaviour would know why a grown man would allow children to become inebriated.

But Henry obliged with an answer. He was numb enough to make a clear statement about his teacher's intention. 'We were compliant. Too pissed to fight him off.'

Without actually saying the words, I knew what Henry was saying had transpired in those training sessions. Max was slower to comprehend the gravity of Henry's revelation. But when he did, his whole demeanour changed. He looked angrier than I'd ever seen him. When he realised that the discipline master had been sexually inappropriate—abusive—Max let forth with a string of invective about what kind of treatment might be in store for Wheeler if we should ever find him. Max's anger barely ruffled Henry, who had slipped into a stupor. He looked out at the river, unmoving, not even blinking. Even when Max left the boat, swearing under his breath, Henry remained impassive. I had no idea where Max was going but he likely had to move to quell the rage, but I had to sit and process the snippet of information Henry had given and then bear the brunt of the details to come.

It became a weekly ritual. Most Sundays after Mass, some Fridays after school the parents would let Benedict, Henry and Miles go to the old presbytery. Archie would not be invited to come in but would walk with the lads through the town to the house. The first months the three boys, who initially thought they were special, teased Archie about not being one of the chosen. Only they had been selected to be in the inner sanctum. Archie was jealous because he felt left out. But that feeling transformed into pity and indignation when his friends were not spared the canings for their minor infractions. Surely, he reasoned, if you had to give up Sunday or Friday night you wouldn't get thrashed on Monday. But The Rottweiler's intentions and actions hadn't been apparent to Archie, and the boys' shame at what had been done to them prevented any disclosure.

Henry had tried to tell his older brothers, but they beat him for saying such disgusting things. They called him a poof for even thinking up such filthy things. The late 1970s were not a time of enlightened thinking in regional Australia. No one had even considered that adults might have nefarious motivations. Cruelty was tolerated; sexual brutality against children was something beyond a community's grasp. And the profound sense of powerlessness further victimised the children.

'He'd touch us. Laughed when we got erections. Said we obviously liked it.' Henry continued to drink from the bottle with almost every recollection at this point. He described the monster in detail. The things Henry remembered concerned his mouth and the red wine-stained tongue. How the man had unzipped himself and what each boy had to do was revealed in staccato storytelling. '*Noli timere.* It was all he'd say to us. Don't be afraid.' Henry's tremulous drunken voice reveal more and despite him being an adult, all I could hear was the anguished suffering of a boy and his friends.

I was floored by this sudden outpouring of detail. I'd expected Henry to tell us nothing but to go away. It seemed he had been waiting for more than twenty years to release the poison inside him. Kitty's death and his letter about the truth killing him made sense. The yielding of the terrible story was unexpected and I had been unprepared for it. Yet in my heart I knew that the story had to most likely proceed to this.

Max had disappeared. Now alone with a quite drunk and traumatised victim I became worried for both of us. I had no skills or knowledge of how to help him. Some instinct took me closer to his slumped figure. I laid my arm gently on his shoulders and attempted soothing words. 'Henry this truth that you have been burdened by is now able to be addressed. This is a crime. He can be punished.'

Henry started to very slightly shake his head. He trembled and his head moved so violently that the boat rocked with the agonised denial Henry seemed to be exhibiting.

'No no no,'. He held his head in his hands as if trying to stop himself from the uncontrolled movement. He then began slapping his head violently and pummelling his body. Henry had become truly hysterical and his cries reverberated against the hills on the far side of the river. I was deeply concerned that he was experiencing some form of psychotic break. Dredging up the past had been too much for him—too painful.

The noise brought Max back to the boat. Between the two of us, we managed to lay him down on the floor of the boat and restrain him.

I kept gently saying that he was safe and that this secret, this truth, would now help us all make sense of Kitty's death. 'It's okay Henry. We won't leave you. This truth isn't a death sentence.'

Henry stopped wailing and thrashing about. He felt clammy with sweat and the stench of alcohol filled the space between us. His rheumy eyes struggled to focus on mine. I was hoping that my face would calm him enough to get him back to a more even keel. He even smiled, somewhat pitifully.

'You think that is the secret?' He slurred his words when he spoke. 'What that scum did to us? That's not Kitty's truth. We could survive the things that shit did to us. We weren't that weak.' Another fit of agonised emotion wracked his body.

Through his shirt, I could feel the narrowness of his body. He was a man in the prime of his life, but the alcohol and the past had withered his arms and chest. The bones felt like they would snap under my touch.

I couldn't image what the truth could be if it wasn't that three little boys had been molested by a monster. What could be worse? Surely not the fact that one of them burnt down the mongrel's house.

Henry became quiet and wriggled from Max's restraining hands to make his way into a sitting position. He swayed and could barely hold his body upright. 'Silly, girl. The Rottweiler couldn't kill Bennie.' His eyes closed and his head lolled. Max shook him a little. Henry repeated, 'Silly girl. It's Miles. It's always been Miles.' A wet burp brought vodka and mucus out of his mouth and down his shirt.

It was revolting and made my stomach heave. But I stayed and tried to make sense of his words.

The boy we had just heard about from Archie. Why was he the centre of the secret? 'What is Miles's surname?'

Henry, nearly unconscious again, spoke again. He shuddered as he said the name, 'Miles Rennison.'

'And where is Miles?' Max's voice bought Henry's chin up one more time. Henry looked at him as if just realising I wasn't alone.

He lifted his arm and pointed in the general direction of the road. 'Up there. In the cemetery.'

Chapter Seventeen

One and half hours of conversation had unpredictably rendered a wealth of information. Maybe Henry might have given us a name or a hint, but his drunken revelation had given what I'd initially expected to be the whole story—a whole appalling story of an evil man who did terrible things to children right under the community's nose. But he also offered up a second chapter. What he called the real truth. Miles Rennison, now dead one presumed, given he was in the cemetery.

Henry was dangerously drunk and couldn't be left on his boat. One stagger and he could fall overboard. Between the two of us, we got him on to terra firma, and Max went through his pockets for an address. Luckily Henry's house was just across the car park, nestled in the forest, invisible from the jetty. We held him upright as he walked unsteadily home between our supporting arms. He made an occasional blubbering noise that seemed to surprise him as much as anyone. Our noisy shuffling and Henry's continued drunken sounds silenced the bellbirds temporarily. The whole forest seemed to become still and watch the strange circus being played out below them.

The house had been left open to the elements. Windows up and door wide open. Inside was dark despite the airing it was getting. Surprisingly the house didn't seem indicative of the chaos inside Henry's mind. It was neat, uncluttered and quite bare. Minimal furniture sat in front of an enormous open fireplace that contained the remnants of the previous evening's blaze. Books were piled up on the end of the couch, several spilling onto the floor. The only indication of Henry's excesses was two vodka bottles that clinked together as we steered Henry towards the lumpy three-seater. His descent into drunkenness was not, as I initially thought, an immediate response to his long draughts from the bottle on the boat. Henry last bottle just topped up his late night and early morning session. The blurting out of his story that kept him drinking was completely a consequence of the volume he'd already consumed. As Max hoisted the slumbering man's legs onto the couch and found a blanket to cover him and a pillow to wedge under his back to stop him rolling off, I had a quick look at what Henry had been reading.

The pile of books included high school yearbooks. In preparation for our arrival, Henry had been taking a stroll down memory lane. I took the top two and moved to the kitchen where there was more light. St. Finbar's College produced a fairly low-budget black and white record of the school's highlights. The two magazines chronicled 1980 and 1981. Kitty and his mates would have been about twelve or thirteen. Still kids, wide-eyed innocents on the threshold of their teens. The books would provide a picture of the boys and hopefully some of the other adults who had been ignorant of the tragedy being played out in plain sight.

Max wanted to get going. A few hours in Henry's company had made him fidgety and angry. He was not comfortable with anything that had been said. While neither of us could have done anything to stop what had happened to these boys, the horror at what they'd endured made us feel impotent and sick with grief. I still hadn't fully processed the whole sorry story. I felt drawn to what Henry referred to as the real secret. It was the thing that Kitty couldn't live with and it had something to do with Miles. 'What do you think this secret is Max?' Max shook his head.

'Nothing good that's for sure. Let's get out of here.'

I didn't want to take the books without Henry's permission, but his laboured breathing meant that we wouldn't be able to wake him to ask the question. I wasn't going to steal the books but thought if Max could drive us back into town, I would be able to find the pictures I wanted and we could photocopy them at the post office. I'd then leave the books with Archie at the pub. It assuaged my guilt in putting them in my bag.

We checked that Henry would be able to sleep off the vodka in-duced sleep safely and left by the front door, that we actually closed. Coming up the drive towards us was a woman who raised her hand in greeting. 'Friends of Ned?' she inquired.

Trying to explain the connection seemed a bit pointless, so we simply agreed with her assumption.

'He's been really bad for the last couple of weeks. Lost a mate and hasn't bounced back.' She introduced herself as Kim Barton, a cleaner at the resort which was literally a stone's throw away but totally concealed by the trees. She'd been watching the decline of our conversation from one of the guest rooms that faced the water. 'Guess you had something upsetting to say.'

I thought it fair to let her know that we were friends of the deceased Benedict Jepp, too, and we thought that Henry—Ned—could give us some information about what had precipitated the suicide.

'I don't think we've been very helpful.' My confession was hardly necessary given the obvious outcome. 'We are worried about leaving him in this condition.'

Kim smiled, sadly. She confirmed that Henry frequently spent a lot of time in this condition. Perhaps not as bad as he had been since the funeral, but she often looked in on him. Others in the community did too. 'Elvis will be up in an hour or two, after the lunch rush.' It was nice to know that Archie was still there for his friend. He must have a great deal of patience. Or a great deal of guilt.

We left Kim making her way into Henry's place. I felt better that he wouldn't be alone. I asked Max to drive so I could scan through the few photos in the magazine. I also wanted to stop at the Gipsy Point Cemetery for a quick look to see if Miles Rennison was in fact buried there or if Henry's statement was some other cryptic signpost.

Our drive away from the river was heralded by the return of the chorus of the bellbirds. It seemed they were also glad to see us go and allow them to get back to the business of electrifying the bush with song. We only had to drive a couple of kilometres to the turn off and the cemetery. In that time I'd found two class photos in the 1980 book. Kitty, Archie and Henry were in the Year 7 class picture. The grainy nature of the photo meant I had to refer to the names listed beneath the image. The three boys stood side by side in the back row. They had been placed in the middle as they seemed to be the tallest boys in the class. The class consisted of only 18 students altogether and the seven girls sat demurely in the front row. Their hairstyles mirrored each other; swept fringes that fell low over the forehead. Their school uniforms were bulky affairs that included a pleated tunic, rounded collars on the shirts button at the neck and a strange plaid cravat that reminded me of my short stint in the Girl Guides.

All the boys had stern expressions. As if they'd been asked to frown into the camera, posing for mug shots. And despite being squeezed into their uncomfortable ties and jackets, most of the boys had bucked the rules by letting their hair grow. Kitty's was the wildest. It was curly and unruly, much as it had been when I first met him only a few weeks before his death. Archie had longer straighter hair that had been tucked behind his ears to appear neater and more compliant. Henry had shorter curls but a rakish fringe that seemed to be moving to cover one eye as the photographer took the picture. Nothing about the bleakness of their lives was evident here. They could have been kids from anywhere living ordinary lives, free of secrets.

The Year 6 photo had fewer students, five girls and ten boys. They sat in two staggered rows, so each child could be easily seen. Miles Rennison sat at the end of the first row. Even the poor-quality photo couldn't hide his fragility. He appeared thin, washed-out and neater than his peers. Miles' hair was cut stylishly short. It had been swept across his forehead and held in place with what might have been a wet gel. He was groomed and set apart from his peers, both boys and girls, by his purposeful pose. Miles looked straight into the camera lens, no smile, knees clamped together, shoulders rigid and his thin fingers interlaced as if he needed to hold on to himself for dear life. And he was beautiful. A pallid angel seated among the lesser beings. It seemed that he had been plucked from a world that did not include the rough and tumble of country-town life. What had happened to him?

As if to answer my question, his photo did not appear in the 1981 journal. The others were there in the Year 8 photo: different places in the grouping but same demeanour and hair styles. A little taller, a little fuller in the shoulders but relatively unchanged. This book also contained pictures of Benedict Jepp in the school play, the football team and holding up a cup won by the debating team. He certainly appeared to be an all-rounder. So much potential.

'Do you want to go in here?' Max's question made be aware that we had stopped in what might have served as the bus bay right outside the cemetery. I put the books on the floor of the car and made my way over to the small gate. I left my door open, with Max making a phone call to Mick. The cemetery was old and barely inhabited. Some old headstones dated back to the 1890s and 1920s, but there were no new graves. The last seemed to be the 1980s. The little graveyard, despite its few residents, was apparently full. It didn't take long to walk through the four sections clearly marked with wooden signs: Anglican, Methodist, Catholic and Other. I wondered what you had to be to get into the "Other" category. A quick glance at the three graves indicated that these lonely few were early immigrants to the area and their exotic faiths could not be signposted by the men who ran the cemetery.

But in the Catholic section there was one grave. Despite being over twenty years old, it was the newest and best kept plot in the block. *Miles Augustine Rennison.* Born on the twelfth of October 1968. Lived only a tiny life and died on the nineteenth of September 1980. It was an extraordinary and quite beautiful grave marker. A large, polished block of black granite that had angel wings carved into the top and swept down the sides as if embracing the young body interned in the soil below carried the final farewell message:

To unpathed waters, undreamed shores.

A quote from The Winter's Tale by Shakespeare. Miles, the son of Robert and Kelly Rennison, an only child. Nestled into the white porcelain pebbles stood a silver urn that held fresh roses. They were pink and recently placed. I knelt beside the grave and bent over to smell them. The scent wafted as clearly as if I'd stood beside them growing on the bush. Hybrid tea roses reminded me of the gardens of my childhood home. These had to have been just cut from the bushes to have remained so fragrant. Someone who loved Miles Rennison had been to see him recently. That person had tended the white pebbles and rid the surface of leaves and grasses. Perhaps they'd even polished the angel's wings. Despite the great sadness I felt at the loss of this twelve-year-old boy, I also had to acknowledge the love evident in the simple tending of his grave. In amongst the birdsong, brittle grasses and forgotten dead, lay one who was still remembered.

'I told you to go home.'

The voice from the road surprised me. I was lost in thought and shaken out of my reverie when the voice boomed the same demand as last night when I'd stood on the jetty at Karbeethong. A man stood almost concealed by the tall grass and melaleuca trees. As I stood, he moved forward slowly. His voice seemed more frightening than his physical self. The man who walked closer moved slowly due to the use of a walking stick. He wasn't elderly, but obviously in pain. He was reed slim and not very tall, with grey hair styled in the manner of a much younger man. As the two of us moved closer together, I couldn't help but see the son in the father. Miles Rennison's angelic, high-cheeked face had been inherited from this man.

'Mr. Rennison?' He seemed somewhat surprised that I knew who he was. 'I'm sorry that you think we are interfering…'

'I know why you are here. Prying into lives that are none of your business. You think you are doing that Jepp kid some big favour by coming down here and sticking your nose into the past.' He turned away only to look back over his shoulder to say, 'I'm glad he killed himself. He should have done it sooner.'

I was so angry at such flagrant disregard for Kitty that I forgot about respect and understanding. 'How dare you! Kitty Jepp and Miles were friends.'

Robert Rennison made his way with awkward haste towards his car.

'Something terrible happened here.' I followed him, my voice becoming more strident and louder with each step.

Max powered towards us.

Miles's father turned on me, raised his walking stick and swung it at me.

Never in my life had I had hand-eye coordination that might be of any use, but on this day I was able to catch the cane and yank it from the man's hand. It shocked me that I managed to unbalance him and he crashed forward into the dust. Max arrived, helped him up and returned his walking stick.

Robert Rennison was sobered by the fall and the apparent aggression between us. But he said, 'Something terrible did happen here. Benedict Jepp…' He faltered for a moment, as if the name was acid to him. 'Benedict Jepp and those other animals killed my son.'

Some words can stop time. The three of us stood in the Gipsy Point Cemetery and that's precisely what happened. The world stopped. The birds stopped. The breeze stopped. All signs of life ceased in the utterance of those words. It seemed this was the secret. The terrible thing that could not be contained was that Miles had been killed. In order to restart the clock and bring the heartbeat back to the world, I leaned forward and vomited. The angry stranger turned his back and limped towards his car. The only thing left to do was watch him go. I wiped my mouth with a tissue I'd had buried in my jeans' pocket. Max put his arm around me and led me back to our car.

We didn't speak. We waited until Robert Rennison's car turned and went in the direction of the highway before we made our way back into the town. Mick was waiting for us, holding a wad of paper and waving cheerfully as we pulled into a car space outside the pub. Mick was the most observant man I'd ever known. Before the engine had been turned off, he'd opened the door. 'What's wrong?' It must have been the shocked look on our faces, my teary eyes, the inevitable sadness that made him realise that something had happened. The three of us had so much to share and I still had the yearbooks to go through. A hot cup of tea and a quiet place to have it seemed to be in order before we set off for Eden. I still had to face Teresa Jepp and ask her even more questions. But we all needed time to put these pieces together before landing on her doorstep unannounced, where I would ask her if her son had murdered Miles Rennison.

Max gave Mick a rundown of the events in the cemetery. 'It ended with me knocking Robert Rennison to the ground.' And before he could ask, 'Not deliberately.' But the information that Miles's father thought that his son had been killed didn't seem like news to Mick. He had spent the morning with the editor of the local paper who had been raised in the town and knew every intrigue and every cover-up. Fred Lewis suspected all kinds of things about the rights and wrongs of his town, but he didn't ever have proof of anything. The things he knew didn't ever make it into print. He was good mates with the ex-police sergeant who was recovering in hospital from a recent cancer operation. While Mick asked questions, Fred rang Angelo di Michele, third generation Italian, second generation cop. While Angelo struggled with pain management, he was able to fill in Fred's story with some details that also never made it into the light of day. The story added more shadows than illumination.

It seemed that in September 1980, the spring rains had come early and the water from the Wallagaraugh River had increasingly looked likely to flood. The storms and gale force winds had forced everyone off the water. But on that Friday in September, for some reason four boys from St. Finbar's College set off from Stringray Point in Benedict

Jepp's three metre tinnie. Henry Kelly, Archie King and Miles Rennison were on board with him. Three of those boys had been with their teacher Mr. Wheeler for the first part of the evening, where they prepared for Sunday Mass. The boys weren't found until the following evening, the nineteenth of September. By then Miles was dead and they found his body floating between Jimmy Point and Gravelly Point in a small basin known as Dead Finish. The irony was not lost on anyone. The three surviving boys were cold and incomprehensible when rescuers found them at Goanna Bay, halfway between Mallacoota and Gipsy Point. Of course there had been a coroner's report, the details of which had not been fully recorded in the public records, and accidental drowning was documented as the cause of death. But the grapevine had a rumour circulating within days of the death that the boy, Miles Rennison, had been sexually assaulted. In the absence of any coherent statements from the others, the gossips had already concluded that Jepp, King and Kelly had done something awful to Miles and drowned him to cover it up.

In all of this, Roger Wheeler's reputation and role in the evening had never been called into question. The boys simply were at his house for a couple of hours and when they left, he'd warned them about taking the boat back to Gipsy Point. Benedict apparently had organised to stay with the Kings, which was why Archie waited for them at the presbytery gate at 7:30. Whatever had taken place between 5pm and 7.30 deemed irrelevant in the investigation, because the boys had been safe in the care of a respected teacher. The two events didn't seem to have any connection. The only scandal generated by the town concerned what those boys had done to Miles. Consequently, Mr. Rennison's belief that those boys had killed his son.

Mick remained impassive when we told him about our meeting with Henry. He simply wrote a few notes and finished with, 'It's what I suspected. There have been other cases of young men surviving the abuse only to fall into drug use, depression and suicide. The call for a Royal Commission will lance the boil.'

Mick often used this metaphor when he meant that the truth came after something painful. Once the whole toxic secret was exposed, people would pay for what they had done. I wondered if that meant that Archie and Henry, as well as Roger Wheeler would have their pasts revealed and wounds opened.

Chapter Eighteen

The trip to Eden was subdued. Mick had managed to get some details about others who had been at the school and I had photocopied the class photos and staff pictures from the two yearbooks. I dutifully returned them to the pub, but Archie wasn't available. Apparently, he'd been called to some family emergency at Gipsy Point. I imagined that Kim had called him about Henry's condition. We left the town and made our way back past the cemetery and the road to Henry's, back to the highway and away from the incessant noise of the bellbirds. I was grateful for the return to silence as it gave me time to think.

Max drove, and Mick had taken the back seat. He hadn't been feeling well since our morning tea discussion and although he had been intrigued by the discoveries of the last twenty-four hours, he didn't look particularly well. He was flushed and fidgety and I wondered if the complicated truths we had uncovered weighed him down. When I asked Mick if he was alright, he merely shrugged off his discomfort blaming the large vanilla slice he had eaten with his coffee. 'I'll just have a small serve of fish and chips at Eden. That'll fix me.'

His joke did not do much to allay my concerns about him. Perhaps I had been unreasonable asking my two friends to join me on chasing down a story that I might never be able to share with Kitty's wife and child.

But that I would share with Kitty's mother. The trip back to Eden took an hour. Mick hoped for a mid-afternoon lunch at the fisherman's wharf where I would be able to add Teresa Jepp's story to the puzzle. Her house was close to the Princes Highway which ran through the town. She had bought a weatherboard house at the top of the hill just off the highway. The white house had minimal garden but looked neat enough to have been manicured by hand and a view to die for. I told my two companions to make their way into town, and I would walk down the hill and meet them in the main street so we could drive down to the wharf together. It was possible that they wouldn't need to meet me anywhere if Mrs. Jepp tossed me out on my behind before I got a word in.

Mick didn't move out of the backseat and Max waited until the front door opened and it seemed that I'd been asked inside. Teresa Jepp simply raised one eyebrow and stood back to allow me to enter.

I started with an apology. 'I'm sorry Mrs. Jepp but there's just—'

'I am sure you are sorry Ms. O'Hara, but it seems the only way to get rid of you is to let you get this out of your system and send you home. I don't want my neighbours hearing anything you have to say.' Teresa Jepp didn't seem angry but resigned to having to listen to a bothersome child tell some fanciful and boring. 'I expect you will want a cup of tea as well.'

I was about to say "no" but she had already turned and left me standing in the front room of her perfect little house. It wasn't at all what I expected. I had images of dank, lightless rooms where she might have a cauldron on the bubble. Teresa was a good-looking woman, tall with chiselled features. Her manner on the other hand left a lot to be desired.

Her absence from the room gave me the chance to look about. The place was too sweet to be called austere, but it was minimalist. An antique sideboard and two rather modern cream lounges filled the space. The mantelpiece held a small vase of fresh flowers and the walls had three miniature watercolours of non-descript landscapes. What caught my eye almost immediately were the two silver framed photos on the sideboard. Perhaps impressions are not everything. One large frame held a picture of Kitty when he was probably sixteen. His hair wild, his school tie undone, and his face more pensive and preoccupied than brooding. He wasn't looking at the lens but off into the distance as if unaware that he was been photographed. A beautiful portrait. The second frame, smaller but also silver, held a picture of Kitty's son, Isaiah. A small crucifix nestled between the photos.

Teresa Jepp had built a little, unassuming shrine for her son and grandson. She hadn't, as I'd assumed, detached herself completely from her flesh blood. Kitty and Isaiah never far from her thoughts.

At least not when she was in this room. I wondered about the distance between them. What had kept a son from his mother and a
grandmother from her only grandchild? I almost feared the answer.
I had complicated and unresolved feelings about mothers and if I was
completely honest, fathers too. Mine had been absent my whole life,
I'd never known who they were and until a few years ago had resisted
knowing about them. As their stories unfolded, an unexpected connection to them emerged. Two flawed and long-dead people were my
flesh and blood, mother and father. Not to mention my poor brother
who died somehow entwined in our mother's madness. It seemed that
the connection between family members could not be fully severed.

'Deep in thought, are we?' Teresa had entered the room without
my noticing. I wondered how long she had watched me delving into
memories. 'You're surprised at the photos, aren't you?' It was more
than a reasonable question. She motioned for me to sit down on the
sofa facing the view. She sat opposite me, sitting back against the
cushions but without looking comfortable. 'So what do you want,
Lily?' Another question, softer this time.

I felt if I spoke quickly, she wouldn't be able to cut me off before
I'd conveyed all I knew about the events that led to Kitty's death. She
poured tea but said nothing. She wasn't even really looking at me. I
had to assume she was listening.

I started with the letter and the obscure references to Henry and
Archie and the truth. I went quickly onto meeting Archie and Henry.
Before I could tell her about Henry's admission, I had to have a sip of
tea. My mouth felt dry, and I wasn't sure that I could get the words out
without crying. I felt my eyes become glassy and I looked away from
her face. If she noticed I struggled with my next revelation, she gave no
hint that she felt moved.

'Henry said that Roger Wheeler sexually assaulted him. And Miles.
And Benedict.'

The room fell to silence as the words pierced the uncluttered and
pristine life Teresa had created here in Eden. But all the imposed order
in the world could not keep the nasty darkness of those words from
sullying the space between us.

I think I had expected her to become enraged and full of harsh
denial. Perhaps I thought that she would tell me to leave. She didn't.
She sat very still for a whole minute. She replaced the china cup on

its saucer with a tiny chinking sound. Teresa stood and walked to the photograph of her son. She lifted it and stared at the boy in photo.

I was too afraid to speak or move. All I could do was wait because I had more to say about the fire and Mr. Rennison's accusation about Miles's death.

'He was probably drunk.' I imagined she meant Henry. 'He is an alcoholic. Hardly a reliable source.' But she seemed prepared to go on with some part of the story. She didn't return the photo to its place but laid it face down on the sideboard and walked back to where she left her teacup.

She said, 'The boys lied to cover up a terrible thing that had happened.'

'Miles's death?' I wanted her to know that I knew what the accusation had been. She nodded and continued to tell me the version of events as she saw them. The three boys had been at Mr. Wheeler's on the Friday night. Benedict was going to stay at Archie's home that night and then boat home the next day. But the four of them decided to get up to some mischief and go out camping somewhere on Top Lake. They had been allowed to camp at Jimmy Point the summer before. But the weather went against them and Miles must have fallen overboard. The investigation drew that conclusion. No charges were laid. The community mourned the loss. The boys lied about something having happened at the teacher's house to cover up their guilt.

Teresa's recount was emotionless at best. She added nothing new except for the fact that she had known that the boys had told adults that Wheeler had done something to them. No-one believed them, not even her.

As she spoke something came to me. Why would the boys, who had grown up around the lake, take a boat out to go camping on a stormy night when a flood warning had been issued. They were just young boys, but they knew the lake. They also wouldn't gain much pleasure from setting up their covert camp on such a night. Where was the fun in that? It was a question worth asking.

'Why would they continue with the camping plan in such awful weather? Does it make sense to you?'

Despite having voiced the questions, Teresa Jepp simply continued with her story without directly answering them. 'Benedict loved the

water. He was as safe on the lake as he was on land.' She admitted
she had been surprised that he would have taken the boat out that
night. The lie about Mr. Wheeler, however, hadn't been invented
on the night just to cover their tracks. According to Teresa Jepp,
her son had implied that something untoward happened to the
altar boys before. A teacher from the school had approached her
six months before the infamous night and told her that she felt
uncomfortable with something Benedict had said. The teacher,
Connie Harlow, was young and inexperienced. An outsider who
had a different notion about education and child protection.
'Naive and had no experience with raising boys.' Teresa almost
sneered. 'Too soft and didn't realise that the boys were all madly
in love with her.' It seemed to Teresa that being tender was more
of sin than being violent.

But Teresa did see someone else after Connie had spoken to
her. The local priest, Father Vic Burrell, had been asked to speak
to Benedict after his teacher had conveyed her concerns to Teresa.
She had asked Father Vic to counsel Benedict about the sin of lying. 'Of course Father Vic was more than happy to help. Benedict
had been one of his favourites.' But according to Teresa the priest
was as soft as the teacher. He listened to Benedict's story about
Mr. Wheeler. He interviewed Henry and Miles the same day, but
the other two boys denied that anything had happened. They
didn't confirm any part of Benedict's story about the drinking or
the beatings or the inappropriate touching.

I was shocked by the sanitised manner in which she described the
indiscretions—the crimes—against her son and his friends. It seemed
that Benedict had been cut adrift at the time of his outcry. His friends
betrayed him and denied consolation and solace from three adults who
had the responsibility to protect him. His mother, his teacher and his
priest had failed to see the vulnerability of this frightened child. If
they had acted then, maybe the trauma that followed would not have
eventuated. Miles would have lived, Henry would not have resorted
to the bottle, and Kitty would not have been so broken that death
became his only option. How many lives would have been changed
for the better? The Rennisons, Archie and Teresa herself. Something
instinctual made me fold my arms over my yet to swell belly. My
child—our child, mine and Phillip's—would not ever be betrayed by

us. Phillip and I would never allow our daughter or son to feel that we would not stand with them against the worst of fortunes.

Anger towards Teresa built up inside me, and she seemed to sense a change in my demeanour. 'You can't believe everything your child says, particularly if they are flawed by nature. Benedict's father was a liar and a cheat and ended up in jail. They say the apple doesn't fall far from the tree.' Teresa had let her guard down for a few minutes, but it was well and truly re-established during my few moments of reflection. And the thought that had haunted me my whole adult life was summed up by her use of that idiom. My own mother had been ill with depression when she took her own life and that of my brother. My father took his own life too. I momentarily feared the implications of my own flawed genetic heritage. But this wasn't about me; it was about Benedict and his mother.

'Did you ever think it was true?'

Teresa responded by merely shaking her head. It seemed that words had eluded her in answering such a simple question.

'Even when Benedict burnt Wheeler's house down didn't you think it might have been possible?' I watched her hands roll into fists and press down on her thighs. The internal struggle to maintain her composure showed. I thought mentioning the fire might jolt her into speaking, but it simply brought our conversation to a halt.

Teresa Jepp got up, replaced the photo to its rightful spot beside her grandson, called time on our encounter, and walked towards the door—a signal that I should follow her.

I tried to mend any broken bridges by saying that I'd hope to see her again should she come up the coast to see Isaiah and I apologised if my questions had been rude. It was not my intention to hurt her.

She said nothing until I was on the other side of the threshold. 'I loved my son Ms. O'Hara. Loved him his whole life. I forgave him everything, but he chose to cut me out of his life. He went away to school for a year and then went away forever.'

She almost closed the door on me, but another thought must have billowed up from memory. 'You think you know everything that happened that year but you don't. You want something to be true so you try to make it so. Your assumptions do not reflect what actually happened. Benedict didn't burn down Roger Wheeler's house.'

'I know you want to protect him Mrs. Jepp but surely it makes sense. You're a mother trying to protect her son from a crime he most likely committed. I do understand that. But surely you see it might support the theory that…'. She cut me off.

'I set fire to that bastard's house. The only thing I regret was that he wasn't in it at the time.' She slammed the door.

I had to catch my breath before I could move. My walk down into the town was something of a blur. Teresa Jepp had refused to believe her son when he revealed the nature and vile proclivities of The Rottweiler and yet she had just confessed to burning down his house. The two events seemed incongruous. If she hadn't believed that he abused the boys, why would she exact a fairly brutal retribution on him? Burning someone to death is vengeance at its best. The fact that she failed in her attempt to kill him still made something of a statement. Was it possible that for all her posturing about the truth of that night and her son's role in Miles's death, she really did believe that Roger Wheeler had done something to her child?

I hoped that Max and Mick could shed some light on this but we didn't get the time to really get into the discussion. In the forty minutes I'd been with Teresa and walking down to meet them, Mick had taken a turn for the worse. That vanilla slice and the previous night's drinking had really taken a toll on his digestive system. He had serious indigestion or possibly food poisoning. He'd actually been throwing up and in a lot of discomfort. I suggested we stop at the Pambula Hospital if he didn't start improving.

'It's only twenty minutes up the road. Can you hold on that long?'

'I'm not going to the bloody hospital. It's just indigestion or some nasty bug. Just drive.'

'Well there's another hospital in Bega which is about forty minutes away. If we miss one there's always another.'

'Great the hospital tour of the south coast.' He tried to make it sound like a joke but he wasn't a good colour.

I retrieved some plastic bags from the boot of the car just in case he needed to vomit again. We gave up the idea of lunch on the wharf; the thought of fish and chips didn't appeal to any of us after the day we had experienced. Getting home was the only item on the agenda. Mick settled into a bit of a sleep. I drove and talked to Max about Teresa Jepp. 'Why would she burn down Wheeler's house?'

'Maybe she was having an affair with him. Perhaps he cheated on her and she was getting him back.' Max's response was not what I'd expected. I didn't think that was the reason for the fire.

'It has to be something more than that Max.'

I checked the back seat at the turn to Pambula in case we needed the hospital, but Mick was sleeping and seemed to be breathing normally. I did the same thing at Bega but by this stage both men were napping. It gave me time to consider the possible reasons for Teresa Jepp's actions. I couldn't reach any other conclusion except the one I started with. She was somehow protecting her son.

We were about one and half hours from home, so while my passengers slept I felt confident that Mick was alright. But twenty minutes out of Moruya, Mick's voice from the back seat brought me rapidly out of my thoughts and into reality. He was grey and sweating and clutching his left arm. I woke Max immediately. Mick was in extreme pain 'I feel like I can't breathe, it's like a huge vice is crushing me'. The symptoms were that of a heart attack. I should have taken him to the first hospital. Waiting can be deadly, and I didn't want to lose Mick. He was more than a friend, he was family.

Max wanted to ring an ambulance, but I was convinced that we had to keep going. Stopping would waste vital minutes. 'No ring the hospital and tell them we are fifteen minutes out and bringing in a man in his sixties with significant chest pain.' My foot instinctively hit the accelerator in an attempt to cut down the minutes between the attack and treatment. If the police were out on the road, they could chase me all the way to Moruya but I wasn't stopping.

The hospital had confirmed that they would be waiting and if the patient stopped breathing to stop driving, start CPR. They would phone for an ambulance that would start making its way to us. It seemed that the delay in stopping and waiting was not recommended. When we saw the ambulance we should pull over, signal them and they would take over the care of the patient and transport to hospital.

The police did not stop us nor did the ambulance get to us. In fact apparently the paramedics were only a few minutes into their journey when we rushed into town. I pulled up in the ambulance bay and, true to their word, several medical staff attended to Mick within seconds. I stayed with him while Max parked the car.

The two of us waited for news. The night would be long.

Chapter Nineteen

At some point in the night, Max and I left the hospital. Mick had been stabilised and he would require heart bypass surgery. The hospital made preparations to fly him to Wollongong. We could do nothing else for him until he recovered from the operation in a few days. He was medicated and dazed when we left. We needed sleep and Max was desperate to see his daughter. Peter and Margaret had suggested that they drive down to the hospital to collect us but neither of us wanted to leave Mick until we knew he had been stabilised.

Despite being tired, my body and mind had switched to high alert. It was only about 11pm when I stopped at the Swan's house to drop off Max. He insisted that I come in with him and stay the night with my in-laws. I had no intentions of staying, but I didn't quite want to be alone just yet. Typically the front door was unlocked and let ourselves in. Max went to check Sarah, who had been put into her mother's childhood bedroom for the night and she was fast asleep. Max decided to sleep in the other single bed in the room. I spoke briefly with Peter and Margaret who were in bed but awake. They tried to convince me to stay too. I went to the kitchen to make us a hot drink, but Max didn't reappear.

I left them asleep. The father and child, oblivious to the world outside, could have at least a few hours of rest. I, on the other hand, felt no need for sleep.

At home I turned on lots of lights and made more tea. I wouldn't sleep for a little while. A spring had been wound inside me and only keeping busy would gradually unwind it. The first thing was to check if Phillip had been able to email in the forty hours I'd been away.

Happily, he had. It wasn't particularly full of news. He spoke of the weather—teeming rain—and things he had eaten—food—ever important. He mentioned the people, Australians, locals and other nationals he worked with, not by name but by the job they were doing. It was intentionally vague and light-hearted. I knew Phillip was dealing with critical issues and while he wasn't confronting dangerous criminals, I did wonder about his safety. These task forces weren't put together to simply discuss the semantics of international crime; they intended to stop the perpetrators. He went on to more personal matters about how much he missed me. He wanted to know how I was feeling and how big my belly had grown. He made ridiculous suggestions about me photographing myself side on so that when he finally got home, he wouldn't be shocked by my increased size. Even in my agitated state he could make me laugh.

I responded straight away. He needed to know about Mick. He would be upset that he wasn't here to help, but it is much worse to be left out of the loop. I deliberately left out the part about where it happened. And I certainly wasn't going to tell him why we went there. It wasn't actually a lie. Merely an omission. Inevitably, he would know the whole story. For the first time I thought it was a good thing that we were unable to have phone contact; even from a different time zone, three and half thousand kilometres away, Phillip would know something was up if he heard my voice. I supposed he would guess anyway when he saw what time I'd emailed him.

I drank tea and stared out at the water. I contemplated going for a walk, but the temperature had dropped and it was not an appealing way to diminish my anxiety. Instead I sat at the dining table with the photocopies of the yearbooks and the pile of notes Mick had from the local journalist. His own notes would be in his notebook which I hesitated opening as it seemed a real violation of his privacy. But if sleep wasn't coming any time soon, I might as well get all the information sequenced and summarised. I was good at this. Taking all the little pieces and making a whole story. I started by again looking at the photos of the four boys.

I'd photocopied numerous pages but hadn't examined any of them other than the class photos. The pile included two lots of staff photos. These pictures were clearer than those of the boys. They were single portraits of each adult employed by the college. My eye immediately drawn to three names—Father Victor Burrell, Miss Connie Harlow and Mr. Roger Wheeler.

Father Victor was a middle-aged benevolent looking man. His hair was thinning and combed forward into a most unflattering fringe. I imagined that priests didn't spend much time styling their hair but this would have taken some time. The side comb-over that most men went for when their hair abandoned them seemed almost stylish in comparison to what Father Vic was attempting. He had a wide toothy smile and didn't appear to be a man deliberately hiding the truth about a wretched situation in which children would ultimately suffer. In the second yearbook the photo surprisingly showed a man much changed. I had to look closely to ensure it was the same person. The hairstyling had been abandoned and his much balder head had been divested of the long sweeping strands that had been positioned ludicrously to give an illusion of hair. But more than that, the big grin had been replaced with a taut, closed-lip smile that didn't reach his eyes. In the year between photos he had aged more than what seemed possible in one year. In the hollows of cheeks the weight loss was clearly evident. The fine lines around his eyes looked less like those created by joy and more like those etched by burden. It couldn't have been my imagination that this was a man transformed.

His transformation by ordeal was corroborated when I looked at the two photos of Connie Harlow. In 1980 she looked as shiny as a new penny. Her long dark hair was loosely tied back, and she wore a pale patterned shirt. She looked so young and happy. Her smile mirrored the priest's, as if the photographer had caught her halfway through a laugh. I could also see why the boys of St. Finbar's might have been in love with her. She was very pretty; full lips and round eyes made up with just enough make-up to accentuate the shape of them. She had smooth skin and full of light. The second photo, only a year later, revealed a more sober portrait. Miss Harlow had her hair cut short and was also infinitely more serious in 1981. She was still the same young woman, but her eyes didn't stare into the camera with the optimism and unmasked happiness of the previous one. In fact she looked exhausted.

The third photo of interest was Roger Wheeler. It was not what I expected. In the 1980 yearbook, he presented in a suit and tie, dark hair neatly parted in the middle, longer over the ears. His oversized tortoiseshell glasses sat on a rather large round nose under which grew a thick, chevron moustache. He gave a rather shy smile to the camera, but only one side of his mouth curled up. He looked innocuous and more like someone who would be a victim of bullying, not the perpetrator. The vicious and lascivious nature of The Rottweiler was not evident here. More telling, perhaps, was the second photo. Where Father Vic and Connie had been made haggard, Wheeler remained unchanged. In fact, if it hadn't been for him wearing a different shirt and tie, I would have sworn it could have been the same photo.

I looked at the other pictures; there were only one two others who had been in the school in 1980 who appeared in the 1981 book. Even the principal had changed. There had been something of a staff exodus in 1980. There were few smiles in the latter pages. But one photo did capture my interest. The little quarter page article titled *Vale*. "Those who have passed away this year, 1980". Two names of past teachers, one of a founding student, and of course Miles Rennison who had died in September. The photo, grainy and taken at a distance, showed the school forming a guard of honour on the main street outside the Catholic Church. The funeral cortege made its way through the lines of students who had been arranged to form a grief-stricken barrier. The children looked rigid with heartache, the teachers stood behind them to, one assumes, ensure dignified compliance. One teacher in the back row was not head forward, eyes down. He looked across at the line on the other side of the road. He was looking at three boys who appeared shambolic in comparison to the neat militaristic straightness of the other students. I couldn't really tell for sure, but the hair styles seemed consistent with the class photos I'd examined earlier. Kitty, Archie and Henry were the focus of Roger Wheeler's gaze. Two of the boys had almost collapsed against the third, who stood between them. Kitty had his arms around his crying friends, but he was returning the stare across the road as fiercely as it was directed at him. And two steps behind Kitty another familiar form remained motionless. Teresa Jepp stood staring across the road in the same direction as her defiant son.

I felt tired and overwrought by the disclosures and Mick's heart attack. Possibly I was seeing things in twenty-year-old photos that simply didn't exist. In the morning I would attempt a more dispassionate examination of these photocopies of poor-quality photos. Maybe I was just making it all up. But in the few hours that I slept, I dreamed I was there at Miles's funeral. In the foggy nightmare images, Robert Rennison shouted "go home". Roger Wheeler left his place in the line to confront Kitty who pushed Archie and Henry to the ground to protect them. From nowhere he produced a homemade toy sword that he brought up in front of himself as if to charge full force into the man now looming ever larger through what appeared to be hundreds of hearses all carrying the white coffins of children. I screamed for help, for someone to help Kitty as he couldn't defend himself with a child's toy. And then there was a noise. Loud enough, even though imagined, to bring me nearer to wakefulness. From behind the boys Kitty stepped out as a man. He was holding his son, and also a gun. As the dream ended, The Rottweiler fell to the ground, blood growing in volume, washing the hearses and mourners in the lake.

The violent dream had concluded with the rising of the sun. I was relieved to be in the light and for the night to be behind me. The day would bring more discoveries and plans would be made to further decipher the puzzle Kitty left us.

Chapter Twenty

The day started early in the other Swan home too. By 7:30 I had visitors knocking at my door. Margaret, Max and Sarah had come with breakfast ready for consumption. The fruit platter, muffins and foil-wrapped egg-filled toasted buns had been laid out on the end of my dining table that didn't contain the evidence of our journey south. I made coffee and tea and a cup of milk for Sarah who had immediately leapt into my arms on arrival. She was getting heavy to carry about, but I wanted to hold her while we busied ourselves with eating. Margaret wanted to hear all about Mick. She had a real soft spot for him.

I had called the hospital for an update as soon as I'd woken from the nightmare. He had rested well and would head north by air ambulance at 7am. He was already on his way by the time we gathered at the table. 'I thought his face had a poor colour the last time I saw him. He wasn't eating well.' Margaret's medical diagnosis stemmed from her belief that the right food would help cure disease and offset calamity. Her ability to produce banquets at a moment's notice was not just about staving off hunger, it curative. Food was medicinal and primarily soothed the soul, therefore where Margaret was, food followed.

If I had been more observant I might also have noticed that Mick was a poor colour and not quite himself over the last couple of days. He was not one to complain or probably even take advice if I had given it. I wish I'd over-ridden his command that we soldier on when he started to feel ill in the car. It wouldn't be a situation I'd ignore again. Beating myself up over the poor decision wasn't going to help Mick's recovery. I'd already decided that after his surgery he would come here to recover. I would look after him and ensure he was going to be safe when he returned to his lonely life on his Gundaroo property. By then

Phillip would be home and we would probably move back into our Canberra house and resume a normal life.

It meant that I would have to finish my dissertation and eventually put Kitty's story out of my head. But not before I knew more about Miles Rennison's death and why Kitty chose this time to end his life.

I must have been pensive for too long because Sarah decided that I wasn't paying her enough attention. 'Eat this Lil-Lil,' she said while ramming a piece of her own apple muffin into my mouth. It was only slightly wet and gross but it certainly dragged me out of my reverie. Max hauled his daughter off my lap and onto her own chair. 'Leave Lil-Lil alone for a bit, she needs to eat her breakfast.'

We spoke about the material we had gathered and decided on our way forward. Max had to go to work. Several contracts were near completion and he had to ensure that he could meet his obligations. He also had to finish off several things in this house, but they would have to go on the back burner for a bit. Margaret would take Sarah and when she wasn't available her other daughters would pitch in. It meant that I would have a day alone to go over the Mallacoota stories, including Mick's notes. I wanted to talk to Henry Kelly again about Miles's death, but I was nervous about triggering another decline into drunkenness. I felt it might be better to ring Archie King and see if he would divulge details about that night on the lake. I didn't want to hurt anyone, but the story couldn't end with Kitty's suicide which meant that meant old wounds had to be reopened. I knew the pain associated with peeling back the coverings that concealed the past. The past is best left in the past many people say. It was advice I had been given on numerous occasions on my own journey of self-discovery, but it was wrong. And in this case, where a monster hurt children, it was absolutely wrong. If I had to lance the boil, then what I knew had already sharpened the scalpel.

With breakfast done and the house quiet again I contacted the hospital where Mick would undergo surgery. As his nominated next of kin I could speak to him briefly. 'I'm driving up tomorrow and I expect to see you looking your best. He tried to encourage me to stay home. 'I'll bring your phone and notebooks, some books and the bag you had packed for our trip south.'

'Lily, look at my notes. There's things there about the Jepp case. And in case things go wrong, you'll find numbers for you to call on my phone.'

He sounded breathless and medicated. His allusion to his potential death made me feel helpless. His life had literally been in the balance. I couldn't catch the last thing he said but I finished with, 'I love you, Mick. I'll see you tomorrow.'

The trip to Wollongong would take me nearly three hours. I intended leaving about 6am. I would ring the hospital again this afternoon to see how the surgery went. Or they would ring me if things hadn't gone well. The only thing to do was to distract myself with combing through the information, ringing Archie, making some notes and possibly calling Angela Flynn if her number was in Mick's phone. I didn't know if she would want to be informed that her ex-husband was critically ill but on the off chance she still cared a bit about him I wouldn't deny her the opportunity to make contact.

Mick's phone wasn't password protected so access wasn't an issue. But that wasn't where I started. I liked the tangible world of artefacts. Things that could be touched and held up to the light. Things that were open to interpretation and required imaginative thinking. Photos, newspaper clippings and relics from the past gave me a sense of time and place and allowed me to make timelines, create narratives and provide evidence for bringing a long-forgotten time to life. In my work, this meant handling things from hundreds, sometimes thousands of years ago. The twenty-year gap between Kitty's death and the events at St. Finbar's was nothing. Living witnesses who could tell their part of the story made discovery and certainty easier.

So did newspapers. Mick had been given some photocopies of the stories that had appeared in the local papers, The Snowy River Mail and The Lakes Post. He had paper-clipped the editor's business card to the top of the pile. Fred Lewis was a local and also a shire counsellor and owned farming land in the district, according to some hand-written annotations that Mick had made on the top sheet. He was also the journalist who had written at least three of the stories that appeared in both papers in September 1980. I briefly wondered why Mick had written down the details about Fred as they seemed to have little relevance. But when I recalled every conversation between Phillip and Mick about cases they had worked, or Phil was continuing to work. Every detail adds to the overall picture. Who said something, the tone of voice, where they looked when they spoke, what movement, what went unsaid, what they touched when they spoke were all details that contributed to the telling of a story. Or a version of a story. Then each account was placed side by side so the truth might reveal it itself. Perhaps Mr. Lewis might add more than his articles from the week of the Miles's death could. Hindsight is a great thing.

The articles provided a timeline of sorts. The weekend paper ran the story of the flooding lake and the four missing boys. The interview with Archie King's parents and Robert Rennison revealed their concern for the boys' safety given the weather and the torrents of water pouring into Bottom Lake. There was nothing from the other two families—Teresa Jepp and the Kellys had not been interviewed or declined to comment. The accompanying photo was of the lake and the water lapping over Karbeethong jetty. Nothing was said about the three altar boys who had been at Mr. Wheeler's for the two hours on Friday evening.

The Monday paper bore the brief but heartbreaking headline—Local Boy Lost to Flood. By the end of the weekend the first version of events was revealed. The surviving boys, who had not been interviewed by Fred Lewis, had given the police a fractured account of what had occurred. They thought they could still negotiate the lake because the rain had stopped. Benedict Jepp was going to stay the night with the Kings but collectively the lads thought that they'd just have a brief trip out to Jimmy Point. No-one, it seemed, questioned the reason why the boys would do such a foolhardy thing. The lake was rougher than expected, and Miles fell in and the others hadn't realised for a few minutes. They couldn't rescue him because they couldn't find him as the light had gone at this stage.

It seemed improbable that four boys in a three-metre tinnie didn't notice that suddenly only three remained in the boat. The only interview in this article was with Sergeant Angelo di Michele who spoke about the tragedy of misadventure, poor judgement on the part of the boat's owner and the scheduling of the autopsy for the following week. This was accompanied by a photo of the locals surrounding the ambulance taking the body of Miles Rennison to the hospital morgue. Some local men were quoted as saying it was a tragic accident and that the family of the dead boy had the town's support. A teacher from St. Finbar's, Roger Wheeler, confirmed the "devastating loss of a wonderful boy". That obsequious bastard and his offensive sympathy made me ill to my stomach. Why had he been chosen to speak for the school? Why wasn't the principal asked to comment?

Another article, dated eight days after the accident, stated that the body of Miles Rennison had been released to his parents for burial. The coroner's report concluded that drowning was the cause of death and that the cause of other injuries could not be confirmed. This included a quote from Miles's father, "Those boys are responsible for my son's death. They should be charged." More from Sergeant di Michele who confirmed that no further action would be taken in the case. Fred Lewis padded out the piece with descriptions of the heart-broken parents who had lost their only child. He concluded with a warning about floodwaters and the number of boating deaths that had occurred in the district in the last five years. It seemed that the things that remained unsaid in all of these reports were the key to understanding the events.

A final report dated 1983 was about the fire at the old presbytery. The fire had been set deliberately and had started at the back of the residence. As a weatherboard structure, it burned quickly and the local rural fire crew struggled to contain the flames. Luckily the resident was not at home at the time of the fire and because of the use of accelerants the place had been gutted. Angelo di Michele was interviewed again and concluded that no local would do such a thing to a respected member of the community, nor the school which would be closing down later in the year. Itinerant vandals seemed to be the most likely culprits.

I had to laugh at that conclusion given Teresa Jepp's confession that she had burned down Roger Wheeler's house.

The three articles confirmed what I already knew and shed little light on the real catalyst for these terrible things. I hoped that Mick's notes might give me a lead so that I could gain more of an insight into Henry's story about The Rottweiler. Other than going back to Mallacoota and getting Archie to reveal what happened on the lake, I had reached a bit of a dead end.

As I opened his notes, I could see that Mick not only had written down the names of potential witnesses he had made preliminary enquiries into their whereabouts. Mick was thorough. His connections always seemed to pay off. Listed were two key players—Connie Harlow and Father Vic Burrell. He had other names too—Samuel Bent, the principal in 1980 and the local doctor, Hugh Smith. They might have something to add.

The last two did not have any contact details but I'm sure Mick had ways of getting them. The most important players did. Father Vic was apparently a parish priest in western Sydney. He would be in his early seventies by this stage. He worked primarily with refugees who required rehousing and support as they adjusted to new lives in Australia. He would be easy to find and within a few hours of the hospital where I'd visit Mick. The day would be busy, but I had planned to stay in Wollongong for a night or possibly two anyway.

The second person, Connie Harlow had kept her maiden name according to Fred Lewis. She had left teaching after a short stint in Melbourne and had moved to Queensland. A little further afield and much harder to get to. Apparently, her parents lived in Sydney and as they were now ageing and living in care, Connie was a regular visitor. He had recorded a phone number and the name of the nursing home where her parents resided, both were a surprising find. Mick had made a little note in parenthesis which explained why Fred had the details. It simply said, "Kept in contact, had a relationship in the 1980s." So a teacher at the school who had suspicions about a fellow teacher was sleeping with the newspaper editor. It appeared that the opportunity to expose Wheeler had been overlooked, or simply ignored.

To my surprise I'd been reading and making notes for a few hours. It was almost 11:30 and Mick would have been in surgery for about an hour. It had been predicted that the operation might take about four hours. There was still a long way to go. Luckily I could continue to focus on what Mick had called the Jepp Case.

I thought the second part of the day could begin with phone calls. I would try Archie first, then Victor Burrell and finally Connie. I had Fred and Angelo as possible calls after the first three. While I made tea and a sandwich, I rang the hospital. Mick was still in surgery according to the staff in charge of placating worried and probably exasperating family members. She was, however, kind yet firm. 'Mr. Flynn is doing extremely well. His surgeon is most pleased with the process of the bypass and little more will be known until your father is in the recovery ward. He'll be in ICU for the following few days.'

I didn't bother correcting her assumption that I was Mick's daughter. Next of kin was usually a relative. It was a relief to know that the surgery progressed without problems and that a strong recovery most likely. I let her know that I'd be at the hospital in the morning and asked if someone could let "my father" know when he was out of theatre. Mick would get a little laugh out of me masquerading as his daughter.

I felt more relaxed knowing that things could only get better for him. I left a message for Max to let him know that Mick's surgery had gone well. And quickly spoke with Margaret to update her too. I had to insist that she stay at home and that I didn't need anything. So with no further distractions, I rang Archie King. It was just before the lunch rush at the pub. He answered his phone on the first ring and didn't sound at all peeved that it was me.

I started with questions about Henry. 'I was really concerned when we left Gipsy Point. Henry seems to have a problem.'

Archie complimented me on my artful understatement. 'It's slightly more than a problem.' Understatements all round. 'I suspect you've called because you didn't get everything you needed yesterday.'

'Yes. There are some gaps and we really need more information about what happened on that Friday night. I know that was you didn't go to Wheeler's house, but you were in the boat when Miles fell overboard.' Archie simply confirmed those two simple facts. I let him know about Mick's predicament, not just to elicit sympathy and hopefully compliance, but because he had got on well with both the men.

It did have some effect on his willingness to speak. But he wanted to get Henry in the room as well. 'Can you wait for a few hours? I'll go to Gipsy Point and talk to Ned about telling the whole story. I don't know it all, even though I was there. Bennie and Ned really didn't say what happened and Miles was incoherent by the time we left in the boat. Only Ned can tell you the details.'

I agreed to wait until Archie rang me back to ask other questions. I wondered what condition Henry would be in and whether he would be ready to talk about what actually happened. I wasn't confident that the facts would be forthcoming but at least I would try to ask some questions that might jog his memory; a memory even if faded by time would help us understand what had happened.

The phone call to Father Vic Burrell was not much easier. Once the priest had been found and brought to the phone, he sounded breathless from rushing.

I apologised for making him run but assured him the subject was important. 'I don't know whether you remember some of the boys from St. Finbar's College and the events of a child drowning in 1980?' I intended to continue drawing the father a picture of Mallacoota and the school but it seemed it was not necessary.

'Miles Rennison,' Father Vic stated blandly. 'How could I forget him? He was such a lovely child and a wonderful family.'

'Well I'm afraid there's more bad news, Father. Benedict Jepp took his life a few weeks ago because of something that happened twenty years ago. He had a wife and baby son and everything to live for.' I didn't mean to sound as cross as I did, nor as accusing, but I sensed that the story hadn't been forgotten by Vic Burrell. The silence at the end of the phone prompted me to ask if he was still there.

'Yes. I'm here. Poor Benedict, so lost.' He paused and then asked, 'How can I help?'

It opened the way for me to introduce my concerns about Henry and Archie and the role of Roger Wheeler in Miles's death. I gave a truncated version of my visit to Mallacoota and my discussion with Mrs. Jepp. Much of this was accompanied by deep sighing at the other end of the phone.

'I would rather speak to you in person Father, if I could.' A request he agreed to. We had a brief discussion about where and how to make the meeting. I explained that I would be in Wollongong the next day and could drive out to his parish if that would help. It was only an hour and half drive, depending on the traffic. Father Vic had a better idea. He had to meet a group of newly resettled refugees in Engadine, only forty minutes from the hospital. He was happy to make his meeting tomorrow so that it fitted in with my plans. In the end he was most accommodating and gave me directions to the parish hall where he would be at 3 o'clock the next day.

He finished the call by saying, 'There's no surprise in this. In any of it. I knew you would come someday. You or someone else. A child shouldn't just drown and nobody ask why.'

It seemed that the priest had been holding on to a secret for long enough. He was right, we should not forget to ask why.

I wondered if Connie Harlow would be as accommodating.

I phoned her and had to leave a voice message. She was unavailable to speak at the moment, but her message assured me that she would return the call. I stumbled over the message I left as I wasn't sure what would encourage her to follow up. In the end I left my name and explained that Fred Lewis from Mallacoota gave me her number and I really needed to talk to her about St. Finbar's.

I'd assumed that if Fred and Connie had stayed in touch she would have already been alerted to the trouble brewing.

When she rang back she confirmed what I suspected. 'Fred told me that an ex-cop might be calling me, but you didn't sound like a Mick Flynn.' A fact easy to confirm, I wasn't Mick but a friend of Benedict Jepp.

With the mention of her former student's name, she burst into tears. Connie immediately apologised for her outburst. She did the same when Fred rang her to say Benedict had killed himself. It took her a minute to gain a semblance of control.

'I know this is difficult to discuss over the phone, and you might not be able to recall much detail as it happened twenty years ago, but I am really trying to make sense of his death.' At that point Connie cut me off.

'I remember every detail and there haven't been many days that I haven't been reminded of what happened to those boys. I have waited for more than two decades to talk. And I'm happy to come to you.' Connie stifled her sobs as she made this statement. She had been carrying a story around for a long time. It seemed she wanted to divest herself of the weight of it. 'I'm still in Queensland at the moment, but I planned to be in Sydney in a week, to see my parents.' Despite my protestations, she insisted that she would drive down the coast to meet me. I offered her a compromise as I was certain I'd be returning to Wollongong the following week to check on Mick. It meant that Max might be able to come too.

'Thank you, Lily.'

It was a strange way to end the call. I didn't know why she would thank me for bringing her bad news or chasing down the terrible days of 1980.

I had plenty of time left to do things, including waiting for Archie's call. I was feeling tired and wondered if this could be a part of being pregnant. There were times over the last few days that I'd forgotten that our child was growing inside me. I felt concerned that perhaps the stresses of the story we were uncovering and Mick's brush with death would take a toll on the baby. The phone rang as I worried and paced. It was Margaret. 'I just wanted to know if you've eaten because you have had a lot to deal with.' And as if reading my mind, 'It's not good for the baby to have this much stress.' Everything I had heard about mothers-in-law did not seem to apply to Margaret Swan. She had an enormous capacity for caring and the love of her family seemed to encompass all of us newcomers. Of course I was carrying her only son's first child which probably made me special by association. I confirmed all was well but did confess to being tired. I managed to put her imminent visit off by saying, I'm just going to have a little nap just to take the edge off things'. She was still happy to come and do something in the house while I slept. Again I put her off with promises to walk over to her place for dinner. The mere mention that I'd be there for a meal had her bursting into culinary action.

Instead of sleeping, I took Mick's notepads and phone out onto my partially completed deck. I dragged one of the outdoor bean bags out there too and a small table to hold all the bits and pieces I needed to record the other conversations I hoped to have. The sun warmed me despite the coolness of the weather. It would have been easy to fall asleep, but I knew I had to make more of an effort to put all the pieces together. I looked down the long stretch of beach which started on the other side of the creek. It formed a near-perfect arc that finished at the tip of the island on the southern end. A few winter surfers tried to make something out of the poor swell but most of them were just sitting on their boards looking out to the horizon. They seemed to be chatting and showing little interest in the waves. It looked more like an opportunity to catch up rather than engaging in the solitary pursuit of the perfect wave. Surf therapy—sit on the sea, chat to your mates, catch a wave, go on with life. I wondered what Phillip and Max talked about when they sat about like those who bobbed about below me.

This distraction didn't help me get things done. I looked through Mick's notes and opened the one titled Contacts and Interviews. Not surprisingly he had written a substantial list of names. The key players were all listed with their names including Connie and Vic who had been listed on the notes he had made from talking with the newspaper editor. Archie and Henry, Teresa Jepp, the police officer Angelo di Michele and Robert Rennison were the only names I immediately recognised. The principal the year Miles died was Samuel Bent. The local doctor at the time, Hugh Smith. Both had last known addresses and contact numbers. There were also names of other teachers who had been employed at St. Finbar's at the time but not all of them had a clue as to where they might be. Twenty-three years was long time but probably not long enough to make it impossible to track people down. One name on the list did make me look twice—Kelly Rennison, then (Morgan) followed by a question mark. Kelly was Miles's mother. The additional name could have been her maiden name or perhaps she and Robert had divorced and she had remarried. I wondered if Fred Lewis might be able to clarify this.

So I called him first. He was an affable man, ready to talk to me.

Fred was taken aback by the news of Mick's heart attack in the hours after we had left Mallacoota. 'Coota usually has the opposite effect on people—lowers the blood pressure being here on the lake.' His tone was quite sincere and his concern for Mick genuine. Again, the misfortune opened a way for people to talk to me. Fred was very informative. He barely drew breath as he spilled the story of Robert and Kelly Rennison. 'The death of Miles was too much for the couple's marriage. He was there only child I'm sure you've realised that. Robert went mad with the grief and his belief that that the other boys had killed Miles.'

He paused briefly enough for me to ask a question. 'What happened to Kelly?

'Robert became violent towards Kelly, who believed that something else had happened to her son but couldn't muster the courage to find out. She was afraid of what the truth might have been.' This didn't surprise me at all. It seemed that a number of people were afraid of what might really have happened. 'She took refuge in her parents' home in Eden a year after the funeral. Robert, on the other hand, here stayed in Mallacoota, poor bastard was constantly on the rampage. He had car accident in 1983. Never really walked without pain since'

It was a big year 1983. The school closed and Wheeler's house burnt down, Kitty left to board in Bairnsdale so he could complete year 11 and 12 and according to Fred Kelly Rennison married Brian Morgan.

'Do you know where Kelly Rennison is now?'

Fred immediately corrected with Kelly Morgan. 'Yes she is up your way. Lives in Tuross, on the lake up there. She and Brian have a son. I think they called him Riley. Must be about 18 now. Kelly was nearly forty when she had him. Robert went crazy all over again when he found out. And I think her marriage to Brian is over too.'

'Fred, would Angelo di Michele be available to talk? I know he's been ill but there are just a couple of questions I'd like to put to him.'

Fred happily let me know that Angelo was bored senseless having to be confined during his recovery and that he'd love the distraction. 'He's got a great memory and can't sit still. Even on the chemo he had to keep doing things. Got to be a cop thing,' Fred concluded. He ended the call by confirming Angelo's mobile number.

Probably a cop thing. I wondered how Mick would go with being told he'd have to take things slowly over the next few months to ensure he made a full recovery.

In the few minutes it took me to get a glass of water and dial Angelo's number, Fred must've made a pre-emptive strike and informed him that the *"little ginger Irish girl"* would be giving him a call. I introduced myself and before I could say why, he validated my suspicions. I couldn't deny much of the description as I was indeed small, red-headed and a girl, but only the name was Irish.

'You are what you are, Miss O'Hara. Irish-Australian, Italian-Australian or whatever your ancestors were when they made this place home.' He was an amiable sounding man and I imagined he had the perfect temperament for a country cop. Clipping recalcitrant boys about the ears and giving their parents the benefit of the doubt on a number of issues most likely his modus operandi. The death of a child must have rocked him and the small town.

'So what do you think you don't know about the little Rennison boy's death?' It was an odd way to phrase the question. It implied I knew lots already and perhaps I already knew the answers to the questions I wanted to ask.

I opened with, 'What do you think happened on that night, Sergeant?'

Angelo talked as if he had his press statement that he released on the weekend of the tragedy in front of him. I let him talk for a few minutes without interrupting him. It sounded rehearsed.

'But I take it that you don't want my official summation, Miss O'Hara?'

He was right. I pressed him to describe his feelings about the night and what he knew about the four boys, the victim and the implicated. I'd ask him about Roger Wheeler last of all.

I struggled to keep up the note taking as he began. He thought the whole thing was pretty fishy. 'I knew Benedict, Archie and Henry from the cradle. They weren't bad boys but hyperactive and prone to being in the wrong place at the wrong time. You know the usual things. Footballs kicked through windows, accidently killing a local spinster's chickens by unintentionally blowing them up with fireworks, under-age drinking, silly stunts on boats and bikes. And the day they "borrowed" Henry's father's fishing boat and grounded it on the sandbank between the lake and sea was another high point in their mischief.'

While inconvenient, these didn't sound like the crimes that might be a precursor to being involved in the death of a child. 'These boys weren't criminals. They were just silly lads who were a bit bored with life in a country town.'

Angelo confirmed my thoughts. 'Was Miles a part of this crazy collective?' 'Well that's the interesting part,' Angelo said. 'Miles hadn't been a part of the gang and his parents never let him out of their sight.'

'So are you saying it was strange that he went out with Benedict that night?

'You're right making that conclusion. He didn't really belong with them.' He said that the boys, however, were always kind to Miles. He was a bit slower at school, looked soft and very young. 'He wasn't fit enough to be one of the group. He had asthma, couldn't run much or play. Some other kids bullied him. Roughed him up once or twice. He wanted to be out with the boys, but his parents never really let him.'

'But they let him be an altar boy?'

The retired policeman didn't respond to my question. He might have been a country cop, but he wasn't naïve. He had heard the whispers, but according to him they were just unfounded rumours that the boys used to protect themselves.

'You mean the rumours that Roger Wheeler was a paedophile.' It was as blunt a statement as I could have made.

And too blunt for Sergeant di Michele. He started coughing and had to put the phone down for a good minute. It gave him time to think.

'I don't know.' It was not a complete denial of the possibility.

I wondered how deep his doubt ran. With prompting and a number of pauses, Angelo di Michele made a confession of sorts. Not a legal one, but one of conscience. I imagined him propped up in his convalescent bed thinking about the cancer he'd beaten or that might be beating him. He was talking to a voice at the end of the phone, a powerless *little ginger Irish girl*, who could do nothing with his information. It seemed that if he told me what he suspected then he might be free of some past sin.

He began by stating that it wasn't really a cover up, which made me think that it was exactly that. The coroner's report, prepared locally, stated that Miles's death was a drowning, but the causes of other injuries could not be confirmed due to the twenty-four hours he'd been in the water. 'The doctor had found damage to the body consistent with assault. The boy had bruises on his waist and legs and tops of his arms. It might have been caused by him being held down. But this couldn't be confirmed.'

'Anything else?'

The tone of my question made him ask if I really wanted the answer. But he spoke anyway. The final bit of the puzzle was that Miles had been sexually abused. Anal tearing and significant contusions in that area confirmed that a terrible thing had happened on that night.

'Who?' I couldn't ask anything more. Angelo paused to cough again. When he spoke he offered an unconfirmed opinion.

'The boys.' And no more than that.

It infuriated me that Wheeler wasn't considered as a possible culprit. So I asked him, 'Why not Wheeler?'

Angelo again hesitated. Then dredging up the last of his confession stated that he was always suspicious of the possibility but to accuse him would mean going against the whole town, including Miles's parents who were great friends of Roger Wheeler. The unwitting parents had given the monster access to their son. His last statement was the most torturous of all. 'Giving the family and friends a sanitised version of the coroner's report seemed to be the right thing for the parents.

They didn't need to know what had happened to that child. No good could come from it.'

But you had the responsibility to tell the truth. It was the law and you and the doctor who wrote the report acted fraudulently and denied the dead child genuine justice. And let Roger Wheeler wander blameless through the last twenty years while Miles decayed under a tonne of earth and lies. And three other children went into manhood broken by your deceit and desertion. I said none of this out loud. It simply rolled about in my mind until I felt sickened by the cloying scent of disgust.

'The doctor who prepared the statement—is he still alive?'

'Long dead. The *Spanish dancer* got him five years ago.'

So the doctor died of cancer, which unfortunately exempted him from facing up to his wrongdoings.

'I'm sorry.' Angelo's final words before he put the phone down.

Not sorry enough.

Chapter Twenty-one

After that I received two calls. One from the hospital and one from Archie King. Mick's surgery was over and he was in recovery. The surgeon had been working on Mick's bypass for four hours; about the average time on the table. The nurse I spoke to confirmed that the doctor found no nasty surprises and that within the hour Mick would be moved to the Intensive Care Cardio ward where he would be monitored for at least 48 hours. If he was stable after that, he would be moved to the heart ward for a least a week or more. I would be able to see him in the morning and he should be able to talk but I'd need to be aware that he would not be able to see me for long. The information made me feel more optimistic than any other I had during the day.

The second call came from Archie. Henry hadn't come in didn't feel up to talking. But he said he would write down what happened as he saw it.

'And what about you Archie? What will you add?'

He didn't respond immediately. 'I'll send you an email too. I can only tell you what I saw. I can't do more than that. It might be better if it's written. We might both be braver if we just write it down.'

Archie didn't exactly say when he and Henry would be writing their accounts, but I felt it was a positive step forward for both of them. I wasn't the police or anyone with the authority to compel statements but perhaps I was someone they felt they could trust with information that they had struggled with for so long. Kitty's death might just have had one positive outcome; everyone could something off their chests.

I intended walking to Margaret and Peter's place. Dinner would be at 7.30. I knew the southerly had blown in and the beach would be colder, so I dragged out an old jumper of Phillip's. It was unlikely to be a much of a fashion statement, but I would be warm, and it would feel like he was closer. I missed him. The madness of the last few days had briefly removed him from my thoughts. But in the quiet times he was all I wanted. I felt the months of his absence would be more awful than I let on. But I had others to think of at the moment and delayed wallowing in my own misery.

I'd almost had enough of sifting through the lives of others, but I wanted to do one more thing, if I could find the number. I opened Mick's phone and had a quick search through the contacts to find it. Angela Flynn. Both a mobile and a home number were listed. I wrote them down and continued to scroll down the list without any real purpose and found a totally unexpected name. Sandra Flynn-McGowan. Mick's absent daughter; the one who had cut him out of her life after the death of her sister. It was a Queensland number and I couldn't help but wonder if it who would answer if I rang it. The phone only rang twice.

'Sandra McGowan.' The voice sounded mature and light.

I hadn't been prepared for Mick's daughter to be at the end of the phone despite me having called the number attributed to her. I cowardly hung up. And instead of ringing her back like an adult I rang the other number instead.

This time it was a voice with less light. 'Angela Flynn.' And then she waited with the expectation that someone would speak. I found my voice and introduced myself as a friend of Mick's. I quickly explained what had happened and that he had been admitted to Wollongong Hospital. Angela was most grateful for my thoughtfulness and pleased that Mick had such a good friend.

I momentarily worried that she thought I might be more than a friend, so I filled in the gap. 'I'm married to a police officer too. It's how Phillip and I became friends with Mick.' I realised the "too" was no longer accurate.

Angela didn't correct me. But thanked me again and asked if I thought it would be okay if she went to see him.

While Mick hadn't been explicit in giving me permission to bring his ex-wife into the picture, she was obviously a person who he'd wanted contacted in the case of an emergency. Perhaps his daughter Sandra was someone else he wanted me to call.

On the walk to the in-laws, I mulled over the day's discussions and findings. The only conclusion I reached was that life was messy. And that mess hurt people. Not just those entangled in Kitty's story but those in Mick's story. Max's story too. I hadn't thought about my sister-in-law Sophie for a couple of days, but she had made a mess of things too. I felt that old sensation of panic stirring around in me. People made messes and someone always had to clean it up. If it wasn't dealt with it just got bigger and consumed everything and everyone.

The table as usual had been set to feed the five thousand. Obviously, Margaret had not only invited me to dinner but the whole family. Of course Max and Sarah would be there, but I hadn't expected to see Lisa and Robert, Jessica and Lachlan and their respective tribes. Wherever the Swans were, there was a party. The discussion started with Sophie, which made Max immediately tense, but he need not have worried, Sophie was made the villain. Her sisters were ruthless, and I could see how much the tone upset her parents. The saving grace was that Jessica had been contacted by her younger sister. Sophie needed money and wanted Jess to ask Max to put money into her account.

Max didn't get a chance to speak before Peter piped up. 'You'll do nothing of the sort, Max. If Sophie wants money, she can go out and work for it.' My father-in-law rarely showed anger and he, like his son, usually played the rational peacemaker. Obviously, Sophie's abandonment of her husband and child had done more than hurt her parents; it had made her father mad.

The shock of it directed the conversation elsewhere. I became the focus when Sarah didn't want to be anywhere else but on my knee.

'You will a great mother one day, Lily,' came the barely concealed revelation that the entire table knew of my pregnancy.

Lisa's comment brought a smile to my face and I slightly shook my head at Margaret. It wasn't really chastising her for revealing the worst kept secret since the beginning of secret-keeping. The table sort of erupted into laughter and happy congratulations. I don't ever like being the centre of attention and I felt flushed and overwhelmed by the excitement. More than ever I wished Phillip was here to deflect the family inquisition.

This time Max came to the rescue. 'Oh settle down all of you. They do this every time a Swan baby is announced. It's not just for you, Lil. It's a thing!'

A thing! A family thing where everyone is genuinely thrilled at the expansion of the clan. They discussed the due date and where we would be having the baby and how nice it would be if it was a girl. Four grandsons and only two granddaughters so far. Robert started up a betting sheet, so the family could put bets on for the gender, the weight and the hair colour. Only one seriously unkind punter put their money on twins. The day had been complicated, the next day would be a strain but the evening was a blessing. While the sadness of Sophie's departure was still raw, Phillip and I had given the family a promise of a tiny bit of happiness in the shape of our future son or daughter. Or God forbid, twins! Or a red head!

Max wouldn't hear of me walking home. Not that he thought that I'd be mugged but that the wind had whipped up fiercely and gusted at thirty or forty kilometres per hour. 'Enough to knock you off your feet Lil.' I didn't really feel like being blown home so gratefully accepting the lift. I helped Max get Sarah to bed first. Having to lie down with her and read two books before she would let me go. Max it seemed was staying over as well. On the way home I asked him about when he thought he would move back into his own home and get Sarah settled there. 'I don't know for sure. It looks a bit too hard at the moment and if Sophie needs money to relocate in Sydney, I'll will have to eventually sell the house and give her half the money.' This was his interpretation of fair play.

'Maybe not, Max. You and Sarah need to take back your life. And I'm here for a little while longer and happy to help Margaret and the other girls take Sarah.' It was not a spontaneous offer. I'd been thinking that I could help out with Sarah, particularly after the hospital discharged Mick and we could put the Kitty Jepp story behind us. A conclusion to his story seemed close.

Max insisted on walking me to the door, hugging me and telling me about ten times to drive carefully in the morning. He wanted to come with me, but I suggested that it might be better if he came with me the following week when hopefully I might be bringing Mick home. It would give him time to finish up some of his work, including getting some doors on my bedrooms and finishing the deck. He made lots of promises as he walked back to his car.

It was only 8:30 and I'd eaten too much to contemplate getting into bed despite the early start the next day. I wrote Phillip an email about the evening and how I'd be seeing Mick in the morning. I had no new emails in my inbox, so I knew there that Archie or Henry hadn't been able to get their stories down. To fill the hour or two before I went to bed I thought I'd try the phone book to see if I could find an address for Kelly and Brian Morgan. It was so easy. The phone directory only had one listing for B and K Morgan in Bridges Avenue, Tuross Head. It was something to follow up when I got back in a day or two. The other thing I thought I might do is to ring Sandra McGowan one more time. All she could do was shout and hang up. The world wouldn't end.

'Sandra McGowan.' The voice as equally upbeat as the first time I heard it.

'Hello, Sandra, my name is Lily O'Hara and I'm ringing about your father Mick Flynn.'

Her intake of breath was audible but I rushed into the void so she could hear the vital piece of information before she disconnected us. She was listening for the minute it took me to get the details of heart-attack, bypass surgery, Wollongong Hospital and that I would see him tomorrow.

'Are you his partner?'

A question I again answered with too many details when the word no would have sufficed.

Sandra then calmly and deliberately explained that there had to be some kind of mistake that I had called her. She had been estranged from both her parents for a number of years and that she had no interest in what might be happening to either of them.

It was something of a slap in the face. I had expected that this call might have been the beginning of a reconciliation between father and daughter. It was most surprising that she had no interest in re-establishing links with her past.

I finished inadequately with, 'He loves you Sandra. It's never too late to know that.'

She put an end to the call at the last word.

I felt disappointed and a bit of a failure. I'd made no inroads into healing this rift, chasm, between Mick and his daughter. I may even have driven her further away. This unfinished business simply had to remain incomplete and out of my hands. When Mick felt much better, I'd consider telling him what I'd done. Maybe.

I slept, better than I expected and got up at 5am and on the road by 6. I'd be at the hospital before 9.

The trip north was pretty uneventful. Some slow points through the little towns that dotted the Princes Highway but no real traffic snarls. I even had time for a hot drink and a bacon roll in the quaint town of Berry. Road works happened sporadically which meant at some time in the future the road would sweep around these towns and people just interested in their destinations would miss the wonders of these places. I loved country towns. Not just the quiet but the harkening back to a time when things seemed easier, simpler, less impersonal and more connected. I grew up in a world like this. And even with all its complications I wouldn't have given it up for a city childhood. It made me think about where Phillip and I would raise our child, Canberra or the coast. It was something we would have to talk about when he got home, or perhaps we might leave it until this little person had arrived.

The two-and-a-half-hour travel time gave me the space to think about the future. Phillip would be home and would make decisions about continuing his career in the force. I would return to my job at the museum, plan to take some time off to be with our baby, change jobs, or go part-time. We could live at the coast, not work, have half a dozen kids and home school them. I couldn't wait to tell Phil about the possibility that we would become a little bohemian on his return to Australia. I'd play music and cook, and he could go fishing with Max and grow a garden. All totally fanciful stuff that Phillip would never subscribe to; and in reality I could never survive the disorder of such a choice.

The hospital was new and I easily found my way from the information reception to the pristine world of ICU. The door in could only be breached by a conversation over the inter-com system. I had to identify myself, who I wanted to see and my relationship to Mick. It was on my mind to say daughter but if he was awake and the nurse said "your daughter is here" it might not be the best for his health. "Next of kin," seemed clinical despite its legal accuracy.

The ward looked busy despite the quiet. An incessant hum of machinery attached to every person in the place contributed to the strangeness. Every bed had a person recovering, or not, from one form of surgery or another.; The nurses and specialists seemed to move soundlessly between patients. Someone directed me to Mick's bed and met the nurse standing guard over him. She nodded at me to move forward and speak to the still form that lay unmoving under the crisp whiteness of fresh sheets. Mick's eyes opened but were unfocused.

'It's likely that he will be confused for a few days. The breathing tube has just been removed and he is on a lot of pain medication,' she said, matter-of-factly but not unkindly. 'Are you his daughter?'

It was too hard to convey how I'd become the next of kin, so I simply said yes.

I was allowed to stay for an hour in which time Mick said nothing but opened his eyes three or four times. He looked at me and half smiled in recognition and then floated away again. I prattled on telling him about the information I had gathered since we left Mallacoota and that I was meeting Father Burrell that afternoon and Connie Harlow the following week. It was just noise really, but it beat simply staring at the beeping machines and tubes that seemed to consume the man I'd come to know as strong, intractable, kind and consistently—and somewhat annoyingly—always right.

'He will be okay, you know,' the nurse's voice cut across my thoughts. She must have been thinking that I was concerned that he would not be.

I nodded. Of course Mick would be okay. A week in hospital, six weeks of recovery he would be as good as new.

I left after an hour, indicating to the nurse that I'd be back in the early evening. I had to be buzzed out of the unit and felt a strange relief as I left the sealed world of the ICU. It felt like I'd been holding my breath under water for an hour.

'I was surprised when the nurse said my daughter was with her father.' The voice came from the row of seats lining the outside waiting area. A woman in her sixties dressed in jeans and casual sweater stood and walked towards me with her hand outstretched. 'Angela Flynn. You must be Lily.' We shook hands and she drew me in closer to her for a light hug. 'How is he?'

I felt a little embarrassed to be the one giving out information to Mick's wife—ex-wife. She seemed genuinely relieved with my report that he would be fine. It was obvious that she wanted to talk a little more before she went into the ward and I was happy to spend time with her. I wasn't really sure what I expected Angela to be like; Mick had said so little about her except for the terrible tragedy they shared when their youngest daughter died.

Angela filled in some of the gaps. She started with, 'I expect you don't know much about me.'

Typically Mick hadn't said much but he could have started with beautiful, calm and warm. She was all of these things and not the least bit disparaging of her ex-husband.

After about fifteen minutes of us trading key details about Mick, I thought I'd ask her about Sandra.

'She thought the two of us abandoned Belinda. Blamed Mick most of all for her death. But it wasn't his fault, nor mine. A terrible thing happened and we could not undo it. It was just what it was.' Angela's eyes watered but she stayed in control. Probably too many tears in the past had been shed trying to come to terms with losing her child. She seemed bewildered by Sandra's decision to excise both parents out of her life. As a mother, she grieved the loss of her child. 'Perhaps I didn't give her enough attention at the time, left her alone too much.' Apparently by the time Angela had found some equilibrium Sandra had moved away and the link had been lost.

'Didn't you try to find her?' A silly question given the fact that I knew Mick had her number and had information about her life. Angela seemed to be ignorant of these facts. She said that Mick had looked and found out that she had moved to Queensland and possibly married. I couldn't believe that Mick hadn't told Angela that she was a grandmother and I certainly wasn't going to drop that bombshell. I also thought I'd keep the fact that I'd spoken to Sandra a secret too. It would all be too much. I asked Angela if she had planned on staying in Wollongong, thinking we could catch up in the evening, but she was driving back to Canberra after she saw Mick.

'Would you mind if I stayed in touch, to keep you in the loop with Mick's recovery?' I asked.

She nodded. Patted my shoulder and walked to the intercom. 'I can see why Mick likes you so much, Lily. He always had a thing for red heads.'

I sat for a minute thinking about how sad it was that these two lovely people had been torn apart by the pressures of a job and the loss of a child. I had imagined that the opposite would occur; that the two of them would have held onto each other to survive the worst of the storm. I hoped Mick would remember that she had been there. I hoped that they could become friends again and together they could bring Sandra back into the family. And that was a lot of hoping.

I continued my journey north, apprehensive at the thought of my appointment with Father Burrell. I had brought the photocopied sheets from the yearbooks and wondered what kind of story he might tell. I wouldn't reveal immediately that I knew the three boys had tried to enlist his support twice during the time Roger Wheeler allegedly abused them. Every time I conjured that image, something hot and boiling raged in me. I had a propensity for wanting to strike out at people whose actions hurt others. I'd never mustered any physical aggression in my whole life, and it would probably be quite bad for the maiden punch to be aimed at a priest. Control would need to be my friend today.

The parish hall at Engadine was fairly modern, something interesting built in the 1970s. A number of churches built by communities in the 60s and 70s, adopted the experimental architectural shapes of the era. This was one of them. A narrow walkway separated the church and hall and the noise led me to my destination. The doors were open, and I could hear the noise of children playing and adults talking, not a language I immediately recognised. As I stepped through into the light-filled room I recognised the people as Hazara Afghans and I assumed the language was either Farsi or Dari. The children were being ushered away by young adults and the parents and other adults settled down into chairs that had been set up in loose semi-circles in front of a table at which sat five people who appeared to be officials of some sort.

One of them, Father Burrell was the first to speak. He welcomed the group. '*Salam va ashnai.*'

He used the assembled group's own language. It may have been the extent of his vocabulary as the rest of the introduction continued in English, translated by a young man who stood to the left of the table. He spoke about the open arms of the community and the ecumenical services available to assist the assembled group. The group looked to the priest with a mixture of expectation and bewilderment. How odd this place must have seemed to them.

By the time the speaker from the Migrant Health Service started her spiel, Father Burrell had recognised that I waited for him at the back of the group. He spoke briefly to the woman seated beside him, made a cursory bow to the room and walked towards a side door. He beckoned me to follow him.

Despite the passing of twenty years, Victor Burrell had changed little from the photos I had of him. He was older, a little weathered, thinner perhaps and still clinging to the same few hairs that now formed a partial tonsure around the sides of his head. He led me across the walkway and into the church where the sounds of the hall could not be heard. And I assumed where my conversation would remain between the two of us.

'Miss O'Hara it's nice to meet you.' He warmly shook my hand and invited me to sit down in the back pew. 'Poor Benedict. What happened to him?'

I described the details of Kitty's suicide, leaving nothing out. I'd decided that no-one deserved to be spared the awfulness of it. My intention had been to rattle the priest and my words appeared to wound him. His brow furrowed and his eyes fluttered closed on several occasions. The sadness looked genuine, but I was not sorry.

'Father, a terrible thing happened at St. Finbar's. A terrible thing that you knew about.' I wanted to add, "and did nothing about".

To my surprise he nodded his agreement. 'A terrible thing indeed.' A long pause. 'I'll tell you everything I can remember.' His story started with a description of Miles. 'Full of light, not a mean bone in that child's body. Kind to a fault. And deep faith.'

None of which had saved him. Even though I wanted to add my bitter asides I kept quiet and let him talk. He spoke highly of Benedict, who he called Bennie. And his sidekicks, Archie and Henry. The boys were bright, and he believed that if they could get out of the town they would all do amazing things. The death of Miles was a tragedy for everyone, but particularly for the parents. They spent months after the death trying to find a reason, something or someone they could blame for the loss of their little boy.

'Towns like that appear to close in on themselves when tragedies happen. They try to deal with it together but more often in causes deep divisions. Rifts like chasms between people.'

I wondered what he meant by deal with it. Cover up the truth?

'But you're not here for that part of the story are you?'

His face was earnest, and I sensed a deep sorrow in him. He wasn't a monster; it would have been easier if he had been. If he had been arrogant and dismissive I could have hated him and deliberately set out to hurt him. But he was just a man who had not been able to predict the consequences of his inaction. To draw him in, I talked about Kitty. His wife and child who had little idea that his past had been corrupted by the death of Miles and what precipitated it. She had no idea that he was at risk of suicide. 'The baby is Isaiah.'

'It means God is my saviour.' Victor looked up at the crucified Christ before continuing. 'Bennie wasn't a particularly religious boy, but he had great faith in God. We had lots of discussions about good and evil.' He stopped talking, looked towards the altar again and said, 'I suspect you want to know about Roger Wheeler.' He waited for me to nod. 'He was a mean son-of-a-bitch.'

'And a paedophile,' I added.

Father Burrell didn't deny the possibility but recounted the time he had spoken to Benedict about his accusations. He thought the boy just wanted to stop being an altar server but was too afraid of his mother to simply say he didn't want to do it. Wheeler was very handy with the cane and the strap and this was, according to the priest, another reason the boys might have made up the stories about the wine drinking and the inappropriate touching. He had given the boys the opportunity to give the real reason why they didn't want to continue in the roles. 'But they didn't say, and they didn't repeat their initial accusations. It's why I thought it might have been a lie.' The priest said he had talked to Wheeler about the boys' unhappiness, but not the accusations directly. He'd suggested that the discipline master be less focused on punishment and more pastoral in his guidance of the students and to be aware that the servers probably drank the altar wine. 'There was nothing in the man's demeanour that made me think that he was doing what Bennie said he was. I did speak to the Bishop, I asked him for advice but little came from that discussion.' Father Burrell's spiritual guide had told him to ignore the assertion because the school would close within a few years and Wheeler would be someone else's problem.

'But they repeated the allegation when Miles died. And no-one believed them for a second time.' I heard my voice becoming more strident. 'And Miles had injuries consistent with sexual assault.'

The priest laid his face into his hands and shook his head. 'We believed that boys might have done something to Miles. That's why everyone covered it up—to save them.'

'Are you sure it wasn't to save Wheeler?'

Victor became more animated than ever in his denial of that knowledge. He was adamant that if he'd known that Wheeler really abused the boys he would have acted and never have allowed the information about Miles to be suppressed.

'How could you condone covering up for the three boys if you thought they'd assaulted and then killed Miles?'

'I believed Miles died as a result of accidental drowning. That night the weather was terrible and floodwater poured into the lake. The other thing was a stupid prank, a bit of experimentation. It would have ruined them all if it got out. The boys would have gone to jail.'

I tried to sound as in control as I could. I willed steel into my voice. 'Sexual assault of a child is not a prank, Father. And the event did ruin their lives. And Roger Wheeler did abuse those children.' I wanted this man to take responsibility for his silence and for his spurning of Kitty's outcry. He could not claim ignorance or that he supported a lie to save the reputations of the surviving boys. He must have had suspicions that Wheeler was not the man the town thought he was.

'It's all in the past.' His last desperate attempt to deflect blame cut deeply.

But he was wrong. The ills of the past cannot remain hidden. The darkness bubbles to the surface and pain is always the price. I suspected in some odd reversal of roles this man, a decent man, wanted me to give him absolution for his sin of silence and the convenience of his disbelief. But the suffering of four children could not be so easily erased. I did not forgive him. There were not enough Hail Marys and Our Fathers that could wipe away this transgression. I looked towards to the modern-styled crucifix of Jesus. He had been hewn from local timber and had taken on a Picasso-esque visage. The face contorted and the limbs barely discernible from the cross. But the eyes looked down into the body of the church, seeking comfort or perhaps a little hope that the pain would soon be over. His suffering to ease our own, his death for our lives. Faith was such a complicated thing and real life even more so.

The priest must have assumed that I was praying as he quietly left my side and walked to the back of the church.

Father Burrell left me sitting in silence but behind me I heard him greeted warmly by a small posse of children who had come looking for him. Their little faces were full of trust. I had no doubt that he was a good man, a good priest, a servant to his people and his God, but his adherence to one lie had cost others their lives. He looked back at me for a moment and walked a few steps to speak to me. 'If I could change the past I would, Lily. I would have been less of a coward. God forgive me for being one twenty years ago.' He left with the children to rejoin the adults. His goodness would make a difference here and now.

If he'd been braver, however, Kitty might still be alive. As I sat there his comment about the bishop's suggestion that Wheeler would be someone else's problem made me feel ill. If he had left St. Finbar's and moved to another school, there could possibly be more victims, more lives ruined and ended because of his actions. If only Mick was well and could advise me how I would find out about his movements over the last twenty years. If there were others we wouldn't have to rely on vague recollections and hearsay to bring Wheeler to account for his actions.

I ate before I went to see how Mick had progressed over the past six hours. The drive back to the hospital was straight-forward. They buzzed me in; a different nurse was watching him. He was awake and a little more aware but not talking. I attempted to hug him, carefully avoiding wires and tubes and the padded wound on his chest.

The young male nurse said they were pleased with his progress and that he would be moved down to the cardio ward in the morning. 'He will be more like himself tomorrow,' he said patting my shoulder.

I expected that these nurses were very experienced at reading the minds of visitors who sat watching and hoping that the silent and still family members who lay in critical condition would somehow get better. It was hard not to worry about what the following days and weeks would bring. But also futile to contemplate all the "what ifs" that might befall the critically ill but impossible not to. What if the operation didn't succeed? What if he wasn't himself when he fully woke up? What if Mick died? I hadn't realised I had started to cry until I felt a tissue placed into my hand. I sat beside him for an hour, listening to the sounds of monitors and watching his heart rate and blood pressure on the screen. The rhythmic reminder of his beating heart became a strange comfort after a while.

The hotel was not particularly busy, and it had a business centre where guests could use computers and print documents. Only a few other guests sat in the area, intently focused on their individual screens. I looked for a seat away from the others and logged on. There were two unread—one from Phillip, full of his declarations of how much he missed me and letting me know that he would be out of touch for the next five days. He wanted an update on Mick and asked if I knew how Max was going and if anyone knew anything about Sophie. I could fill him in on all the news I had, continuing to omit the issue about the investigation into Kitty's suicide. I had promised myself that when I could contact Phillip in five days' time, I would tell him what we had been doing, and hopefully all the chasing down information was at an end. I would be getting ready to bring Mick back to the coast and settling into my study and doing my bit to look after Max's little girl. Sometimes promises are hard to keep but they are worth our best efforts.

The second email came from Archie King. It started by telling me that Henry was in a very bad way. The two men had met up and Henry had started to tell Archie what had happened that night in Wheeler's house but he couldn't continue. He went back to his boat and locked himself in the cabin. Archie sat sentinel for a few hours making sure that the boat didn't leave the moorings. But Archie was prepared to explain what happened after the boys met and took the boat out.

He started by describing how the rain had eased off by the time he saw Benedict and Henry approaching the boat. They held Miles between them. Miles's head lolled forward, and his legs weren't touching the ground. He seemed barely conscious. The front of his shirt was covered in vomit; sour red liquid had soaked his white t-shirt. Miles groaned occasionally. Benedict and Henry were ashen, and it was obvious that the other two boys had been crying. Their eyes, wide and unblinking, and pallid skin made them look like ghosts emerging from the dark. Archie had expected to meet the two older boys and simply walk with them to his house where they would settle in for a night of talking, eating and playing games. He hadn't expected the sight that greeted him.

Henry said that they had to get away from The Rottweiler and that they were taking the boat over to Jimmy Point. Archie didn't question the logic or danger of the situation he just knew that a terrible thing had happened, and his friends needed him. The boys loaded Miles into the boat and Archie took off his coat and wrapped the sick Miles in it. No one said anything in the few minutes it took to get the boat away from the jetty and out onto the lake. At that point Henry started crying and Archie put his arm around him and let him lean against him. Benedict focused on getting the boat as far away as he could.

Within minutes they made it through The Narrows and about to skip across Top Lake to the landing. Benedict cut the engine and the little boat floated about in the strong current that pushed them closer to eastern side of the bay. Miles seemed to come to in the lull and sat up, leaned over the side of the boat and vomited again. Benedict held onto the Miles's shoulders as he wretched and heaved. In the foggy moonlight Archie could see Miles's back as he knelt with his head over the side. There was blood on the back of his blue jeans. And a smell that made Archie think that Miles had diarrhoea as well as vomiting. Benedict said that they would have to get Miles in the water to wash him. He had a towel in his backpack and clothes for the night he was spending it with the Kings. He said we would clean him up and dress Miles in his clothes and then spend the night out on Jimmy Point in the camp shelter where they could light a fire.

They were just kids Archie wrote. They thought it the right thing to do. When you're a kid the worst option could seem logical, could appear to fix the problem. He continued writing about how Benedict got out of the boat into the freezing water. It was about 15 degrees Celsius, not enough for hypothermia to set in quickly but cold enough to hurt the body and affect the control of breathing. Too long in the water at this temperature would eventually become dangerous. Miles cried out when they lowered into Benedict's waiting arms, the water immediately making him more alert. Benedict told Miles that they needed to clean him up and that he would be okay. "*Noli timere,*" he repeated over and over. Everything was going to be okay. Henry started to cry while he waited in the boat. He had the towel out ready to help change Miles. Benedict walked away from the boat; the water level reached his shoulders. Both boys shivered with the cold. The sound of chattering teeth and Benedict's soothing words could be heard above the swirling relentless noise of the floodwaters being sucked back through The Narrows.

The boat had to be moved or it would have drifted back into the fast-moving floodwaters. Archie started the boat and moved it about twenty metres away from the two boys wading in the neck-deep lake. There was another camping spot on the same side where the two boys struggled in the water. Archie decided to take the boat up there, moor it and run back along the bank to help Benedict get Miles back onto land. In the few minutes it took to manoeuvre the boat out of the dragging water, Benedict and Miles had moved away from the shallow water and had been separated from each other. Miles had wrenched himself out of Benedict's supporting arms and simply swum away into the deep water between the two points. Within a minute Miles could not be seen and Benedict, now shivering and blue, dragged himself to the shallows where Archie waited.

The three boys got back into the boat and searched the water between Gravelly Point and Jimmy Point. The rain began to fall, the milky moon hid behind even more threatening clouds. Archie took the boat over to the camp area, dragged Benedict to the shelter, made Henry light the fire in the pit with the dry kindling that had been left by the rangers. He helped Benedict out of his wet clothes and into the dry ones they were going to put on Miles. They called out for Miles missing in the water, their eyes straining to see the white t-shirt in the dark green water. But Miles had gone. The police search and rescue found the three survivors huddled around the embers of a fire that had burned all night and had kept Benedict alive. It seemed like a dream. Like they had all imagined that Miles had been with them. It didn't make sense that that frail little boy could have simply disappeared.

Archie made it clear that Benedict was not to blame for losing Miles in the water. It was impossible to think clearly in freezing temperature of the water and he feared for his own life as he began to struggle in the ever-increasing depth and strong current. It was not what they had said to the police that night. They hadn't been blithely speeding along in the boat when Miles simply fell out. Kitty was washing Miles clean of the brutal assault. His motives, both tender and innocent, could not placate him. His whole life had been shaped by his inability to save Miles. His guilt finally overwhelmed him.

Archie had promised at the end of his email to get Henry to talk about what had happened at Wheeler's before Miles went missing on the lake.

It seemed obvious what had transpired at Wheeler's house in the hours before the boys' misguided flight to what they thought was a place of safety. Archie's description of the child's condition made it clear that he had been shattered both physically and mentally. It seemed to be that Miles's disappearance into the dark and unforgiving water of Dead Finish had been precipitated by something infinitely darker. Miles's death was a tragedy. The shadows that consumed Kitty and Henry that night in Wheeler's house were an equal tragedy that had continued to play out for over twenty years. My heart broke for the children they were and the men they had become.

If Wheeler was alive, it was time for him to pay.

Chapter Twenty-two

I could not sleep after reading Archie's email. The images of those four boys battling against the water, the night, the cold and the corruption meted out to them made sleep impossible. Reflecting on the cover up provided no comfort either.

The morning couldn't come soon enough. I'd see Mick and then drive home for a few days of rest. I'd be back in five days and meet with another player in the story, Connie Harlow. I wondered if anything she had to tell me could be as soul-destroying as Archie's account of the night Miles's death or Father Burrell's confession of his inaction. Would meeting her have any merit at all?

As predicted, Mick was more like himself when I tracked him down on the cardio ward. He looked a better and although still on lots of pain medication, he sounded lucid and talking about getting out of the hospital. I asked if he had remembered his visitors in ICU.

'Do you mean Jesus?' And he laughed. 'Seriously I thought I saw him.'

I countered with a joke about him checking that Mick was staying put, he wasn't ready to be grilled by Detective Flynn.

'No I meant Angela.' Mick was surprised that I'd call her and that she had driven down to see him.

He deflected how pleased he felt by saying, 'Was she just checking to see if I was dead?'

'She was worried. It seems she cares about you.'

Mick closed his eyes, feigning sleep for a few minutes. His way of controlling his emotions.

During the rest of the visit I talked about driving back to Broulee and how I'd return within the week and make arrangements to get him home with me soon after that. He didn't want me fussing about and made ridiculous assertions about being able to look after himself, which I simply ignored. 'You're going to be with me whether you like it or not, Dad.'

He looked surprised at that so I explained how the hospital was under the impression that I was his daughter.

He laughed.

I didn't want to worry him about the investigation into Kitty's life but he wanted to know what had happened in the last few days. I gave a brief précis of the conversations and emails and who I had planned to see next—including Connie Harlow—when I returned the following week.

Mick said that he would be well enough to sit in on that conversation, which I let slide, neither confirming nor denying the likelihood of that. He thought following up with Miles's mother was a great idea, particularly since she lived so close. He also advised me not to push Henry for his story. 'Just let him come to you now. He obviously needs time.'

As I got ready to leave, I asked one last question. 'Mick how can I find Roger Wheeler?'

The question upset him, and his answered, 'Stay away from that line of investigating until I get back on my feet. You don't know what might happen.' I was almost ready to argue with him. It's not something you should do on your own.' I thought I'd have Max for company if I managed to track him down. Mick could see that his warnings had fallen on deaf ears despite me saying nothing about what I would or wouldn't do. 'The electoral roll is your best bet. You're not meant to use it find people but everyone does it. If he is alive you will find a record of him there.'

It meant a trip to Canberra, but I could do that in a day. I'd stop at the cemetery in Bungendore to check out the family graves, catch up with Helena and Brendan for lunch in the city and spend an hour or two at the house to make sure everything was fine after being shut up for the last few weeks. It would be another day out of my writing schedule, but time well spent.

On returning to Broulee I found myself exhausted and in need of quiet time. I rang Margaret to let her know about Mick's operation and subsequent recovery. Texted Max to see if he could drop in the next day to discuss availability to come back to the hospital. Emailed

Phillip even though I knew he would not be able to respond for several days and then curled up on the couch to sleep. I hoped that keeping the lights off might mean that Phillip's well-meaning family would leave me alone for the night. It didn't work. The lack of light and movement seemed to trigger Max's emergency response mode and thinking that something was wrong, he just let himself into the house.

I woke to find him sitting at the end of the couch peering at me under the beam of a torch. 'Shit.' Involuntary swearing seems to happen when I'm startled. 'What are you doing, Max?' I tried not to be exasperated by his alleged well-meaning intrusion.

'I just wanted to check on you and if you were asleep I didn't want to wake you.'

Apparently breaking in, not turning on any lights and blinding me with a torch was his attempt at not waking me.

Defeated by his version of caring, I sat up and gave into to the questioning about who had said what, how Mick was travelling and what our next move was going to be.

I had already written down the week's timetable of activities. A rest day. A day in Canberra. A day tracking down Kelly Morgan. A return to Wollongong to collect Mick and speak to Connie. And at some point after that, going to see Jean and Isaiah at Congo to let her know what had happened in Kitty's life when he was a boy. It wouldn't be a definitive answer as to why he'd chosen this time, or it had chosen him, for his life to seem unworthy of living. In this case pain could not be avoided. This part of the story could be passed on to her baby son when he was old enough to ask what had happened to his father. It was not a story that I would ever want to tell but I also knew that being spared the truth had greater repercussions. At some point in the coming days I also hoped that Henry Kelly might find a way of revealing what had happened in Wheeler's house that night. We all could guess but only in the telling, out loud, could he be freed from the nightmare.

Max and Sarah stayed with his in-laws. They would return to their own home in a couple of days and start his life as a single father. Sophie still insisted on money and had made a fairly abusive phone call the previous day. The family had gathered to discuss what to do about Sophie in my absence. The outcome was that her sisters, Lisa and Jessica, were going to Sydney to meet her and try to work out what she needed, who she had left with and why. One way or another, the entire family were involved in some form of hide and seek investigation. We all looked for answers to a strange set of questions.

Max left early after he convinced himself that I was going to eat and then sleep. We decided to catch up with each other at some point the following day.

As always I checked my emails just in case Phillip had managed to get to a computer but there was nothing there. I felt too tired to do anything but go to bed. Sleep came, dreams followed. All peculiar in nature and unresolved. But by dawn I had rested and happy to be in my nearly finished beach house. For the first time in weeks, I really looked about the house in the process of transformation. It was a simple renovation that had left us with plenty of room and a sweeping view of the beach. The main part of the house was filled with light and when completed would be a wonderful place to live and raise our child. It wasn't the first time that it occurred to me that Phillip and I might choose to live and work here, have children who could grow up with cousins, and grandparents and ever watchful aunts and uncles. I always wanted a house where friends could come and go, stay a while, or longer. The possibility of Christmases and birthdays, christenings and maybe even marriages being celebrated here made me smile. The thought of the happy life ahead of us made me feel better than I had for weeks. I hadn't realised that all the attention I was paying Benedict Jepp's life had cost me my happiness. It motivated me to be more focused on getting this problem solved. I decided to see this through and then put it behind me.

Chapter Twenty-three

The day of rest had been much needed. I spoke to Mick and he said he felt much better. Determined to get out of the hospital sooner rather than later.

The following day I got up early and left for Canberra. I had let Helena and Brendan know that I would meet them for lunch at our favourite Chinese restaurant in the city centre. I'd spend some time at the electoral office scouring the rolls to see if I could find a record for Roger Wheeler. I'd already checked the phone book but it had been a dead end—too many Wheelers and no Roger Wheeler specifically. I would also look at the historical electoral records at the National Library if I could find nothing at the AEC. It would be a busy morning.

With little traffic about I made good time. I had a cursory look at the cemetery where my family were buried saying out loud that I'd be back in the afternoon to visit them. I wasn't particularly superstitious, but I didn't like to think of the rows of ancestors and loved ones lined up and seeing me whiz by without a simple acknowledgement. Again I blamed the pregnancy for such an over-active imagination.

It took me three hours to look through dozens of records in the two locations but other than his registration in the electorate of Gippsland East in 1985 with an address in Mallacoota, it seemed that he hadn't re-registered in any other electorate. I knew for sure he didn't live at that address anymore. Henry and Archie would have said something if he had been still living there. It was possible that he used a different name or simply using that old address to vote in elections. Or he may have been dead. The latter most unlikely given a quick search had revealed that no-one of that name had died in Victoria or New South Wales in the past twenty years. Another dead end. I really did need

Mick's expertise and resources. Finding the dead seemed to be easier than locating the living.

I felt frustrated that I'd wasted a whole morning trying to find The Rottweiler. I didn't really even know why I wanted to find him. I had no real idea what I'd do if I knew where he was living. Confront him about his actions? Go to the police? Burn his house down? Without Henry's story about the night of Miles's death, no one could make a coherent case against him.

I walked through the lunch-time crowds in the city mulling over the possible ramifications for Wheeler if Henry could add that final puzzle piece. I had no idea what I could do to help him bring the memories forward.

Deep in thought initially I hadn't noticed Helena and Brendan waving wildly at me from the outside dining area of Jimmy's Kitchen. They both called my name as I was about to walk past them. As always I loved to see them. Being with old friends is a reminder that all is well with the world and that the best things in life don't change.

They were as pleased to see me too. The conversation focused on Mick. Helena in particular was deeply concerned and keen to see him. I suggested that she come down the weekend after I rescued him from hospital. We had an excited discussion about the baby. Tears and laughter as the two fought over who the baby should be named after. Both of them offered a range of frivolous and impossible names for both boys and girls.

'I'm not naming my child Birdie. Seriously Birdie Swan? It will condemn my child to a lifetime of school yard bullying.' I also vetoed Sweeney, Ermengarde, Star-cruiser and several names spelled backwards such as Nadnerb and Aneleh. It was ridiculous but also very relaxing to be silly for a while. Over the past weeks very little light-heartedness had made its way into my life.

After several tasty dishes and numerous cups of jasmine tea, Helena finally asked what we had been doing when Mick had his heart attack. I explained Kitty's suicide and Max's request for help in understanding the letter he left. Brendan and Helena exchanged looks of concern as both of them remembered my last experience with exploring the past. Helena immediately went into her protective mother mode as the story began to unfold.

'I suppose there's no way you can be persuaded to let this go, Lily?' She knew the answer before she had finished asking the question. She said, 'Please look after yourself,' and kissed me on the forehead.

I walked them back to Helena's car. They had to get back to work and they'd already extended their lunch break to an hour and a half. I also wanted to get on the road so I could check the house and then spend an hour tidying up the family plots in the cemetery.

'You know Lily, a Royal Commission into child abuse is about to start. Every state is conducting some sort of investigation into institutional violence and the definitive final step is a nationwide inquiry. Your friend's story can be told, and the perpetrators will be exposed.' Brendan's matter-of-fact tone was also tinged with sadness. 'This country will be shocked by the number of stories that are revealed when the time comes.'

Perhaps the promise of revelations and legal retribution would be enough to prompt Henry to talk about the events of 1980. Maybe the hope that he and others could be healed when their stories were told would help him find his courage. The thought that one day, should he still be alive, Roger Wheeler would be exposed for the monster he was. The monster he continued to be whether he acted on it or not.

I'd confirmed that Helena would be down in a week or so to spend some time making a fuss of Mick before heading back to my own car. She seemed pleased to have made the date.

I stopped by our house—only ten minutes from the city—and it remained in perfect condition. I just walked through, checked windows and doors and left after I re-set the alarm. I could tell Phillip that the house was secure and surviving without either of us.

I drove to the cemetery after a detour down Lake Road. I'd grown up here and only a few years ago had sold the family land to an American family who wanted a life away from city living. I was surprised to see a serious fence separating the property from the dirt road. A locked gate would keep the most earnest visitor off the land. The dwellings that once housed my extended family had been renovated and extended. The front house where I lived for several years after university had been painted a rather dull green and the old roof replaced with black tin. It seemed to have merged into the dark ridge behind it. It looked slightly like a military compound with its big fence and camouflage colouring. I had a little twinge of regret in seeing the strange changes that had been made. It also made me realise that there was nothing left for me here; the home I'd known now buried beneath a modernised exterior. My Uncle Darcy's orchard that I'd tried so hard to save in the last year I lived there had been ripped out for a tennis court. Life had moved on. The past would have to live on in my memory.

The cemetery, however, hadn't changed. It still struggled from a lack of water and looked as forlorn as ever in places. I walked through the main entrance and up to the Catholic section where several generations of O'Haras rested. My mother, father and brother lay beside my aunt and uncle. A little un-named grave of my aunt's illegitimate stillborn girl nestled in amongst family who would have loved her. I wasn't sad here despite the loneliness these tombstones indicated about my own life. The graves really didn't need my attention as they had been recently neatened, but I liked to sweep away dry leaves and pull out any weeds that encroached on them. I gave each of the new plaques a little polish with a cloth I'd brought from the car. Each one had a small faux plant in a mosaic pot centralised in front of the inscriptions. These I'd have to change at least twice a year as the extremes in temperature would fade the foliage. I was about to clear away a piece of cardboard from a plant on the little baby's grave when I noticed it had something written on it. "*Lily*". On the other side of the card was an almost completed faded message. "*Thank you for this. All the best, Roland Devine.*" I could not have been more shocked.

Roland Devine had been my Aunt Billie's boyfriend and the father of her child. He had abandoned her and before she gave birth to and then buried the baby. I had wanted to hate him for the hurt he'd caused her but when I finally found out about him, and nearly confronted him, I discovered that he was not a bad man. He too had been young and had made a decision that perhaps he regretted, but he hadn't forgotten the little child who had been long dead. He had been here, perhaps many times, to wonder at what might have been. The past was never completely done with us, with any of us. A filament always linked the present to the events often thought forgotten.

On the drive back I thought about the future, rather than the past. Thoughts about my own child who began to make his or her presence felt in my belly, filled me with calm. Only a few weeks ago, I felt concerned about my ability to be a mother, to be a good mother, but something had changed. Perhaps the hormones had kicked in or the slight tightening of the waist band of my jeans that made think that parenting might work out. Or it could have been holding Kitty's son Isaiah or becoming Sarah's favourite auntie. Even my intensified feeling about Kitty, Miles, Henry and Archie and their suffering as little boys could be part of the change. Whatever caused these feelings, I was more certain than ever that the unplanned conception was a wonderful thing. Whether normal or not, I already felt protective of our unborn child. By summer there would be no hiding the fact that I was pregnant, by autumn he or she would be born.

I arrived home late in the day. The sun was low in the sky creating a yellow streak across the sea. I looked forward to being able to sit on the deck and watch the changing colour of day fading into night. I would relax with a hot drink, a little dinner and rest easy despite my inability to find Roger Wheeler. But the possibility of a quiet day's end was rendered impossible when I noticed a car with Victorian number plates parked outside the next-door neighbour's house. Even more so when the occupants of the car emerged and walked towards my front yard. Archie had driven Henry from Mallacoota to Broulee to see me rather than attempting to get the story down in an email or letter. They had driven three hours and had waited most of the afternoon. I was surprised that they hadn't called to say that they had intended to come up.

'I hope this is okay, Lily.' Archie's tone was neither apologetic nor questioning. They probably would have waited all night too if need be. 'Henry has to talk about the night Miles died.'

Much of the sense of calm dissipated with those words. Henry, sober this time looked worse than the last time we saw him in Gipsy Point when he was blind drunk. His skin looked ruddy and his eyes sunken and his body stooped. I've seen people look defeated before, but Henry looked as if he had been beaten down several times. Of all the things I didn't want to do at the end of the day was endure Henry's confession. But I could not turn them away.

They had booked into the hotel at Moruya and wouldn't stay for a meal, which was just as well because the fridge had been emptied. Coffee was all they'd take. I got them settled into the big chairs by the window and left them to look at the view that I'd hoped to enjoy alone.

Henry's hand shook as he sipped his coffee. 'I had hoped I would be drunk when I had to dredge up the memory of that night.' It seemed that this was the first time he would speak of it. Archie would hear for the first time what preceded Miles's death. They agreed that it should be taped.

It was an arduous fifteen-minute story. Henry fought to keep his emotions in check, occasionally holding his hand over his mouth, almost attempting to stem the flow of awful information. Archie did not look at him. His eyes stared off across the sea in front of us. He expected the story to be the terrible thing it was. For my part I simply let the tears flow. The effort to restrain them would have been too great. No words of comfort I might offer would suffice. There was nothing but shocked silence and pain.

Henry reiterated the parts of the story about the drinking and the repugnant nature of The Rottweiler's touching, but the night Miles died, the vile escalation of his behaviour had ruined the boys' lives. Henry and Kitty had as usual pretended to consume more wine than they actually did. They behaved in a giddy sleepy fashion that seemed to amuse Wheeler. But they were vigilant and safer than the intoxicated young boy. Wheeler unzipped his fly and began to touch himself. He pulled Miles on his knee and undid the child's jeans. Henry and Kitty pretended to be asleep, feigning being non compos mentis but they were fully aware of what followed. Roger Wheeler raped Miles Rennison. The child screamed out to his sleeping friends but out of fear, confusion, disgust, they did nothing. Miles's screams turned to sobbing and whimpering until the monster had finished with him. Wheeler kicked the little boy away from him as if he was repulsed by the broken child. He walked out of the room to the bathroom. As soon as the shower started, Kitty and Henry dressed Miles, who was conscious but deeply shocked. He couldn't walk or talk, so the two boys carried his frail body between them. When they got to Archie, the rest of the night unfolded. Miles drowned after he had been brutalised and Henry and Kitty would spend their lives carrying the memory of the appalling assault and, more damaging, the guilt of doing nothing to stop it.

They were only children themselves and weak in the face of the abusive and dangerous Wheeler. I could only imagine the weight of the memory. Kitty said that the truth could set them free, but I could not imagine how. Perhaps he meant that if Wheeler could be punished for his crimes against them, against Miles, the agony of their inaction might be resolved.

Henry made no fuss in the few minutes he spoke. A crime had been committed, a disgraceful sin had gone unpunished and a burdensome guilt had snuffed out a life. The boys had not saved Miles, not stopped Wheeler and gave up trying to find help.

At the end of his story, Henry downed the remains of his now cooled coffee, and if it was possible he looked older and more crumpled than he did when he first sat down. But his chin lifted a little higher as he too followed Archie's gaze out across the near darkened sea. Archie said nothing, but I watched his hand wipe away the tears from his face.

We three, now linked by the heavy truth, sat in silence for a few moments until Archie asked the inevitable question. 'So what now?'

I had no immediate answer for his question. The initial response was to scream out loud and demand retribution, but I knew of nothing that could possibly help Henry. It was too late for Kitty. It felt as if all was lost.

When the men left, I rang Mick who sounded like his pre-heart attack self. He desperately wanted to get out of the hospital and counted the days until I'd return to spring him from what he described as institutionalised hell. I didn't want to burden him with Henry's story. When he was home I'd let him listen to the recording and he would know what could be done. Mick's endless contacts with serving and retired officers never failed to turn up a possible lead. Someone would know how to bring The Rottweiler to account for his crimes.

My job was to speak to Connie Harlow and hear her version of events and to let her know what had happened the night of Miles's death. Perhaps I could encourage her to see Henry and Archie. She was their ally once and possibly she might stand by them again if the time came. I also planned to visit Kelly Morgan and tell her what Henry had said. If she had been living with the notion that Kitty was responsible for Miles's death and assault the time had come to bring the truth to light. Once I had all the participants' versions I'd write to Teresa Jepp and visit Jean and Isaiah. Everyone would then know that Kitty's suicide was directly related to those terrible Friday nights in Mallacoota. We might never know why he had chosen this time to take his life. What had happened in those days before he left home and curled up in the rocky crevice at Bingie? Why had the past suddenly broken him?

Chapter Twenty-four

Max came with me to retrieve Mick from his hospital prison. He had several visitors in my absence. His ex-wife had returned and spent a lovely few hours with him. They had talked about Sandra and whether they should make a united effort to re-establish contact with her. Both suddenly felt life was very short. A number of ex-colleagues had also made the trip to Wollongong to see him. He hadn't been bored but he hated being looked after. He was slightly cross that I'd organised to meet Connie at a time when he would still be held captive by his cardiologist who needed to give him the "change your lifestyle" talk. Max stayed at the hospital with Mick and I walked the short distance to the café where I would meet Miss Harlow.

I sat at a centre table so I could see her when she came in. Still lovely and somewhat reticent to update her look it seemed. She still styled her hair the same and despite the odd kilo or two around her tummy, I immediately recognised her as the young teacher who had been photographed for the school magazine. Now in her late-forties, Connie still had that look of an optimist; a shiny lightness that all good people seemed to have. I waved to her from the table I'd selected. She took my hand in both of hers and greeted me warmly even though she knew the conversation would not make either of us happy.

We ordered coffee and brightly coloured French macarons. She opened the conversation with, 'Poor Benedict. I thought if he got through his teens he'd be okay.' She had a lovely voice, soothing and low. 'They were total little rogues you know.' Only an English teacher would refer to naughty boys as rogues. It made me sad to know that when I told her Henry's story that the shiny glow would tarnish. That all the wonderful words in her vocabulary would never be able to put right the malevolence of that night in 1980.

'I'm sorry that you have to hear this.' And I meant it. I was sorry for everyone who was now going to hear about Roger Wheeler's crimes against those boys.

As predicted, Connie's face fell with each awful detail. Despite her fairy godmother face, Connie had a core of steel. 'If that fucking bastard is still alive, I'll kill him myself. Her eyes, voice and words reflected nothing but pure hatred.

She recalled some of the broken memories she had of St. Finbar's. Her first meeting with Wheeler made her uncomfortable. He was disparaging about her ability to control students, particularly boys. He made some vile comment about how her breasts would only distract them momentarily and then they'd eat her alive. Connie had simply thought he was a chauvinist pig, misogynistic and a bully. She had a degree in psychology and a Diploma of Education and she believed in positive reinforcement not punishment. Hitting children was draconian and cruel. 'I remember saying to him that surely there are smarter ways than having to hit children to make them do the right thing. He raised a cane above his head and whipped it down onto the desk in front of me. He liked the fact that it made me flinch.'

Poor Connie, in those days she was fresh from university and full of new ideas. So keen to bring the world to her students and encourage them to have big dreams. But thwarted by a monster who hated everything young teachers like her stood for. She talked about the relationship she had with Fred Lewis. He was older, but he well-read and a writer. 'Well a journalist.' They had a common interest in books and writing. And a common enemy. Much of the discussion centred on the punishments meted out by Wheeler. They both hated his archaic attitude to moulding children. The two of them mocked him behind his back but neither actually confronted him about the nature of his "training" methods.

She had, she stressed, spoken to the principal and the priest. Father Burrell had listened to her concerns but counselled her against speaking out. He assured her that he would inform the parents, speak to the boys and the bishop. Connie was certain that these things had been done.

I asked a final difficult question. 'Did you think he had been, or was capable of sexually abusing those children?'

She couldn't answer for moment. It was as if she was trying to remember if that had actually been something she feared. She sipped her coffee and only then answered. 'I was so appalled by his disciplinary measures that I didn't really consciously think he or any adult could do those things to children. We weren't negligent but naive. Just couldn't imagine that a respected teacher could be so deviant.'

But you were negligent. I didn't utter these words. They had all been negligent. Every teacher, family member and adult who did nothing to prevent the tragedy was in some way culpable. The fact that no one spoke out or spoke up with any real vehemence relegated the boys to a lifelong battle with shame, guilt, pain and fear. I didn't want to blame her. Connie looked as if she would be weighed down with the facts for a long time to come.

To bring our meeting to an end, I asked if she knew what had happened to Wheeler after the school closed. I explained how I couldn't find a reference to him in the electoral rolls.

'He moved on to teach in schools further north. Maybe even around this area, or further south, down your way.'

Down my way? Was it possible that Wheeler had moved interstate after St. Finbar's? In those days their teacher registrations and police checks didn't exist as they were deemed unnecessary. A teacher like Wheeler could move from school to school without any record of concerns about him being noted. In some cases people like him were recommended to other schools because the encumbered employer wanted to get rid of them.

It might be something Mick could follow up. If the abuse happened at St. Finbar's it was possible that it happened in other schools too. There might be other victims, other boys like Miles and Kitty, whose deaths could be attributed to abuse. Men like Henry and Archie who lived with the consequences of those memories.

Connie asked for the contact details of both Archie and Henry. 'I want to let them know that I haven't forgotten them. And if they need me I'll stand up for them this time.' Better late than never.

We parted without any recrimination on my part. I didn't think I had expected too much of these people. Wanting them to have done something, anything, to have changed the course of events. Or if the crime could not have been halted, to have ensured Wheeler paid for his actions. The burning down of his house seemed paltry in comparison to his sins. I thought about what should have been done as I made my way back to the hospital. People, unfortunately, would have found it difficult to prove Wheeler's crimes. He had the community's respect and in those days few listened to children. Fewer believed in teaching children about their rights.

* * *

Mick was coming home.

He virtually ran to the car. I kept telling him to slow down or we'd simply be turning around and dropping him back in emergency. Despite the pain the considerable incision caused he was, without doubt, renewed. He wanted to know all about the meetings I'd had with the priest and Connie. We were all sobered by the retelling of Henry's story. Max's face told the story of his feelings. It was the second time he had heard the details of that terrible night. It took a great deal of restraint to stop himself from smashing his fist through the car window. Even though at the wheel and talking to Mick, I still put my hand out and squeezed his arm to let him know that we all felt the same way.

The trip took no more than three hours. The traffic headed in the opposite direction to us. I'd set up the spare room, despite being unfinished, for Mick. Max had a mate come around and put in power points and set up a television in the space. The second bathroom had been completed the week before and was now functional for my convalescing patient.

Margaret's sixth sense must have been operational as she appeared soon after with Sarah and dinner. Dinner for approximately twenty. 'Hospital food is no good for patients.'

Mick gratefully hugged her for being so thoughtful and so right. His appetite had returned, and he was desperate for real food. Something with flavour. So our little party commenced, the usual faces around the table. We didn't discuss Kitty while Margaret was there; I didn't think it fair to distress her or Sarah with the ghastly details.

Max and Sarah left with Margaret when it seemed that the day had been considerable for Mick. While he wanted to sit up and discuss the case, as he kept calling it, he really needed to sleep and continue his recovery. He didn't want me to fuss over him and I didn't want to have to intrude on his privacy. I simply made him promise to call out for me if anything should happen during the night.

An email from Phillip kept me up. He was back with his team and had a few days off. They had been in South Sumatra and flew to Bali for a rest. I couldn't begrudge him a break from work but part of me felt jealous of not being the one who would be with him at a tropical resort. He'd been sick with some sort of stomach bug that had been prolonged by his refusal to fast for a few days to clear his system. Typically, he might have been ill but couldn't be kept from food. I replied with news only about rescuing Mick from the hospital, news of his ongoing recovery and stories about his family. I let him know that Max was doing better and had moved back into his home with Sarah. I had little to tell him about his sister's exodus from the bay. She obviously had no intention of returning any time soon. To save him from worry and me from inquisition, I told him nothing about the information I'd gathered about Kitty Jepp.

Fifteen minutes after I sent the email, Phillip rang. It was a pleasant and unexpected surprise. It was only late afternoon in Jakarta. I loved the sound of my husband's voice even though the light-heartedness of his usual conversation was missing. 'I'm so happy to hear your voice Lil.' He did sound very tired. He confirmed that he had been really sick and that he'd lost weight and had little energy. The trip to Bali would hopefully strengthen him. 'You'll have to watch what you eat there Phillip. Bali Belly on top of being unwell won't do you any good.' I kept the conversation fully focused on his life and health. 'The baby is beginning to make an impression on my belly. I might need to send you that photo so you can tell it's me.'

Inevitably he asked what Max and I had been getting up to. 'I know you've been looking into Kitty Jepp's death.' I truly had no idea how he found things out. It was unlikely to be Mick this time, but perhaps Max or the Swans had spilled the beans. Nothing seemed to happen around here without the whole town knowing.

The call ended with Phillip's emphatic suggestion that I leave things alone and he said twice that nothing could be done to undo Kitty's death. 'Please leave it alone Lil.' Phillip was right in that Kitty's death could not be changed. He was also wrong in that there was something that could be done to right the injustice of the past. None of which I disclosed during the phone call.

I finished with, 'I love you Phillip. Please look after yourself and call me when you get to Bali.'

After the call I felt restless. I couldn't help but worry about Phillip. He just didn't sound himself and he rarely complained of feeling ill. I felt tired from driving and wearied by the weight of the information I now had but sleep seemed impossible. I sat at my computer and instead of attending to my thesis, I simply wrote down in order everything that had been said and by whom. I created a timeline of events and a "to do list". I had desk jobs for Mick to complete and a list of people I wanted to see. The first person was Miles Rennison's mother. Whether it was for wrong or for right, she deserved to know the truth of what happened to her child. Kitty, Henry and Archie deserved their names to be cleared and their voices heard. It would be an awful conversation that might not contribute anything to the solution. But there had been too much silence already.

Chapter Twenty-five

The next morning I left to find the Morgan's house in Tuross, leaving Mick sitting at the computer looking over the notes I'd made the previous night. It was another beautiful coastal town bordered by the sea, river and a lake. The wide isthmus that separated the village from the busy highway formed an entrance into another world. The world of people going up and down the highway to possibly thousands of destinations seemed far away from the homes and holiday cottages that either perched high above the lake or sat close to the beachfront. Tuross was known for its fish. Flathead and bream plucked directly from the water arrived at the jetty where tiny restaurants hovered metres from the river's edge. A tangle of streets wove their way between the three water sources.

The Morgans lived on the avenue above Coila Bar. The camping ground and holiday cabins separated the residents from the beach. The view was lovely. I parked in the visitor car park at the end of the road and looked back up the street to the house I had to visit. I watched the house for a while. The outside was very neat and well-kept. It seemed that the weatherboards had been recently painted and new plantation shutters fixed to all the front windows. The front garden contained several timber plant boxes filled with coastal and salt-tolerant plants. The mild climate had ensured some pre-spring growth so lots of colour contrasted with the grey of the weathered treated pine. Someone had put a lot of work and thought into the plantings.

Parked in the driveway was an ageing Toyota tagged front and back with P-plates. I assumed it belonged to Riley, the Morgan's son. And as if on cue to confirm my suspicions, a young man with long dark hair exited the front door letting the flyscreen slam into place. He was of small build and not very tall. It may have been my imagination, but

I thought I could see the similarity between him and his long dead half-brother. I had hoped that this boy had been told about Miles and despite never knowing him, he had a sense of loss, connection or maybe concern about his death. He manoeuvred the car rather haphazardly out of the drive and moved past me. I noticed his skin was ravaged by acne and that his thin lips were drawn into a near grimace. This, by fleeting glance, seemed to be an angry boy, or man as he probably preferred to be called.

I found it interesting that he didn't see me ambling by his house and that he had no cognition of being watched and his life speculated about. He was of course oblivious to the impending bombshell that I was going to drop on his mother. I had not rehearsed my speech. I thought it best if I introduced myself as Benedict Jepp's friend and see where that took the conversation. Possibly Kelly was at work, or out shopping and that the manner in which I started the conversation would be irrelevant. I hadn't been very pragmatic in my planning. Driven by urgency, I hadn't allowed myself to consider any conse-quences of appearing at her door. I hesitated momentarily at the now empty driveway, losing confidence or gaining common sense. But the front door was open and the radio blared inside, so I pressed on up the front steps.

Luck, however, was apparently on my side as Kelly Morgan an-swered the door in a harried state. Her eyes looked sore and weary, perhaps from crying. For a few moments I remained silent as a second flash of doubt about this undertaking rushed through me.

'Can I help you?' she asked, concern etched on her face.

Probably because a dazed and mute woman had knocked on her door. I doubted that she could help me; I was certain that this con-versation wouldn't help her at all.

I stumbled through the first few words of greeting and she tried to stop me in my tracks with a hand wave and an emphatic statement about her disinterest in whatever brand of door-to-door religion I was selling. Before she could close the screen on me, I managed to utter her son's name and Mallacoota.

She stood still and instead of retreating came closer to me. 'Do I know you? Are you from Coota?'

Her momentary interest helped me find my voice and I began by saying that I'd been talking to Father Burrell and the ex-police officer

Angelo di Michele. I thought these names would add authority to my unexpected visit. Kelly should guess that I arrived at her door to talk about Miles. They weren't in coherent sentences but made enough sense to spark her interest. A light came on in her eyes and I was afraid that she looked too hopeful about the information that I brought. It was, however, enough to get me in the door. By the time she had shown me to the kitchen table and poured tea that had already been made in the pot I'd gathered my wits and began a more articulate rationale for my visit.

I started with how I had met Teresa Jepp at Benedict's funeral and that I'd also talked to Henry and Archie there. The mention of their names had her immediately recoiling. But I pressed on with the story of the investigation prompted by Kitty's letter. I spoke for five minutes, setting the scene without really getting to the night of Miles's death. I spoke about Kitty's family and the life he'd made here, only kilometres from where she lived. It seemed quite shocking to her that he had been nearly a neighbour living only fifteen minutes away.

When I paused she began to speak. 'When Miles died I thought I'd never survive the pain. There is nothing in the world like losing your child. You can eventually recover but you never really heal.' She was not angry or sad; she simply stated a fact. She had a new life and a grown-up son but the little boy whose death was never adequately explained had never left her. She still carried the injurious wounds of tragic loss, even twenty-three years later. The mention of her son's name took her back to that night and following day when she believed that the discovery of his body and the manner of his death was the worst thing she would ever hear. Now, this day, she would hear something equally as awful.

I hadn't really questioned the notion that Kelly would refuse to believe me. I simply thought that the evidence would be undeniable. But as I got closer to disclosure I began to doubt my own motives and the strength of my evidence. I spent time weaving the possibility of the sexual assault that allegedly occurred and once Kelly cottoned on to what I was implying, she took up the story.

She had wondered about the rumours that eventually filtered to her and Miles's father, Robert. She knew that nothing in the story the boys concocted on the night made sense. But Kelly had mistakenly thought I'd uncovered some terrible truth in Kitty's letter. A confession that the older boys had hurt Miles terribly and drowned him to cover up these awful things. 'I have nightmares about him being tortured and crying out for me.' She had to breathe deeply and wipe away a tear. 'The thought of his pain is unbearable. You know in 1993 I wrote to the mother of James Bulger to tell her about Miles and that I knew how she felt.'

It took me a minute to remember the story of the child who had been led away from a shopping centre in England. Two ten-year-old boys had beaten the small child to death. It was a story that haunted every parent, and law enforcement agents across the world. Terrible, terrible things happen. Sometimes children perpetrate crimes against others but this time it was an adult. One who had been trusted.

'It's just unbearable,' she reiterated.

She was right. The thought of that little boy's pain was intolerable but unlike James Bulger, Miles's pain had not been inflicted by the children who joined him on that night. They were also victims, whose nightmares stayed with them in the same way that Kelly Morgan's had. We talked for an hour about Miles and the life they led as a family. She took me further away from my purpose in coming there, but she seemed to be unable to stop the flood of memories. There was no outburst of hatred or desire for retribution against Kitty and the others. She pitied them and spoke about what terrible damage must have occurred for them to have done such a wicked thing.

It was as if I'd somehow pushed the play button and Kelly had to divest herself of the many thoughts she had buried deeply. During this time I really saw her. She had a ruined look that the passing of time couldn't cure. She also seemed desperate to talk and I wondered if she was too fragile to hear about The Rottweiler's betrayal. He had been their friend according to Vic Burrell and others.

And then, as if we faced each other in the confessional, she brought me, a stranger into the darkness of a hideous twist of fate. A similar thing had befallen her second son Riley. The child, when he was nine, had been sexually assaulted. He was so traumatised by the events that he had never been able to fully explain what had happened to him. A stranger had taken him. Riley apparently had never seen the man's face. The injuries were sexual in nature, but Kelly wouldn't or couldn't confirm exactly what had happened to him. It went unreported to the police. For some inexplicable reason the Morgans didn't want to put Riley through an investigation.

'We thought it best just to push it all away and never speak of it again. He was young, he'd forget.' Even as she said the words, we both knew that was a lie.

At this bizarre revelation I almost lost my temper. 'Why wouldn't you go to the police? The perpetrator could have been caught and punished.' I wanted to call her a stupid woman for such an error in judgement. I knew that name calling would have been of no benefit and would have halted our detailed conversation. But I couldn't help wondering at the unlikelihood of both her sons being abused. As if she read my mind she said, 'It is as if I was being punished. It's like I'm cursed. Both my boys. Miles dead and Riley never the same.'

Of course the child could never be the same. He had been traumatised by some foul stranger and his parents felt it was better to smother the truth under the weight of denial. Riley's angry demeanour as he left the house indicated the cloud under which his life had been lived. It seemed that a pattern of concealment had become a way of dealing with things. It was as if the stigma of being a victim had to be avoided. And in doing so the perpetrators marched on, untouchable.

'Your husband agreed to this? That it was best to cover-up Riley's assault.'

He had agreed after a much relied upon friend had given them his counsel. This friend had knowledge of these matters; he had been a teacher and had known what had happened to Miles.

As Kelly spoke a dark thought took hold. It made me breathless and the fear of what she might say next led to a light-headedness that had me gripping the table edge.

My descent into near unconsciousness frightened Kelly out of further revelation. She helped me to her sofa and brought me water. She questioned me about my health.

'Pregnant actually.' A paltry reason for my collapse.

I almost decided to take the coward's way out and keep my fears and revelation from Kelly. But then I saw the photo of Miles on the dresser beside a similar photo of Riley at about the same age. Being faint-hearted was not an option. The victims of the past and the men still suffering had to have their voices heard. This was a time for bravery. There was no room for cowardice.

'Your friend. The one who suggested you keep quiet about Riley's attack, who is he?'

The answer I had guessed. Roger Wheeler had moved north and had stayed in contact with Kelly, celebrated her marriage to her new husband and remained a trusted friend who had been involved with Riley. He still lived two streets away. I wanted more than anything not to tell her about Henry's story about the night of Miles's death, but Wheeler had to pay. Good fortune or simple dumb luck had The Rottweiler within grasp. All my searching had rendered few details, but it seemed he was hiding in plain sight.

The words were raw and unavoidably cruel. There was nothing else I could do but describe the agonising scenario of Miles's last night at the hands of Kelly's good friend and trusted confidante.

In the end only silence remained in the room. I had no other words and Kelly had no response. It seemed that we two were waiting for the last tick of the clock before the detonation of a bomb. Something explosive was coming and it started with the familiar sound of the screen door slamming. Riley stared at his mother and the stranger who had wrought chaos on their home.

The tableau was motivated to action when Kelly simply said, 'Get out.'

I so desperately wanted to take everything back. The faces of the Morgan family mirrored one another's shock. But once spoken, words cannot be rewound, and another version recorded. I had started a course of events that would not end with the Morgans deciding that a mad woman had come to visit and told fanciful lies about their friend Roger. When a spark illuminated the dark memories hidden in the sub-conscious, it could not be extinguished. Doubt would turn to knowing and knowing would provoke action. Even with more than two decades of concealment, a terrible thing would come to light.

I don't remember leaving the house or getting to the car and driving away. I knew Roger Wheeler lived somewhere near me. Somewhere near Kitty, the cause of his nightmare had emerged and been revealed. I had to stop before the highway to open the door and throw up. I felt frightened and panicky. It made no sense that having met the objective of my visit to Kelly that I felt that I'd made the worse mistake of my life. It had been my own belief that the past must not lie in shallow graves without acknowledgement. My own experience with my family's secrets reared up and I questioned why I thought I had the God-given right to drag anyone else to this conclusion. Perhaps I was wrong in claiming that we can't live in perpetual denial of what has happened in the past. Those who suggest you can draw a veil over your mistakes might actually be right after all. The past is the past and nothing can be done to change it. I cried for the pain I'd caused Kelly Morgan and her son Riley. I also cried for Kitty, Miles, Archie and Henry. Nothing I'd done would help them.

I'd drawn some strange looks from people driving by, but thankfully no-one stopped to seek an explanation of why I sobbed slumped over my steering wheel. I needed Max or Mick to help me overcome the conflicting sense of regret and rage I felt.

Max picked up on the second ring. 'Are you okay?'

With my voice steadier, I confirmed that I was all right, but only just. I told him that I felt appalled by what I'd done. That in chasing down what I believed to be right, I hadn't considered the ramifications of my actions.

Max, not known for his deep philosophical understanding, made me see some sense when he said, 'Lily, you were not doing this for yourself. You did this for Kitty and his friends.' He paused. 'Truth hurts but at least you know what the cause of the pain is when someone tells you what you have already suspected.'

And that was the truth. I knew it from experience. I knew that because I'd spent my whole life refusing to examine what had caused my family's suicides and silences. When I met Phillip I finally had the courage to look back, open the wound and finally look at what had happened. The thought that I had eventually recovered from my own revelations gave me the strength to start the car and head home.

I wanted to talk to both Max and Mick. Together with this next puzzle piece we might be able to finally do something about Roger Wheeler. The Rottweiler was in our midst. Despite the havoc I'd wrought in Kelly's home, I would try to have a renewed sense of purpose. Instead of focusing on the victims, I now would go after the architect of this pain.

I'd obviously been crying. They told me I was ashen and smudged. We had some tea as we sat to discuss what would happen next. In my absence, Mick had been in touch with officers assigned to SOCIT units, the Sexual Offences and Child Abuse Investigation Team. They had a lot to tell him. While these special officers investigated current instances, they were also able to bring charges in indictable cases concerning historical sexual assault against children. Mick's contact also gave a cautionary warning. She said many prosecutors would not press charges because of the intervening time between the assault and the disclosure if the evidence could not be sufficiently substantiated. Memory is not always strong evidence. Corroborated stories of events don't always stand up well and more than likely it comes down to who was most believable in court. The scenario of Henry speaking against Wheeler in court looked like a David and Goliath struggle. I imagined Wheeler being supported by one of the victim's mothers versus the known alcoholic Henry Kelly and realised that a judge would deem the accusations as the ravings of a drunk. It was, in my mind, an impossibility. The officer did, however, offer a glimmer of hope. The Royal Commission into institutional child abuse had already gathered strength. Police forces across the country considered creating specialist units to investigate the historical child abuse stories. While she believed it would be some years before federal and state police had the resources for what would be a mammoth undertaking, the children, many of whom were now adults would have their voices heard.

The day had been a roller-coaster of hope and despair. I'd inflicted pain on the unwitting but as the afternoon wore on, I was more convinced of the rightness of my actions. Max had gone back to work and Mick was having his afternoon rest, which I'd insisted upon. I tinkered around with the key paragraphs in my thesis but had little interest in improving any of the expression. The sound of the phone ringing provided a happy distraction until the caller started speaking. Jean, Kitty's wife. She sounded distressed and frightened. Apparently a woman had been to the house yelling all kinds of accusations about Kitty. She was afraid for her baby's safety and wanted me to come out to the house in Congo. The woman, who didn't identify herself had mentioned my name in her ravings. Jean's description had left no doubt in my mind that Kelly Morgan had tracked down the Jepp's little piece of paradise and brought Hell with her.

Chapter Twenty-six

I had no intention of going to Congo alone or telling Jean the story of Kitty's past just yet either. But it seemed that the ball I'd started rolling that morning had gathered momentum and was now unstoppable. I didn't want to wake Mick or put him through what would no doubt be a stressful visit. It would fall to Max to make the journey back down the highway with me. My garbled explanation of what had happened made sense to Max. He had to finish a small job he at the local aged care facility and he would swing by at four to pick me up.

We were both nervous as we set off for Congo. The tangled overgrowth of vines provided a curtain that cut the community off from the noise of the outside world. Jean's house stood still quietly clinging to the side of the cliff where Kitty had built it and she was still swinging in her chair with Isaiah at her breast. It looked as if she hadn't moved. But time had begun to bring her back to life. Her colour was better and her hair had been cut and tamed into a long plait that fell over her shoulder. The baby, as beautiful as ever, had grown and begun to fill out. His sleepy demeanour only occasionally stirred by his mother's movement and voice.

Relief showed on Jean's face that we were there. I didn't know who was going to speak first. But Jean got underway after putting Isaiah down in his own little hammock that had been fashioned out of rainbow dyed canvas, his momentary protests arrested by a slight swing and slow rocking motion.

Jean had apparently been washing up when the woman made her way down the side of the house. It was nothing new for Jean to have friends and strangers wandering onto her property. In general she would greet everyone in the same relaxed manner. But Kelly had no interest in friendly greetings. She opened her rant with the fact that she was glad that Benedict Jepp had done the world a favour and killed himself. 'I was so shocked and thought Issy might get hurt by her. At first I couldn't even understand her she was so hysterical.',

While much of Kelly's words were hard to follow, her outburst included details that I had been to her home and told her that her son's murder wasn't Kitty's fault but that no-one would believe that. 'She thought that Kitty had something to do with her son's death when they were boys and that you wanted to cover it up by accusing some man who had been a teacher at the school.'

Jean had no idea about what the woman said. She didn't know anything about Kitty's life except that he had become estranged from his mother because she was a religious nut. It seemed perfectly normal to Jean not to know about her husband's childhood or the troubles he experienced as a boy. The crazy visitor picked up the nearest thing to hand and threw it at the small brazier situated in the middle of the patio area at the back of the house. It explained the strewn ash and charred wood that littered the area.

Rattled, Jean retreated with Isaiah to the swinging chair when Kelly left. Jean didn't ring the police and instead waited patiently for me to arrive and make sense of the madness she had just witnessed. She may not have known much about Kitty's past, but she knew he wasn't a killer. 'Kitty wouldn't harm anyone, not ever. What did she mean?'

Jean's question was not easy to answer. But the truth that I'd hoped to keep from her a little longer was the only way to make sense of the mad woman's visit.

Jean sat very still as Max and I reconstructed the events of Kitty's childhood. The people we had visited, the stories they told. Henry's account of the night Miles died was the penultimate part of the story. The final chapter was that this man call Roger Wheeler lived nearby and one might surmise that Kitty had encountered him. That every memory that Kitty had stuffed deep down, bubbled to the surface and overwhelmed him. This part I had no clear evidence for; it was the most likely conclusion I could make. Only a discussion with Roger Wheeler could confirm my suspicions. The thought of which made me physically ill. I consider myself a pacifist and I truly deplored violence, but I could not guarantee that my hatred for this unknown man would not drive me to act against my nature. The idea of hurting him, perhaps even killing him, crept into my mind.

I worried about Jean being in the house by herself, but she assured me she had nothing to fear from that woman. Now she understood that her son, indeed both her sons, motivated her rage, she felt she could handle her if she came back. Jean's great sorrow for Kitty's pain and her own inability to protect him was upper most in her mind. 'Mothers seem to get the raw deal, don't they? I mean Kelly, even Teresa and now me. We all have to wear the pain.'

I thought she was right but as I looked at Max and thought about Mick, I knew that the pain didn't just hurt mothers, it injured fathers too. Parents had inextricable connections to their children even when things go wrong. I was so sad for Kitty. His love for his son had been so obvious. So much so that he thought taking his life would be better in the long run for Issy. It renewed my faith in the course of action we had begun. I felt sorry for Kelly, but she had a chance to save her second son. Riley, whatever his story might be, was worth the risk. This constant belief gained strength with each new part of the story. The silence eventually proved too great a burden. These boys, these victims could survive the assault and violation of their bodies but the injustice that comes with silence damaged that part of them that could not be so easily repaired. It was odd that it would be words that saved them. Those words would include accusations, charges and hopefully a recorded history that showed Roger Wheeler abused children and was a paedophile.

We hugged Jean and I leant down and kissed the still-sleeping baby. Max put his arm around me and we walked to the car, with a strange sense of relief. This was not done, not completely. The end of the story hadn't come as I had hoped it would when Jean heard about what had happened in Kitty's past. The end of the story had taken shape. But there was still Wheeler. And Henry and now Riley.

Max didn't ask me if what we did next was a good idea. But when we turned left towards Tuross instead of right to go home, I knew we were going to look for Wheeler's house. Kelly had said that he lived two streets over and had pointed away from the beach and towards the lake. I had no idea of how to find him, but Max was a little more like Mick than I'd realised. His work ute provided the subterfuge we needed to find him. Max would tell the people on whose door he knocked that he had to do work for Roger Wheeler but that his office had only written the street name not the number. It seemed like a reasonable plan provided we found the right street. People generally were unsuspecting, more so in small towns. What could be the harm in telling a tradesman in which house their neighbour resided?

As we turned into the street we realised that our deception would not be needed. Outside number 23 a still-distressed Kelly Morgan sat in her car. An older man who might have been in his sixties appeared to be comforting her. We were able to hide behind another builder's vehicle parked in front of number 18. From this point we could see much of the encounter but not hear the conversation. Kelly looked like a spent force. She allowed the man to help her out of the car and down the path into the house. He patted her back, familiar and paternal. As he opened the door to let her enter first, he turned and looked up to where the two utes had parked. Without doubt, the man was Roger Wheeler. Still in glasses, still impassive and now greying but not balding. The monster in person looked less terrifying than I imagined he would. He looked weak and small. The Rottweiler was not invincible and my loathing grew stronger.

Max wanted to leap out of the car and head down to the house and tear him apart. Despite the immediate desire to agree, I realised that we would be fighting off Kelly and only end up being arrested for assault. I didn't want Phillip to come home to bail me out, nor did I want to have my baby in jail. I convinced Max that waiting at this time would be advisable. There would be other ways to bring Wheeler down. I didn't know what those ways would be but an image of running him down on a dark night came to mind.

We returned home. Mick had started dinner. Max left to pick up Sarah and I filled Mick in on the day's discoveries. 'Glad you decided not to attack anyone, Lily. No matter how much someone might deserve it.'

Max returned. Sarah fussed about eating because she had already eaten, settled on the couch and fell asleep. She had been busy all day with her grandmother, and just needed to sleep.

The adult conversation returned to Wheeler. 'How would you get away with murder?'

Max's question left me uncomfortable.

'Make sure they don't find the body.' Mick seemed unflustered by the question but looked over at me. 'Sorry Lily.'

Mick must have realised that such a thing made me feel uncomfortable. After all, the bodies or, more correctly, bones of my own mother and brother were not discovered for twenty-seven years.

Max would never deliberately hurt me. And he was right. Not finding the body was a distinct option. 'Killing Wheeler and whatever you do with the body doesn't really solve the real problem. The survivors still don't get to tell their story. His death does not equate with their healing.' I remained focused on the living victims. Particularly now that I suspected, without anything but gut feeling, that Riley might also have been Wheeler's victim.

'You need to get the boy to talk.' Mick was right. But if Kelly was correct in saying that Riley couldn't remember what had happened to him, he wouldn't be able to confirm or deny my suspicions.

Before he went to bed, early as directed by his doctor, Mick mentioned that he was contacting a group of solicitors who had been looking into a class action against a school in Sydney. According to the outcry, the officer who first heard the accusations against a group of teachers who were integral in a child pornography ring, six ex-students had sought damages against the school that employed the men. 'Your mate, Roland Devine is one of the solicitors. It's a small world Lily.'

Max showed interest in how Roland Devine was a mate of mine. The story took a reasonable amount of time to tell. He laughed at the part where I had decided to go to Sydney to confront Roland because of the terrible injustice he did my Aunt Billie. The note he left on the baby's grave seemed a sign that our lives were destined, for one reason or another, to intersect. After Max left and Mick was deeply asleep as attested by his snoring, I search his day's notes and found Roland Devine's number. I would ring him in the morning. We could talk about the past but there was also the future. I was interested in hearing about the men bringing a class action against a school, a possible Royal Commission and a reckoning for the wrong doers. I had hoped that my second impression of Mr. Devine was right. I first saw him as a selfish, spoiled egotist and this had been proved wrong by the work I knew he was doing and the note he left at the Bungendore cemetery. If Billie had once loved him, he couldn't be all bad.

I slept well, disturbed by only one dream. I woke as Roger Wheeler's body thumped into my imagined windscreen and bounced away into a tangle of weeds on the side of the road. By dawn I'd had enough sleep. A shower and breakfast would help dispel the thought of murder and death. To my surprise Mick was up and had been out for a short walk. It had been suggested as a part of his therapy, but I didn't think the doctor had meant for him to start so soon after being discharged from hospital. I wasn't sure what the day would bring for me. I would ring Roland and introduce myself. I would take a long walk to clear my head and later in the day I'd ring Jean to make sure she felt safe.

I would not drive to Tuross and lie in wait for Roger Wheeler, no matter how strong the inclination to do so.

Mick had a medical check-up the hospital in Moruya. His specialist flew into the region for several appointments and then flew out again at 4:30 in the afternoon. I wanted to drive Mick, but he had already organised for Margaret and Peter to take him. It made me smile to think how much a part of our family life he had become. My in-laws and friends saw Mick as a father figure and collaborator. He had simply come with the territory. Phillip had enormous respect for Mick, not just because of his police work, but because of the man he was. If Phillip trusted Mick, then the whole family did. I was pleased to be exempted from nursemaid duties and happy when Mick said he'd spend the day with the Swans as after his appointment they were going to have lunch at the local pub.

'A salad and lean protein? That kind of pub lunch Mick?' He laughed off my nagging but knew I meant it.

Finally on my own, I made my first phone call.

The receptionist at Roland's office asked for my name and reason for calling. 'I'll check to see if Mr. Devine is able to take your call.'

While on hold, I thought that perhaps he wouldn't want to speak to me, after all, as far as he knew, what would we have to say to each other?

'Lily O'Hara. How lovely to hear from you.' His voice sounded sincere and warm. The slight country boy twang of his childhood had not been completely polished off by his working life in Sydney.

'I wanted to thank you for the special touches you've made to the cemetery in Bungendore.' I was sure he was busy and as much as I wanted to talk about Lake Road, I did want to get to the key point about the class action he had undertaken.

He was momentarily surprised by my enquiry but immediately interested in the brief outline I gave him of Kitty's story as I now called it.

'I think this is something we need to talk about in detail, Lily. I don't want to give advice out over the phone. And I would love to talk about Billie too.'

Liking him even more, I agreed that we should meet and told him that I was happy to travel to Sydney but, luckily he had organised to be in Bungendore for the weekend. I could drive up on Saturday and meet him at the Lake George Hotel. Fortunately Helena was coming down to see Mick, so I could get away for a few hours knowing that she would keep an eye on him. We decided to meet at 12.

With that out of the way and everyone busy, I decided to go for a short drive. I was drawn to Wheeler. I didn't even take my car. I took Mick's. It had been in the driveway since we had that fateful journey to Mallacoota. His keys still in the bowl on the table at the front door. It seemed deceitful, but if Kelly Morgan was around she might recognise my car from the other day.

The street was full of tradesmen's cars. They were working on a big renovation in the street. So one more unfamiliar car parked on the road wouldn't attract much attention. I put on a hat and tucked my distinctive hair up under it. With dark glasses on I could have been anyone, even a man at pinch. I first drove past the Morgan's house where Riley's car was parked in the drive, and then slowly made my way to Wheeler's street. I pulled up at the very end of the road to have a good look at the house, a neat, rendered brick single storey house. Unremarkable and probably hard to burn down. A car drifted by and I ignored it until it turned into his driveway. A blue Honda Accord, maybe a couple of years old. Wheeler didn't open the garage but parked in his driveway and let himself in the front door.

My curiosity got the better of me and I got out of the car and casually walked past, pretending I was interested in the new house being built opposite. When I became level with his car his sudden reappearance took me by surprise.

'Good morning, nice day for a walk,' he said. Nothing remarkable in that voice.

I could have ignored him, but I was concerned that it might be notably odd to do so. I made a brief comment about the building happening across the road, told him I'd come by to have look at the renovation.

'The noise is driving me crazy. I go out every day to get away from the sound of hammers and builders' radios.' He gave a little laugh as if it wasn't really something to complain about. 'Do you live near?'

I wanted to yell in his face, but I was invested in the role now. 'I'm from Victoria, visiting a friend.' I so wanted to say Mallacoota. I didn't stop to further the conversation to see if a perceptible change registered on his face. I hadn't wanted to see him let alone be congenial. I wanted to scream at him and tell him I knew what he'd done. I felt I could push him to the ground and smash his head on the cement. My legs trembled, and I felt dizzy by the time I got back to the car. I felt hot and ripped the ridiculous hat off my head letting my hair fall down onto my shoulders. I'd checked that Wheeler couldn't see me and that he had in fact gone back inside. I had been undiscovered or so I thought. But then a face appeared at my window. An angry, confused face. Riley Morgan had recognised me from the day before when I'd upset his mother.

'What the fuck do you want?' A reasonable question.

'I want to speak to you, Riley. It's important.' But the boy had no interest in conversation. He slammed his hand into the front window of the car and stomped away, hands jammed into his pockets, head down. I didn't know if any of what I'd done could help him. I got out of the car and called out to him, but he didn't come back. I returned to the car and drove away, slightly guilty at having used Mick's car for a somewhat covert reason. As I left the street, I noticed two builders watching what had happened between Riley and me. I hoped that they hadn't really taken much notice and would soon forget the encounter between the sulky teen and strange redhead who had been in the street two days in a row.

Chapter Twenty-seven

I said nothing of the events and my encounter with both Wheeler and Riley. Not sure whether guilt or fear kept me from telling either Mick or Max about my return visit. Friday was busy, and I had no time to be worrying about it. Helena was arriving in the afternoon and on Saturday I was abandoning them to drive back to Bungendore to meet Roland Devine. This plan I did share. Max wanted to come with me, but I wanted to go alone. The discussion about the past was something *I* had to do, and it had little bearing on anything currently happening. I thought Max should spend the time with Sarah and make time to talk to someone about his absent wife. Sophie wanted money; Max inevitably would cave in and send her as much as he could. It would be unlikely to stop there. But the tribulations of Max's marriage would have to wait until everything else settled. It might even have to wait until Phillip came home and took his sister's mad behaviour in hand.

The thought of Phillip still being sick worried me a little. He rarely got ill so the bug he picked up must be fairly virulent to lay him low. I brightened as I imagined him taking it easy in some beach resort in Bali. If he could stay away from curries and beer, he might have a chance to recover.

Helena had taken the afternoon off work and had driven down after lunch. She was, as always, a breath of fresh air. Still not showing her age, and full of excited talk about the antics of our two friends Jimmy and Brendan, who was working hard at the museum and looked ready to take on more responsibility when things changed at work.

'What changes?' I was on study leave so I had not been around when discussions about changes had taken place.

'Well you are pregnant, Lil. No doubt you'll need a week or two off don't you think?'

Of course she was right, and it would obviously be more than a week or two. I had in my head that I'd like to be home for the first year with the baby.

'And I'm retiring.'

Helena retiring! 'It's not possible. What will the place do without you? What will I do without you? She was as dynamic and energetic as ever.

'I'm sixty-two, Lily. It's time. And I want to go to London and see my son and grandchildren.' While her only child, Louis, had been estranged from her for most of his life Helena never gave up hope that she could forge a relationship with him. Her ex-husband had been a monster when the marriage ended. Her punishment was to lose her son. Louis had been so poisoned by his father that he had always seen Helena as the wrong doer. Every year she attempted to right the wrong and every year he rejected her. She had planned to go and take a flat in London near him and wear him down with her presence. 'Life's short and I don't want to die without letting him know how much I've loved him.'

A sentiment that couldn't argue against. Mick listened and nodded with both her decision to go and the importance of trying one more time to let her child know she loved him.

In that instant I knew I'd have to tell him that I rang his daughter Sandra and that it didn't go well. But it was no reason to give up.

The Friday night was reminiscent of the partying we once enjoyed. The entire Swan clan, Max included, arrived with platters of food and enough alcohol for several parties. Naturally, I didn't drink, and I made sure that Mick would be cautious about his consumption. The others went full tilt. There was music and inevitably singing. I hadn't been singing or playing for months. The rapid changes in life had swept the joy of music out of me. It all came back when one of the brothers-in-law started playing *Hotel California*, an irresistible number and one that everyone seemed to know the words. Without pausing, we went into a rousing version of The Proclaimers' *500 Miles* and then some ballads in which we each took a turn to lead. Mick sat out the solo round but Max, whose singing was borderline tuneless, decided *Bohemian Rhapsody* was his song. It had been a long time since I'd laughed like this and enjoyed the noisy mayhem of a party to celebrate nothing but life. Mindful of the neighbours, we quietened down at about ten. The children, except for Carrie, all asleep curled up on comfortable surfaces throughout the house. The low point of the night was knowing the Phillip was far away and absent from this happy troupe. He would have loved the singing and mad antics of his family and friends. He would have held my hand or stroked my face. Kissed me at every opportunity. But he was not here. He was in Bali.

Mick and Helena spent time chatting quietly on the deck. Max and I stayed in the kitchen discussing the possibility of leaving Kitty's story alone. We both wondered now that Jean knew what had happened was there any point in continuing. Was the road forward one that might only cause further hurt to people like Kelly and Riley? Would more information have any effect on Henry's self-destructive path? Could we actually bring Wheeler to account for his crimes? Neither of us had answers.

The night ended with the family wandering off with sleeping children and tipsy adults. Only Peter remained sober enough to drive and he did two separate runs to various streets in the neighbourhood. Max and Sarah left last with Margaret. Mick went to bed as the final few left.

Helena followed soon after, hugging me tightly. 'This is a great family, Lil. I bet you are missing Phil.' Truer words never spoken. She held me away from her and brought her face close to mine. 'Watch Max. I think he might be falling in love with you.'

I was shocked that anyone would think such a thing. Max and I developed a deep friendship. We were very close and had come to care very much for one another, but I doubt Max felt that way about me. He was my husband's best friend. He wouldn't betray Phillip, and neither would I. But I was not so naive to think that perhaps others could misconstrue the relationship. We had spent a lot of time together; left town and been away overnight, late evenings and long days trying to work out the problems we inherited when Kitty left his letter. With Sophie gone and Phillip overseas, I began to see how our friendship might look to others. I would, in the next week or so, begin to put some distance between us. Not because I thought Max might love me but to prevent the gossips in the town getting hold of the story and making it into something it wasn't.

The following day, leaving Mick in Helena's capable hands, I left for my meeting with Roland Devine. He was a complete stranger to me, and yet he wasn't. Roland had grown up with my father's family around the land and town settled on Lake George. Bungendore was a sleepy rural town with a history that went back to the 1830s. The O'Haras and the Devines took up the opportunity to settle the land in the region as New South Wales grew and the population spread out from Sydney. While the O'Hara clan struggled, the Devine family thrived. When my father, his sister and brother befriended the landed and wealthy Roland, Mr. and Mrs. Devine felt concerned. When he struck up a relationship with my Aunt Billie they must have been almost hysterical, and when at eighteen Billie became pregnant with Roland's baby they were vengeful.

I looked forward to meeting him. I wanted to hear his version of events and ultimately talk about his current work. I arrived in the town in plenty of time, so I made a quick visit to the cemetery. A small bunch of white roses had been placed on Billie's grave, a matching bunch on her un-named baby's. I suspected Roland had placed them there. Leaving my car on the highway, I walked the short distance to the pub in Gibraltar Street. A tall, ageing but still very handsome man, stood as I walked in. He recognised me in an instance despite the fact that I looked more like my mother than the O'Haras, who had all been dark-haired and statuesque. In comparison I was small and red-headed. He had obviously done his homework.

Roland took my proffered hand in his. 'You're an O'Hara, alright. I'm so glad you didn't decide to run away this time.' He smiled, and I blushed at the thought of the insane dash I made to Sydney several years ago to confront him after I learned that he had abandoned Billie and his baby. A bit of common sense had me leaving his office before I conducted some awful kind of shouting match.

Over a pre-lunch drink I told him why I went to Sydney that day and why I left without speaking to him. 'I was overwhelmed by information. I hadn't really come to terms with the discoveries I'd made that summer.'

Roland did not make light of the awfulness of that strange season where past secrets had ruptured my life. He was a good listener and fully aware that learning that my mother and brother had died in the lake just after I was born had brought changes both good and painful.

We then spoke of Billie. I had not been blessed with a mother or a father, but I had Billie who raised me in the absence others. Her brother Darcy played a part as well. Since her death, I had strangely come to know her better than when she was alive.

As he started, he took my left hand in his and said, 'You're wearing the ring I gave Billie when I asked her to marry me.'

'I loved it from the moment I found it.'

His story was not the one I'd imagined when I read the callous letter tucked away in Billie's personal things that I had combed through after she died. Roland had not written the letter, his well-meaning mother had. Before Mrs. Devine put an end to the relationship Roland had proposed to Billie and given her the ring I now wore to mark my engagement to Phillip. He had planned to take Billie and the baby to Sydney after he delayed his university studies for a year. They would go to Sydney as a young married couple with a new baby. They imagined that they would both get work and he would study part-time. The prospect of it filled him with joy. 'It wasn't a well-thought-out plan. Just two kids really trying to make something of the future.' Billie's parents had agreed and while they were sad that their first grandchild would be raised in Sydney they gave their blessing to the young couple. But the Devines had other ideas.

The letter, the separation and the heart break ended any hope of a happy ending. Roland had been told that the baby had died soon after childbirth. A little girl who was too frail for much more than a few breaths after her birth. 'My first daughter.' He had, intended to return to Lake Road and insist that Billie marry him despite the little one not surviving. He had been in love with her and even without a baby, he felt his life would be better if Billie was in it. But then other things intervened. 'Billie was heartbroken and unforgiving. And I was busy with university and opportunities for a big career in law.' Roland said. The hope of a simple love dissipated, and he lost touch with the girl he adored.

It wasn't the story of a high-flying Sydney lawyer who had chosen money and prestige over the girl who bore his first child. 'Did you tell your wife, your kids?' I wondered if it was part of the youthful misadventure tale that he shared with his family. He hadn't. They still didn't know that the life Roland now lived was not his first choice.

'What are you smiling about?' he asked.

It wasn't a happy smile, just a wistful one. He smiled too when I explained it. It had been my intention to put a different plaque on the baby's grave. It now read *Quis enim dolorem*. One for sorrow. 'I had originally intended it to say *Infante Divina*. Baby divine. And despite the obvious difference in spelling I felt if you ever saw the little tombstone, you would know that your secret was out.' To my surprise Roland laughed loudly attracting the attention of lunchtime diners around us.

'Oh God you are just like Billie.' Despite his laughter, his eyes filled with tears and this part of our conversation finished with him saying, 'Let's do that anyway. It's probably time to let my family know my story. We can't continue to live with secrets.'

Secrets and the revelation of them held our attention for the next hour. We had eaten and having a second coffee when Roland got on to explaining the work he was doing with the class action. It seemed that across the world and in Australia inquiries into systemic institutional abuse of children had gained momentum. As the new millennium commenced, the sins of the past no longer could be assured of concealment. The thousands of Australian children who had suffered abuse at the hands of religious, educational, and charitable institutions would eventually be told. A groundswell of outrage and political motivation to investigate these historical cases.

Roland was working on a class action in which many young men were making claims against a Sydney school; details that he couldn't disclose to me. 'It is simply the tip of the iceberg. These stories will come from every corner of the country.' He talked about the ravaged lives of victims of child abuse. The drug use, alcoholism, recidivist crime and suicide that followed periods of abuse were well known. 'Until now there has been no forum for the stories to be told, no promise of prosecution and worst of all, no recognition of the damage done.'

What he said made a clear link to Kitty's story. Henry's alcoholism, Miles's death and the guilt and shame that followed the boys into manhood was not an uncommon story. The brutal truth was that those who abused children walked free, but the victims were punished for life. I told Roland everything that I knew about the abuse at St. Finbar's. I even told him of having tracked down Roger Wheeler and that I suspected that Riley Morgan had also been a victim. The thought that Wheeler had raped Miles and then inflicted some kind of abuse on his brother a dozen years later angered me beyond words. What kind of person would do that? I hadn't realised that I'd voiced the question.

'A criminal.' Roland's simple answer was undeniably correct. 'Wheeler committed a crime. It is, if proven, punishable by law.'

It renewed my belief that all was not lost.

Roland had to drive back to Sydney, so the afternoon had to end. His final bit of advice. 'Try to get this boy to a support group. There's one near you in a town called Milton. I've got the number for you. And Lily...stay away from Roger Wheeler.'

While I couldn't promise to do the latter, I was interested in the contact he gave me for the survivors' group in Milton. The RISE Foundation had been developed for adult survivors of child abuse. The contact was John Laughton.

The drive back to Broulee took just over an hour. I arrived at 3:30 to find the house empty of guests. Helena had left a note to say that she and Mick had gone for a drive and that they would be back to take me out for dinner. I was so glad that the two of them got on well, but I equally glad to have the place to myself for a little while. They had cleaned up the house and the signs of last night's excesses were no longer visible. The day was warm enough to risk sitting outside. Max must have been about earlier in the day as he had left signs that he had been working on replacing the temporary balustrade with the wire rope we had ordered before Phillip went away.

In the quiet of the afternoon I rang John Laughton. He answered almost immediately and listened as I explained how I got his number and that I needed his advice about an abuse victim. His tone inspired confidence and only after I'd ended the call I imagined that he thought that I was the victim. Everyone probably rings on behalf of someone else trying to test the waters. Regardless of who he thought was the victim, I'd been invited to meet with him in Milton on Monday. They held group meetings at 5 on Monday afternoon but he was free to talk to me at 4 and had invited me to stay on to meet the others. I felt uncomfortable not disavowing him of the fact that I really wasn't the victim but I'm sure I could make him believe when we met face to face.

Over dinner I filled Mick and Helena in on the encounter with Roland Devine. I couldn't hide my new-found affection for the man I once considered my enemy. Mick was interested in the class action and how it would proceed. I couldn't give him much information about it. I also revealed Roland's last instruction about staying away from Roger Wheeler. 'Absolutely the best advice he could have given you.' Mick was emphatic in supporting Roland's advice.

The weekend ended. Helena sadly returned to Canberra. Mick talked about returning home too. I persuaded him to stay for a least a few more days to ensure he really was well enough to look after himself. Although Helena would probably seek him out and keep an eye on his wellbeing.

The night came and ended. I worked on my thesis Monday morning while Max was busy with work. Mick was keen to make the short journey north to the meeting with me, but I suggested he make us dinner. 'Show me your culinary skills are good enough for you to return home and I'll consider releasing you.' I didn't add that there was no way I was going to let Mick drive himself the two hours back to his property. He would have to wait until Max could drive with us so that I'd have a way to get home after we dropped Mick and his car at his house.

I met with John at the town hall, where several small rooms branched off the main auditorium. John waited on the steps of the building and welcomed me like a long-lost friend. I suspected that his warmth was part of the process of settling first timers into the meeting. But nothing else suggested that his kind demeanour was anything but genuine. Before I said anything other than my name, John explained what the group did and how meetings were run. He dispelled the notion of any religious affiliation with any church and stressed that it wasn't therapy, it simply provided a chance to talk and share. 'Too often victims think they are the only ones because nobody talks about it. For years victims think that it was somehow their fault because there is never a contradictory voice. That's what we provide.'

'It's not me I've come to talk about.'

John nodded but was hardly convinced.

I began to tell the story of Benedict Jepp. I omitted names and places but finished with how I'd discovered the perpetrator and my concerns for another young victim. By the end of my recount it seemed that I'd persuaded John that I was not here for myself but for others who at this point were unable to help themselves. I thought he would suggest that I not attend the meeting, but he seemed confident that I would be welcome. 'It might be good for you to get some other perspectives on what people are living with.'

The meeting ran like Alcohol Anonymous gatherings as had been portrayed in films. We all had polystyrene cups of tea and formed the inevitable circle. Several men and two women made up the group. I was introduced as Lily who'd lost a friend and was supporting another victim. The greetings were hospitable.

The participants were invited to speak about their situations and how they had coped over the previous week. A woman started the ball rolling. Petra would have been forty or thereabouts and looked like an everyday woman you'd pass in the street and imagine that she was living a normal life. But not so. Petra had been the victim of child abuse at the hands of her father and uncle. It had started from when she turned seven and ended at thirteen when she attempted to take her own life. No charges had ever been brought against them and the rest of the family, her mother and siblings included, had distanced themselves from her. She had been hospitalised after her suicide attempt and went and lived on the streets after the authorities thought she was well enough to go home. Homelessness was a better option than returning to abuse.

Lynn spoke about being abused by a boarding house matron for six years; Tony about his local parish priest; Terry about his scoutmaster and Sandro about a group of older boys at the school he attended. Each victim had gone on to destructive practices and relationships. Not one of the victims had been able to prosecute the perpetrator of their abuse. Some of them continued to have contact with the men and women who had violated them. For years they said nothing, until one day the story could not stay inside them anymore. It usually occurred after something catastrophic happened and their lives were at risk. Some had been in jail, others institutionalised, most living on the razor's edge between sanity and madness.

If a benevolent God existed, he had been absent from these lives for a long time. But the thing that struck me was the absence of bitterness and the lack of vengeful hatred. The acknowledgement of their torment was enough. The opportunity of being believed when they spoke of unimaginable suffering had begun to heal them. It was the silence that made it unbearable. When Kitty and the others cried out against their teacher, no-one believed them. Adults chastised them for telling lies and labelled the boys as troublemakers. When the abuse got worse there was no-one they could turn to. Wheeler, and abusers like him, held all the cards. For the men and women in this group it had been the same; their abusers had power over them their whole lives until, in this case, a stranger believed them. Someone acknowledged the truth of their stories and their genuine pain.

I drove away promising John that I'd stay in contact as I tried to work out what I could do next. Henry had finally been able to tell his story and if he was willing he might be able to be the stranger who saved Riley from the silence in which he was imprisoned. I could forgo revenge against Wheeler, but I could not abandon Riley. I would not abandon him.

Chapter Twenty-eight

I spent the next few days mulling over what I had learned at RISE. I couldn't help but think about the handful of victims who had somehow found each other in this small part of the world. The cover-ups started to consume my headspace. Mick had been able to find Wheeler's trail. He had left St. Finbar's had taken up a position in another regional school in Victoria for eighteen months. After that he went to Sydney to work in the administration of systemic Catholic schools choosing to return to teaching after a year behind a desk. He was, indeed, drawn south and his last few years of teaching he had been employed in the Shoalhaven area. An accident at the school saw Wheeler take a payout for an injury that allegedly disabled him.

'The accident is something you are going to want to hear about.' Mick was well and truly alive again. According to an ex-principal of the school, Wheeler had been set upon by an unidentified group and beaten so badly he had a broken femur, dislocated shoulder and fractured skull. The attack took place in the carpark at the back of the school one evening when Wheeler had been leaving after a meeting. The beating went unobserved and only when another teacher had finished marking at her desk and left at 6:30 that the unconscious man had been found. 'There was no sympathy for him though. The contact told me that the payout was the only way of getting rid of him. He said that the generally held belief was that he got what he deserved.' The man who spoke so freely to Mick had suggested that the beating had been meted out by a group of students who had a big axe to grind. 'But the diocese covered it up saying it the attack had been a robbery gone wrong by a gang who had nothing to do with the school.'

It seems Wheeler had been allegedly punished then by two random gangs. One burnt his house down and the other nearly beat him to death. The coincidence of such arbitrary events was the most unlikely explanation of chance that I'd ever heard. 'Did the ex-employee say anything else about the gossip at the time?'

Mick had two more things to add. 'The privately held opinion of most of the school community was that Wheeler was weird. There had been a rumour, unconfirmed, that he had touched one of the Year 7 boys when he supervised the child on detention. The child was absent for much of the following term, refusing to go to school because he was sick. 'There's no evidence, but we might be able to find the boy if we look hard enough. And I'm sure you're interested in what happened after Wheeler recovered from his injuries?'

Mick hardly had to say the words. Kelly Morgan had taken the monster in. His payout from the church gave him money to buy a property close to his most dedicated supporter. Unwittingly Kelly had paved the way for Wheeler to have access to her second son.

So Riley remained the key to bringing Wheeler undone. But the boy was so wary of me and my motives that I'd have to think of another way to get him the help he needed. Kelly's response to my revelation left me a little bewildered too. She had certainly thrown me out of her house once she realised I was the enemy. Her disbelief and dismissal of such claims should have been the end of it, but it wasn't. She found out where Kitty Jepp's wife lived and went there in a state of rage to ensure the blame for Miles's death was placed back on the boys who were with him that night. She went to defame Kitty so that Jean would know the sins of his past. It seemed irrational and immaterial. Why hadn't she just gone to Wheeler first? Maybe Kelly knew more than she had revealed through her actions.

I didn't think I could make her an ally in the fight against her friend. Archie and Henry on the other hand might be able to help. I also thought of Teresa Jepp's actions when she burned down Wheeler's house in Mallacoota. Teresa would have known Kelly, no doubt quite well; possibly they were even friends before the child's death. If she spoke of her suspicions, the ones that led to arson, maybe Kelly would believe. And possibly Riley would find the courage to speak out.

There were many improbabilities in all of that. I had, however, to start somewhere. And Henry was the most likely candidate.

He surprised me when I called his number by answering immediately. 'Kelly's fishing tours.'

Of course it was his work number and when sober enough, his business was thriving at Gipsy Point. I hoped he wouldn't hang up when he realised it who he was talking to. 'Sorry to bother you Henry, it's Lily O'Hara here.'

The friendliness of his tone was more of a surprise. It was as if he had forgotten the last agonising conversation we had. I explained that I wanted to check on him and to talk obscurely about RISE Foundation and how it might be good for him to find a support group. Then I started to tell him about Wheeler and my encounter with him and Miles's mother.

Henry was shocked that Wheeler had been living so close to both Kelly and Benedict. 'Do you think Bennie saw him? Is that why he killed himself?'

I thought that was exactly the reason. 'But there's something else, Henry. Kelly has a second son and she told me that he too had been abused but couldn't identify the man who did it.'

Henry's silence confirmed that our thinking was aligned.

'Henry, I think you can help Riley. I know you have spent your life thinking you should have saved Miles, but it wasn't possible then. But it is now. You can save his brother.'

I let him think on this for a while and waited for him to respond. 'I can try Lily. But I ...' He couldn't finish the sentence.

'But you can Henry. You're not in this alone. We are all here with you. You are not alone in this anymore.'

'I can try.' He repeated with no more confidence but at least he'd agreed. I rang Archie immediately after Henry put the phone down, fully expecting that what I'd done might have sent him on a bender.

Archie swore a lot. Not about me upsetting his friend but about the swathe of damage that Wheeler had cut through the lives of children everywhere he went. 'I'll bring Henry up as soon as we can get away. And if he can't do it, I'll just come up and put a bullet in Wheeler myself.'

Archie's threats were nothing that Max and I hadn't voiced ourselves. The Rottweiler had survived two assaults on him, two near misses. Maybe he wouldn't be so lucky the third time.

The last call I made was to Fred Lewis, the newspaper editor. I told him that I'd met Father Burrell and Connie. 'She's a lovely person and so sad that she hadn't been able to protect the boys from Wheeler.'

'She called me after you spoke. Told me about Henry's story.' Fred said that it he was now realising that covering up the story had been misguided and in doing so they had all given Wheeler a way out. Fred and Angelo, who was now out of hospital, had planned to visit Robert Rennison. 'He deserves to know. Poor bastard has been hanging onto the hatred for so long it'll probably kill him to realise he's hated the wrong person.'

Poor Robert. I did feel so sorry for him despite our altercation in the Gipsy Point cemetery. I didn't blame him for wanting to hit me for seemingly siding with the boy he saw as the enemy. All those years he has spent in anger and loathing for the wrong reason, all that wasted time. I hoped he would be soothed by the image of his son being tenderly held in the winter water of Top Lake by a boy who understood his pain. A boy who didn't harm Miles, and two other boys who tried to help. Kitty had to live with the guilt of his inaction until it reared up and swallowed him. I couldn't imagine how Miles's father would react.

All parties had been informed about the past and the current situation. I had been reluctant to ring Teresa Jepp after her frosty dismissal of me when I went to her home in Eden. It was cowardly of me to put it off any longer, so I dialled her number. She didn't answer. I felt relieved. I would put it off until the next day to bring her into the murky web.

But I didn't ever have to make that phone call. Jean left a message on my voicemail to say that her mother-in-law was coming to Congo. Jean had called her and told her that things had been discovered about Kitty's life and that the man who abused him lived close by. It seemed that Teresa Jepp too had guilt to assuage and maybe a grandson to protect. I was moved and simultaneously amused by the thought of her astride some kind of broomstick rushing to the rescue. I had seen, however, just a fleeting glance at the mother inside the "old bitch" when I looked at those photos she kept of her son and grandson. Her confession to being the arsonist both comforted and concerned me. I wondered momentarily whether Wheeler would survive the gathering of angry mothers. In the same moment I hoped he wouldn't.

The business of the day ended with a lovely phone call with Phillip. He was still in Bali, rested and recovered enough to be going off to a Balinese banquet that night. We missed each other terribly. I missed feeling his body beside me in bed and making love, and watching him eat, and hearing him talk. I wanted him to come home and make jokes about how his tummy was expanding with mine. I wanted to laugh at how he'd put his mouth close to my belly and talk to the baby as if he was in some conspiracy with him or her against me. More importantly, I wanted to feel safe from the world that had begun to make me feel afraid. I had seen for the first time that monsters are not things that hide under your bed and lurk in darkness; they wander about in the light and take the joy from everything they touch. I didn't cry when I said goodbye to him, I couldn't leave him with the worry that I wasn't able to cope. But I cried afterwards. I curled up on my bed and simply let the tears soak my pillow. I hadn't heard Max come in and didn't realise he was in the house until he lay down beside me.

'Don't cry, Lil. It'll be okay.' I ignored Helena's advice about Max's feelings and turned to him, putting my head on his chest. He rubbed my back and held one hand. 'We really have to stop sleeping together.' He laughed.

It made me smile. It felt good to be close to him; good to have a friend who knew what it was like to miss Phillip.

Max did not stay for dinner or for the night. He went home to look after Sarah. I slept well.

At breakfast Mick announced that he was going home and that I didn't need to fuss about anything as Helena planned to catch the bus down the next day and she would drive him back to Canberra. He would be continuing to track down witnesses against Wheeler and asked if I minded him contacting Roland Devine for advice. I was not happy that he was going to be on his own, but I needed to have the silence of my home back. And also secretly happy that two of my best friends had made such a connection. My thoughts must have been evident in my smile.

'Stop getting ahead of yourself there Lil.'

It made me smile even more.

The following day I gave a dozen instructions about how Mick should take it easy, eat well and ring me should he need anything. Helena joined the chorus of maternal warnings and Mick must have felt henpecked as well as much loved. They left with Helena playing her usual triumphant farewell of horn-tooting long after she had driven up the street. I couldn't help but marvel how opposites definitely attract.

The day was mine. I had left a text message with Jean that I'd come down in the afternoon and speak with her and Teresa. I thought that Kitty's mother would want to hear the whole story from someone involved in the uncovering. It would be nice to again see Isaiah, who had captured my heart with his dear little fat face and chubby limbs. It was probably hormonal, but I was drawn entirely to the world of babies and children.

The day didn't quite turn out to be entirely mine. A few hours into writing a critical chapter on indigenising museums I was interrupted by a knock at the door. Expecting it to be Max or Margaret, who regularly came to check on Mick and whether there was food in the fridge, I simply called out for the visitor to let themselves in. I turned to greet whichever family member had popped in, only to find Henry Kelly standing there.

He said he simply had to come. Felt he couldn't put it off any longer. The last time Henry was at my house, he revealed the shocking events that took place on the night of Miles's assault and subsequent death. He looked no better on this second visit. I didn't realise that skin could be that colour of grey and for eyes to sink so deeply. Henry was sober but suffering terribly from dehydration and withdrawal. 'Two days without booze. It's killing me.' And he was right. Detoxing without medical supervision can be deadly. Henry's hands trembled, and he winced at the light in the room when he took his glasses off.

'Henry, have you been sick, do you have any pain?' Rapid un-medicated detox could lead to seizures, hallucinations and sometimes brain injury. He needed help right now, and if he were to have delirium and fall into unconsciousness, he would be of little help to Riley.

'I'm coping. It's terrible but I wanted to be sober when I spoke to the boy.' Henry had driven three hours in this condition to do as I'd suggested. He was here, in this dreadful state, to save Riley. I wished Mick had not left. I needed help with him. I couldn't in my wildest dreams take Henry to the Morgan's house like this. If we ran into Wheeler the damage would be catastrophic. I couldn't leave him alone or let him return to Gipsy Point in this condition.

Max came immediately. He dropped what he had been doing much to the displeasure of his co-workers. They had stirred him about running when the girlfriend called. He was flustered and unhappy when he arrived. When he saw Henry though, he realised why I'd insisted he come.

Henry wouldn't or couldn't eat but did take long drinks of sugary cola. It seemed to help with the nausea and allowed him to be more focused. He slept on and off in ten to fifteen-minute time slots. In one episode of fractured sleep, he seemed to stop breathing. I was terrified. When he woke, he sounded confused and slightly aggressive as he didn't immediately recognise who we were. Max held my hand for a bit after Henry went back to dozing. Together we decided we had to ring Archie and then an ambulance. Archie was relieved to know that Henry was in Broulee. He'd thought Henry had simply gone missing. He agreed that the hospital might be the best place for him until he could get here.

The paramedics treated Henry patiently and calmly. They asked questions we were not fully able to answer. Next of kin, type and amount of alcohol from which he was detoxing, how many detox sessions had he tried, was he taking any medication. His blood pressure had become dangerously high. The two young men suddenly became very concerned for Henry; this wasn't a case of the Friday night drunk reeling from a hangover. He was at serious risk of having a stroke and dying. Panic started to well up. Not just because I'd hoped that Henry could help Riley but that he might just become another statistic in Wheeler's reign of destruction. This poor man had lived with a painful secret that he kept trying to drown in the bottom of the bottle. I wanted to cry for the injustice of it. The tears would have to wait though. I had to stay focused on the current problem. Henry had to live.

We explained that one of us would follow and that his best friend would be at the hospital some point in the afternoon. Henry was whisked away, sirens blaring and lights flashing.

I sent a message to Archie to say that the situation had become critical and that he should make his way straight to the Moruya Hospital.

'On my way, already passed Eden.'

I would be glad to hand the responsibility back to Archie. I sent Max to back to work, went to the hospital to wait for Archie, and then I'd go on to Jean's for my scheduled meeting with her and Teresa. My hopes for a coherent telling of the story of Henry had dissipated with Henry's decline into delirium tremors.

For the second time in the past three weeks I entered the Emergency Department. One nurse recognised me. 'Jinxed, are we?' She patted me in a friendly and concerned manner.

The GP I'd been seeing was also on duty as an emergency doctor and saw me sitting in the waiting room. 'Lily. You okay? Baby alright?'

'Here for a friend. He's in a bit of strife.'

The same nurse put her two cents worth in. 'Doing her friends in one at a time.' It wasn't funny, but the attempt at light heartedness was probably all that got emergency staff through long days and nights.

The doctor couldn't help but add, 'This kind of stress isn't good for pregnant women. Take it easy will you. Phil home yet?'

I nodded for the first part and shook my head for the second. She was right, this running about and constant stress wasn't good for anyone. Now, of course, I'd be worrying what kind of terrible things might be happening to my baby because of the incessant and relentless stress I'd put my body under. This simply had to end. After this afternoon I'd put this behind me. I couldn't help Kitty anymore. And it seemed that my plan to help Riley had also failed. It was time to let go.

The medical staff couldn't tell me much except that Henry had been sedated and his blood pressure was not yet under control. He would probably need to be moved to a bigger hospital after they stabilised him. The next of kin was becoming an issue as decisions had to be made. Henry had a daughter, an ex-wife, brothers somewhere and a best friend. Archie would have to sort it out when he arrived.

Within two hours he had. I spoke to him briefly before heading off to Jean's. It wasn't the best news—Henry was very ill and the social worker approached Archie immediately to ask for family to be notified. I felt bad for leaving him, but I could do nothing to help Henry, but my mission to protect Riley was something I didn't want to give up on. Archie promised to ring me periodically to report on Henry's condition.

Jean and Teresa were seated at the dining table, drinking tea from the beautiful crockery that I first noticed when I came to the house just after Kitty died. To my surprise and great pleasure Teresa had Isaiah on her knee. She smiled down at him, and he at her. I had not noticed that how truly attractive she looked until I saw the affection she felt for her grandson on her face. I marvelled at the transformative nature of happiness and unconditional love. Teresa seemed reborn.

She greeted me warmly. 'Looks like we are destined to be friends after all, Lily.' Even in the midst of the awfulness of the information we were all now aware of, a small glimmer of hope existed that something positive could be gained. Jean warmly hugged me and poured me tea. We needed to fortify ourselves before launching into the decisions about our next step.

Teresa asked about the pregnancy and how I was feeling. She offered a little story about how she felt when she was pregnant with Kitty. She only ever called him Benedict, never Bennie, and certainly never Kitty. Hers had been an easy pregnancy all the way until labour. At that her son started to cause trouble. He had to be delivered by emergency caesarean after twenty hours of labour. 'He had a big head, even then.'

I had thought little about labour; thinking made me a little scared. It never ceased to amaze me how women, when in the presence of babies and the pregnant, the talk always included birth stories. It was a good tactic to delay the topic of conversation to come next.

Jean led. 'Poor Kitty. The terrible things that happened. I wish I'd known.' It wasn't a criticism of her mother-in-law and now ally. It was a wish we all harboured. Teresa felt the invitation to relive those days in Mallacoota. She talked about how she felt she had to be fairly stern with Benedict. Without his father, she took on the role of both and perhaps she had been too strict with him. She had thought that faith and religion would help shape the boy into a good man. 'He was a good man.' Despite the terrible things that had happened to him. Her voice faltered only once when she explained why she hadn't believed him when he first revealed that Wheeler had been giving them alcohol and touching him. It was easier to make Kitty a liar than a villain out of the well-liked teacher. It wasn't laziness or even misguided religious fervour. It was fear. Fear of being further ostracised and that something worse might happen to her son. 'I felt safer not believing.' She couldn't really fully explain this feeling. It was as if not acknowledging a terrible thing, not really seeing it, would make you immune from the nightmares of reliving it.

'So why did you attempt to burn down Wheeler's house?' I started with a bold question but provocative enough to make Teresa delve deeper into her memory.

The night the boys went missing filled her with grief and horror. She sat with the other parents in the rain and chill of the night, while rescue vessels went out calling the names of each boy. 'It was like something out of a horror movie. The sound of voices calling each boy's name through the fog and drizzle seemed prophetic—it was like the end of days.' When three were found alive and Miles's tiny body recovered, Teresa had vowed to do something about the suspicions about Wheeler's behaviour towards the boys. But the days that followed were full of grief and agony. Then recriminations and accusations; interviews, denials and division. The town was simultaneously torn apart and shut down. Factions formed and inevitably people took sides. Teresa had decided that to take her son's story further would have done more damage than good. She had a real enemy in Robert Rennison, whose behaviour had become a danger to Kitty. He threatened to kill the boys who had, as he believed, taken his child's life.

Kelly, Miles's mother, did not outright reject the Jepps. She believed that the boys were possibly innocent, and Robert's behaviour became completely irrational. Roger Wheeler had been on hand with Father Burrell to counsel and support all the families. Wheeler had aligned himself with the Rennisons, and Father Burrell took on the job of looking out for the other boys. But rumour and innuendo had made its mark on all of them. While the situation was eventually buried, it would never be forgotten.

Teresa got up to put her now sleeping grandson into his rainbow cot. When she returned to the table, she brought a plate of tiny sandwiches from the fridge. We ate for a moment in silence, the three of us lost in the past. I waited until she had washed down a mouthful of food to ask why she had burned down the presbytery.

She paused and explained. 'Benedict was never the same you know. From that night, maybe even before, he lost his spark.' She had initially put it down to becoming a moody teenager and then on the company he kept. After he confessed that Wheeler made them do things he didn't like, and she rejected his claims, he withdrew almost completely from her. In her words he had become a ghost who wandered in and out of the house, silent most of the time. When the school was about to close and Benedict was off to boarding school, he made a comment to her. 'He said that Wheeler could go off and rape other children now because nobody cared.' A tear ran down her face. 'He wasn't bitter or angry. Just deadpan. As if he'd stated the most immutable fact about the most mundane thing.' This ignited Teresa's desire for her own retribution.

The first person she went to on the night was Kelly Rennison. 'I told her that Wheeler had done something to the boys and I was going to make him pay for it.' Kelly listened patiently to Teresa that night; she didn't blame her or Kitty for Miles's death. She also didn't believe that her friend Roger could have done anything to her own child or others.

Kelly rang Roger that night to tell him that Teresa Jepp had been making all kinds of threats and the perhaps Wheeler should not be alone that evening. 'I didn't know she had warned him, when I poured the petrol around his front and back doors I'd truly hoped he was inside.' Teresa had lit a match at the front door and then one at the back, escaping through the school grounds undetected. The house went up in minutes. The rural fire brigade could do nothing to stop the heat swallowing the little timber house whole.

Kelly said nothing to the police about Teresa Jepp's threats that evening. Wheeler had been saved. Kelly's marriage ended, Benedict moved away and the past it seemed had been eradicated in the flames. Kelly could have easily accused Teresa but didn't. She might have made the case that Benedict killed Miles and the mother was trying to do the same to the man who many believed was a saint. But she remained silent. It was a strange choice for someone so convinced of Wheeler's innocence.

By the time the story ended and the food consumed, we three had decided that we would drive the short distance to Kelly Morgan's house. Three women would be a more formidable force. Jean's friend Maggie arrived to stay with the baby. She was an extraordinary contrast to the neat as pin Teresa. Maggie's dark dreadlocks and pierced face only just overshadowed the rose red and green tattoo of a flowering vine that emerged from between her breasts and wound its way around her throat. Teresa looked somewhat disapproving, but I was fascinated by how someone could bear that kind of pain being inflicted on the tenderness of breast and throat. I had a strange admiration for her bravery.

I left my car parked outside on the lawn. Jean drove us. Teresa insisted I sit in the front and the three unlikely musketeers set off with a poorly conceived plan to force Kelly into believing that her two sons had been victims of the friend she had so unwittingly protected. I was unconvinced that we would make a difference and equally unconvinced that we could not draw attention to ourselves as we turned into the quiet suburban streets. A mother earth in a cheesecloth frock, a middle aged, sensibly dressed grandmother and a somewhat bewildered red head in baggy jeans and hoodie would not go unobserved if someone had to report a strange alliance of women descending upon Tuross.

But there we were. I took a quick phone call from Archie who called to say that Henry had stabilised but that he wasn't out of the woods yet. The medical staff could not get his blood pressure under control and that it seemed that he had undiagnosed Type 2 Diabetes. A very bad combination for an alcoholic. I promised to drop into the hospital on my way back and offered Archie a place to stay the night. I didn't like the thought of him feeling that there wasn't someone who cared about him during this difficult time. He politely declined the offer because he had already booked into the local pub. 'How about you? All okay with your current company? Or have you and Mrs. Jepp become best friends? 'We had a sad little laugh at that.

Kelly answered the door and while I expected her to be full of rage at the intrusion, she was most sedate. She recognised Teresa immediately and put her hand out to her in an act of friendship rather than an enemy. Her eyes took in Jean and me, standing a little behind Teresa. Her face reddened, perhaps recalling the last encounters she'd had with both of us. The house was quiet but in a state of chaos, as if a whirlwind had ripped through the home since she last welcomed me inside. Kelly burst into tears and attempted to apologise for her mess, for her behaviour, for everything. A confused babble of words and names that was only contained when Teresa pulled her into her arms.

'It's alright Kelly. We are friends and we are going to help.'

The hysterical woman slowed her sobs and nodded into Teresa's shoulder. She motioned for us to sit down in amongst the strewn piles of clothes and half unpacked boxes that had seemingly been taped shut for decades.

'My husband and I have been separated for a while, and I am trying to finally sort things out.' I looked closely at what had been flung in all directions—baby clothes, and toys and school uniforms.

Nearest to where I perched on the end of a well-worn two-seater was a little white shirt. I picked it up to fold when I noticed the logo on the pocket. St. Finbar's College, *Liberatas in veritate.* Freedom through truth. Miles Rennison's school uniform had the most compelling motto. The boxes that Kelly had strewn about the house belonged to her dead child's. The dusty cardboard had the held the memories of the little boy whose life and death were at the centre of the chaos that Kitty's suicide had brought. Perhaps somewhere in the disruption and pain of my early visit, a light had been turned on for her.

'I was looking for a little diary that Miles used to write in. He always wrote wonderful stories. I couldn't help but pull everything out and try to remember everything about him.'

It didn't explain the disregard with which these precious items had been pitched about.

'It was Riley. He came home in a rage and just kept emptying things out of boxes and kicking them about. He said I cared more about a dead son than a living one.'

'I hope Riley is wrong, Kelly.' Teresa called a halt to the maudlin self-pity. 'We have both lost sons because of one common enemy. Roger Wheeler raped Miles. Benedict, Henry and Archie tried to save him. Wheeler is a paedophile who has stolen our sons from us. He has most likely tried to hurt Riley too.'

'I know.' Her answer was simple and profound.

I hadn't predicted that Teresa would be so brutal in her explanation. But it was the shake-up Kelly needed. It was the metaphorical slap that she required to shake lose the suspicions she once held.

The monster Kelly had protected because she could not believe that he was anything but her well-meaning friend had assaulted both her babies. One had paid with his life, the other with rage.

The conversation that then transpired was the turning point for everyone. As we gathered the trinkets, mementos and memories, fold-ing them back into the boxes from which they had been ripped, we talked like conspirators.

When Henry recovered from the delirium tremors which now held his life to ransom, we would support him as he spoke to the police to bring charges against Wheeler. Riley would be told the truth about his brother and if Henry was strong enough, he might be able to sit down with Riley and unlock the memories of his assault and quell the storm inside him.

Kelly took John Laughton's card and promised to contact the RISE Foundation and seek an appointment for herself and Riley with a psychologist who might be able to help them both. The tone of the conversation was so bland and indifferent, we might have been swapping recipes. The emotion had been spent, the chaos of fear and disbelief had been consumed in the explosion of things from boxes. Once they had been restored, the only thing on our minds was retribution.

I thought of the legal recourse. But the talk had turned to revenge and although the powerful hysteria had left us giddy, I was a little uncomfortable about the topic.

'I could burn his house down again.' Teresa's open confirmation of her previous crime of arson brought a smile.

Jean made me most concerned when she said, 'I'd happily shoot him.' It reminded me that Archie had said the same thing about putting a bullet in him.

I brought the conversation back to reality by reminding everyone that they had very good reasons for staying out of jail. That the law would take care of Wheeler and that our most pressing concern should be for Riley. They agreed, and all talk of vigilantism ended.

With the afternoon's quota of tea consumed, I had to use the bathroom urgently before we left. The house had a long hallway that took the visitor right to the back of the house where the woman's voices could just be heard. In the room just before the bathroom, sat a boy on an unmade bed. His face wretched and wet. I guessed Riley Morgan had been witness to the lounge room revelations. He had heard his mother's confirmation that she had held suspicions about Wheeler's innocence regarding Miles's death. He too had heard the things we had said about Henry's recollections of the night and that we had all suspected that the assault on Riley had been perpetrated by the same vile man.

The child, although technically a man, didn't know me. I was a stranger. But he let me sit beside him and take his hand. The job I thought Henry would have, became mine. I would be the person to hear Riley's first utterances about what had happened to him.

Wheeler had been a frequent visitor. Riley called him Uncle Roger. He had some vague memories of things happening when he was in the bath as a little boy and a strange dream about being touched when he was asleep, to then wake and find Uncle Roger sitting on his bed. But the night when all memory seemed to have failed him happened when he was nine.

Wheeler had picked him up at the shops and said he'd drive him home. Riley had taken a sweet drink from this familiar friend—he was not a stranger. The world became a dream, he dozed and drifted far away. They parked near the campground, but no-one was around. Uncle Roger had pulled the boy's pants down and put something inside him. 'It hurt. Terrible pain. But it seemed like it was not real. I woke up on the sand. Mum found me and I was bleeding. She took me home and put me in the bath. She said I'd had an accident. What really happened just disappeared.' Again the terrible silence once more had buried the unbearable truth. All I could offer was the chance to talk to people who knew what it felt like to be so betrayed and the hope that soon he would be charged and imprisoned.

'Riley you have the power to make him pay. Your assault and memory of it, despite the fact that you have only just remembered, is evidence against him.'

Riley looked at me for a moment, wondering if he should say what he did next. It seemed that he trusted me enough to say, 'I've known for a while it was him, but I just couldn't tell Mum. I thought it would kill her to know that her one friend was scum.'

I had to leave him for a few minutes; my bladder wouldn't wait any longer. By the time I got back to him, Riley had gone.

In his place Kelly sat. She had heard what he had said when she came to see if I was okay as I'd been gone for several minutes. 'He left, just pushed passed me and drove off.'

'He will come back, Kelly. But you will have to be strong for him. This is just the beginning not the end.' I thought that was the end of the conversation, but I felt I should add the same advice that I'd been given by both Mick and Roland Devine. 'Stay away from Wheeler. He will be dangerous now he knows we are coming for him. Keep him out, no matter what you have to do, keep him out of your life and away from Riley.'

Chapter Twenty-nine

As we drove away, I couldn't help feeling a little guilty about the awfulness that had to be faced by Kelly and Riley. I also assumed that Kelly would contact her current yet estranged husband and enlist his support for their son.

I declined Jean's invitation to go in and have more tea, explaining that I really wanted to get back to the hospital to check on Henry and offer Archie some support. The two women, once distanced by their love for Kitty, now a united as a pair. Jean put her arm around her mother-in-law as the two wandered through the overgrown garden to the back of the house. A common enemy often makes friends of the least likely allies.

I hoped that Teresa would be able to see Henry and Archie in the coming days to finally validate her belief in their story. I had thoughts of contacting Father Burrell and Connie Harlow to do the same. Life could be rebuilt; the truth would restore hope that the future could be much better than the past.

I was exhausted from the showdown at the Morgans and very concerned for Riley, but despite these draining feelings, I felt very optimistic for the first time. Being involved, digging out the facts had made a difference and Phillip's warning about not getting involved was invalidated. There was only one person who would pay the price for the concealed past.

That optimism and slightly self-satisfied feeling lasted only until I found Archie. He sat alone in a stark visitors' room for family and friends who waited for news. Henry had taken a turn for the worse and was experiencing seizures associated with acute alcohol withdrawal. Henry's brain had haemorrhaged, possibly because of the complications associated with high blood pressure. The rapid detoxification he had undertaken to come north and bring down Wheeler had triggered a savage spike in his underlying health problems. Archie had been advised to get Henry's family immediately if they wanted to see him as it was expected that time was short.

Archie and I sat with Henry in the closing of the day. Even though unconscious I wanted Henry to know that Wheeler's days were numbered. 'We've got him Henry. Riley knows that Wheeler raped him. And together we going to bring him down.'

Archie's last words moved me. 'You've won mate.'

Just before 7 that night Henry's body succumbed to the years of toxic punishment he had inflicted on himself. It was his attempt at sobriety that had hastened the end. The doctor confirmed that Henry probably had shortened life expectancy given the alcoholism and untreated hypertension and diabetes. Death had long been knocking at his door.

Archie was silent but angry. A vein pulsed in his forehead as we sat, almost strangers, trying to take in the news. 'He wanted to do something for Bennie and Miles. He wanted to feel that he had seen justice done. Eventually.' Archie stared at the floor. 'He couldn't protect Miles. He couldn't face Benedict. And I couldn't save him.' He turned to face me. 'I tried to save them that night, I wanted to make it alright for all of them. I tried to tell Henry over the years that the past didn't matter, it couldn't be changed.'

Poor Archie. Another unwitting victim of Roger Wheeler. Wheeler preyed on the altar boys and eventually destroyed the three of them and Archie could only stand by and watch the poison take hold and down them one by one. I expected he knew that Henry's death had been preceded by a darkness that took him long ago. The alcohol became a balm to images that played out in his head year after year. Numbing himself to the sickening vision of Wheeler raping Miles, attempting a normal life as a father and failing, and then a lifetime drowning himself in vodka was a price too big for anyone to pay. The only solace was that Henry's story had been taped. It might not be admissible as evidence against Wheeler, but it would stand as a record of Henry's courage to finally dispel the lies of that night in 1980. Too tired to cry, all I could do was the practical stuff. Get Archie to the hotel, ring the players in the vile drama in which we found ourselves, and go home to sleep.

Teresa and Jean were distraught at the unexpected death of Henry. Mick was shocked and full of advice about what needed to be done. He would speak to a friend he had at the Department of Public Prosecutions about how to proceed with bringing charges against Wheeler, advising me to make copies and keep safe the recordings made earlier. I also wanted to talk to Roland Devine. He would have advice as to how we should proceed. Max waited at home with food and comfort. When he held me, I finally broke down and cried. Not for myself but for Henry, Kitty, Miles and Riley and every other child whose life had been infected by Wheeler. I wept for the mothers and fathers, the teachers and bystanders who had to accept the dreadful certainty that these children had suffered humiliation and damage and then expected to be silent. That poison could only be contained for so long. In the end it must be rooted out and laid bare. Only in the light could a wound that deep begin to heal.

Sleep came. Max stayed. Sarah was safe at her grandparents' home. The wrongness of him being beside me outweighed the distress caused by the last few weeks. A dreamless, calm sleep proved restorative. When I woke late, Max had already gone. I should have called Archie to check he didn't need me, but I just wanted to have a morning where I could disengage from the sadness for a little while. In my head I imagined that I would, with Max and perhaps Jean and Teresa in tow, attend the local police station and talk to the most senior officer on duty. The story would unfold. Perhaps Kelly and Riley, in the best-case scenario, would join us too. Revelation would bring peace.

At 11am a sharp knock on the door indicated that the visitor was not family or friend. I thought it might be Archie. It wasn't.

The uniformed police sergeant and a suited detective asked if they could come in. I was dwarfed by the two of them and slightly apprehensive at their stern demeanour. I knew in my heart that this had something to do with the Wheeler case. Had Kelly already taken Riley into the station to make claims against The Rottweiler and indicated that I was in possession of a big part of the story? It was plausible, but I wondered at the reason Senior Sergeant Kim Clarke and Detective Sergeant Bryce McWilliams had arrived at my door.

'Ms O'Hara it was reported that you had an altercation in Allenby Road in Tuross Head last week. You were driving a car owned by Michael Flynn.' They both waited for confirmation. I nodded my agreement that this was in fact true. My phone started ringing and as I glanced at the screen I could see Mick's number. 'Would you mind not answering the phone at the moment.' It stopped and immediately started again. Mick obviously had to tell me something.

'You were seen in the area several times in the last week.' I didn't know by whom I'd been seen but I couldn't deny the fact. 'You know or are acquainted with a Roger Alexander Wheeler?'

I couldn't nod assent to that. 'I know about him. I've been looking at his past—' I was cut off by the detective who virtually cautioned me at that time.

'Ms. O'Hara I think you are probably aware that Mr. Wheeler's house was subject to an arson attack last night.'

I was not aware but all I could think of was the coven of women who had grievances with the man, and one who had history with burning his houses. My mind now alerted to what was happening led me to something akin to panic. I'd been seen, allegedly lurking in his street twice. I'd had some kind of run in with a young person and I'd been at the Morgan house on two separate occasions. It might look like I was stalking him. And now they believed I burned down his house.

'A woman matching your description was given to police by several witnesses. You were seen having a heated discussion with a friend of Mr. Wheelers from a car registered to Michael Flynn. Mr. Flynn confirmed that his car had been at your place in Broulee but he had not driven it to Tuross.'

Mick's incessant phone calls now made sense. He'd been contacted when the number plate had been reported and he unwittingly had made the connection for the police. My silence did not go unnoticed by the two officers who had walked further into the house moving me with them through Sergeant Clarke's gentle but firm hand on my arm.

'I can explain.' It immediately sounded like an admission of guilt. What could I explain? That I'd undertaken an investigation into an alleged paedophile's actions that resulted in the death of a boy in 1980 and a suicide this year. That I'd been consorting with the victims and their families and that I was about to go to the police with my suspicions. I had files on my table detailing the material Mick and I and gathered and Detective McWilliams was obviously looking about for something that might be construed as evidence. Two folders of cuttings and photos might just tip the scales completely against me.

The material, if it went unexplained, would be as incriminating as if they'd walked in and found an incendiary device with Wheeler's name written on it.

'I'd like to explain something. Could we sit down over here, I'm pregnant and a bit weary.' Yes, I sensed them thinking because you were out late burning down respected a citizen's house.

It made them move away from the material on the table, but it had caught their eyes. 'Busy with paperwork?' McWilliams asked.

'Studying. Finishing my doctorate.' Perhaps it made me sound more learned and less mad. I thought I'd launch right in and tell them everything that happened, but McWilliams interrupted me again.

'Lily.' Making friends by using my first name. 'It's not just the fire we've come about. A body was found in the house when the firefighters got the blaze under control.' He waited for this to register. But my mind was processing too many possibilities. Was it Wheeler? Surely Kelly or Riley hadn't gone there. Was it Teresa, making good her last attempt at burning him down?

My inability to respond didn't do much for my protestation of innocence.

'We would like to question you at the Bay Police Station. It is a formal line of inquiry and you might like to ring a lawyer.' Sergeant Clarke pulled me to my feet and McWilliams went back to the table to gather up the folders.

Mick had neatly written the names Wheeler on one file, St. Finbar's on another. It had been done in pencil and was barely noticeable, but McWilliams had seen the names as he cruised passed the table. He hadn't flinched when I steered them away and encouraged them to sit. At that point he knew he'd be taking me to the station; nothing I could have said would have deterred him.

I stayed calm. I thought of Phillip getting this news as he rested in Bali. It horrified me. Yes, I was embroiled in an issue that had resulted, possibly in a fire and a death but I knew when questioned I could explain my connection to the case. I had an alibi; I had been with Archie at the hospital. Several witnesses saw me there. And then with Max. All night. It was an alibi that might raise a few eyebrows but none-the-less an alibi. Of course I'd slept like the dead, so I may be a less convincing defence for Max who had gone well before I woke that morning.

As I was assisted into the back seat of the waiting unmarked police vehicle, I wondered how I could explain the comings and goings to Tuross without casting suspicion on the whole group of potential arsonists. I'd start at the beginning and work my way to last night. There was something comforting in the logical unfolding of the events that cast Wheeler as the enemy—the criminal. I secretly hoped the body was Wheeler's and ventured asking who had died in the fire.

No answer came immediately from the two men in the front seat. 'Hasn't been identified but it is the body of a man.'

I had my phone in my pocket. It hadn't been confiscated so I managed a quick text to Mick. *I think I'm being arrested. Ring Max.*

Chapter Thirty

My husband was a police officer-officer, my best friend too. My father had been considered a murderer of my mother and brother. This, although substantial, they were my only contact with the law. Being ushered into the station through a back door, into a place where real criminals were interviewed, was terrifying. The two officers were joined by a female constable who searched me and took my handbag and phone from my pocket. When she was certain I'd be no threat to her fellow officers, they took me into an interview room. Then everyone disappeared for twenty minutes. On return, McWilliams had a take-away cup of coffee and two paper strips of sugar.

He sat opposite me and the female officer sat beside me. She took up a lot of room and I felt myself trying to shuffle my chair to make way for her long and considerable thighs. In a moment of madness I thought if it came to the crunch, I might be able to outrun her. Probably not the detective who had opened his note pad to write down pertinent points.

He started with, 'Are you actually pregnant?'

It seemed an offensive kind of question but I answered in the affirmative.

The big woman beside me moved away as if she thought it might be contagious.

I couldn't help but say, 'You can't catch it.' My tone had a brittle edge. I was not happy. The questioning started for real.

McWilliams wanted to know how long I'd known Roger Wheeler and what sort of relationship I had with him. I'd assumed that in their twenty-minute absence, the police had confirmed that the body in the burnt house was him.

'I had no relationship with Roger Wheeler.' Statement of fact. 'But I knew a great deal about him.' If McWilliams and his skittish friend would let me talk I'd be able to make clear the circumstances of my connection to the man and unfortunately, the crime. 'If I could just tell you how things unfolded, you would understand more about last night's crime.'

But McWilliams had a series of questions designed to make, what he thought, inextricable links between me and the dead man. He started with, 'How long have you been living in the region?'

'My husband, Detective Sergeant Phillip Swan grew up here. I moved here to be near his parents while he was seconded to an overseas task force.' I wanted most desperately to add, you total arse. But common sense prevented such an indiscretion.

'We know who your husband is Mrs. Swan, and your friend Michael Flynn has already been in touch with the regional superintendent. Neither relationship precludes you from questioning.'

I felt a little like a chastised child and became more petulant because of it. 'If you would just let me speak and then when I'm done come back to your inane questions, perhaps you would have some chance of understanding.' Casting aspersions against the detective's intellect probably wasn't my most sterling moment but I felt trapped by exigent circumstances.

McWilliams sat back and regarded me with that same impassive look that Phillip and Mick frequently used.

In the stillness I launched into the first part of the story. I talked about Max and how he had been distraught over his friend's suicide. Benedict Kitty Jepp had unexpectedly taken his life and had left a letter for Max. It was somewhat cryptic but led to the two us trying to work out what might have happened to drive him to abandon his wife and new baby son. At the funeral we made contact with two of his old friends from Mallacoota. I realised that McWilliams might have known some of this because he would have perused the files he'd taken from my house. These things would have been explicit in the timeline I'd created which identified who we met and how they were linked to Kitty. Of course he would already have known that Wheeler's residence in Mallacoota had been burned down and if he had read all of Mick's notes, that he had also been a victim of assault in another town. What McWilliams didn't have was Henry Kelly's account of the rape he had witnessed in 1980. I'd been very careful about securing the recording and had it tucked away in the bedside table drawer. I'd need to get that detail to Mick or Max.

I thought at this point telling the detective and his hovering sidekick what kind of man Wheeler was would clarify the whole situation. 'Roger Wheeler was a paedophile who raped a child and possibly assaulted dozens of others. There are witnesses.'

'A good reason to want him dead.'

I couldn't deny McWilliams' logic. Before I could add what might be construed as fuel to the fire, a rapid knock came at the door. The female officer stood and opened it and leaned out to hear what had caused the urgent interruption. She called McWilliams outside too. They closed the door and left me alone for another fifteen minutes. It gave me time to reflect on the importance of keeping the rest of the story to myself. Perhaps I really should have asked for a lawyer. It would have at least delayed further questions until one could be found.

McWilliams came back in alone. 'Your lawyer has called. We are unable to question you further until he's present. It won't be until tomorrow morning. You can go home but please stay there.'

I had no idea who my lawyer was, probably someone Mick had organised. When reacquainted with my belongings, I saw that I had fifteen missed calls. Max, Mick and Archie King made up the bulk. But two came from Roland Devine. One from Phillip.

I had no intention of making a return to call to Phillip in the police station. But I did ring Roland back immediately. Mick had contacted him and then the ball had started rolling. He was on his way south and would be in the bay at about 3:30. 'You are not to say anything to the police until I get there.' I didn't want to say that the advice had come a little late, but I was able to tell him that I'd been sent home and they wanted to speak to me in the morning.

The big constable was designated to return me to the house, but her duty was not required as Max waited in the reception area pacing back and forwards like a demented animal. Losing his temper was not really going to serve the situation well.

I silenced him with a look. We left without making any eye-contact with anyone in the room. On the walk to the car we said nothing.

Max was furious, yet I felt strangely calm. He swore about how bloody stupid the cops were to think that I could be involved. 'Bunch of morons.'

Before he could continue maligning the collective intelligence of the New South Wales Police Force, I reminded him that Phillip was one of them.

It stopped the ranting and raving. 'Are you alright?'

'Yes. I'm okay.' Rattled and somewhat shocked. Two terrible things happened in the space of one night. Henry died from the ongoing sorrow of his life and someone murdered the perpetrator of his misery.

Within a few hours of my return home, which Max insisted on calling my release from prison, the team had reconvened. Mick had, against my express instructions, driven from Gundaroo. We were joined by Roland Devine who had arrived right at the time he said he would. More surprising were two others, possible suspects as McWilliams might see them—Archie and Teresa Jepp. They had somehow connected and arrived together. Both shocked that I'd been taken to the station for questioning.

Roland wanted to speak to me alone. He wanted to know exactly what I'd already said and explicit details about my movements in the last twenty-four hours. In that time I'd been in Tuross, upset Kelly and Riley Morgan, taken Henry to hospital where he subsequently died, had spoken to Archie who had come to spend the last hours with his old friend. In fact I'd been with nearly everyone who had a reason to kill Roger Wheeler.

'So when I said stay away from Roger Wheeler, what did you think I meant, Lily?' Roland's question sounded benevolent but had a chastising edge.

I could have answered with a dozen reasons but most importantly was my motivation to make Wheeler pay for what he had done.

'For God's sake don't say that to the police when you're questioned next.' Roland went out to talk to the ensemble of witnesses and suspects.

The phone rang and I was too scared not to answer. 'When I said don't get involved, what do you think I meant?' Phillip reiterated Roland's very question. He wasn't completely angry, mainly just concerned. I told him everything that had happened in the last few days and weeks since Kitty's death. He kept exasperatingly sighing with every new detail I gave him. He felt better knowing that Mick and Max were with me and impressed that Roland Devine had come to the rescue. 'Lily you are amazing and I love you so much but I told you that this would end in tears.'

He was concerned for my health and the baby. Wanted to know every detail about how I was eating and sleeping. Could I feel the baby move and was I terribly fat. In the midst of the drama, Phillip had to make a joke. I had come to understand that this was his way deflecting his fears and worries. Who couldn't love that? His main point was that he would be home a month earlier than expected. The gastric problem was playing havoc with him and the doctor in Bali thought he needed less stress, more rest and antibiotics. 'I'll be back in eight days. Please don't be in jail when I get there.'

I had a week to get this over with and behind us.

When I emerged from the bedroom, the entire room turned to look at me. There was obviously more news.

Forensics had identified the body as Wheeler. It hadn't been fully burnt by the fire that had started at the front of the building. The assumption had been that he had succumbed to smoke inhalation and overwhelmed by heat. But Wheeler was dead before the flames engulfed the house. He'd been shot.

It added greater complexity to the story but made me less likely to be the lone assailant. I had no access to guns and Phillip didn't keep weapons in the house except for his police issued firearm which he kept in a lock box in our Canberra house when he was home. The gun had not gone with him to Indonesia and had been secured at his work during his absence. So someone or some people had made a very personal statement about their feelings for Wheeler.

'A shotgun most likely straight through chest from fairly close range.' Mick gave a clinical explanation of the cause of death. 'It has to be officially confirmed but this is what sources are saying.' Mick always had *sources*.

So out of the assembled group, who might be guilty of shooting and burning Wheeler? Archie had said he would put a bullet in Wheeler and he was deeply distressed about Henry's death and would be unlikely to have an alibi for the hours between me leaving him at the hotel and the time of the murder. Teresa Jepp had form for arson, but I couldn't imagine her owning, much less firing a shotgun. Max would not, and Mick wasn't even here. The spotlight might shine on the Kelly or Riley Morgan or Jean. I couldn't imagine that it would have been Jean, a peace-loving mother earth type who would be the least likely to own a weapon. A stranger then? Someone unknown to us who may have been deeply disturbed by a previous encounter with Wheeler. Someone who witnessed the events unfolding at Mallacoota back in the 1980s.

It was not hard to see that all of us had some reason to rid the world of The Rottweiler.

We spent the evening in deep discussion. Roland Devine made us all go over the entire story twice. He made notes and highlighted key points. He wanted the files that had been taken by McWilliams returned and spent some time alone listening to the harrowing story that Henry told that had been recorded. I didn't want to hear it ever again, but Teresa did. She wanted to hear firsthand the details of the night her child's life was changed. When she came out of the room it was evident that she had been crying. Weeping for the deep damage inflicted on Benedict, on all those boys. The past cannot be changed, but its pain can always be felt. In one way, Teresa had lost her son twenty-three years ago, and completely when he took his life. How bereft of hope he must have been. At least Teresa would now have time with Isaiah and Jean. Through Jean and Kitty's friends, she would be able to build a picture of the years he remained estranged from her. It was something akin to a silver lining, provided she wasn't the killer.

We managed to feed everyone. Max and I made pasta, resurrected bread from the freezer and filled wine glasses. I had boxes of chocolates from when I stopped work to study that hadn't been opened. Coffee followed. No-one particularly worried about the caffeine keeping them awake. There was so much to be talked about. By midnight, we were exhausted. Roland had written and re-written the story in preparation for my return to the police station in the morning. Roland had booked himself into a hotel in town, opposite the actual police station. Mick would stay with me, Teresa returned to Jean's and she dropped Archie back at his hotel in Moruya. Max would sleep once more at his in-laws as that was where Sarah had spent the day and night.

By 1am the house was quiet. Sleep eluded me. I tossed and turned, moving from one side of the bed to the other. Sat up, lay down, got up and had a drink of water. Wandered about the house and stared down the long expanse of beach that had been lit by a full moon. The light marked a path across the barely moving water. The tides were turning but the waves were non-existent. They broke in tiny ripples against the sand. I walked out into the moon-bathed night and down to the beach. It was cold but the chill kept me focused. I felt claustrophobic in the house and weighted by the grief of all the losses. In the confusion of the police arriving and the house being full all evening, I'd thought little about Henry. His death was only twenty-four hours old and we had not had time to mourn him. It wasn't a shocking death, I suspected. Not to Archie and not to his estranged family who had no doubt been alienated by his drinking and self-destruction. The fact that he had died on the same night as Wheeler was ironic and cruel. If he could have lived to see Wheeler eliminated, perhaps he could have taken something of his life back. In the years to come he could have enjoyed his life on the rivers and lakes of his birthplace. He might have been sober and reconnected with his daughter. Maybe he could have fallen in love again and died an old man happy in his home.

If Kitty hadn't had some unfortunate recent encounter with Wheeler, perhaps he would be rocking his son to sleep in his rainbow crib this night. He might have taken his secret to the grave, but he'd have given Isaiah his love and watched him grow to be a man. Or maybe in time he might have found the courage to tell his story and have been able free himself of the burden of those terrible nights. Perhaps the men might have reunited and found a way to release Kelly and Robert Rennison from the great affliction of their loss.

The many and useless *if only* scenarios. If only men like Wheeler did not exist. If only someone had stopped him then. Well someone had stopped him now. Someone who had that much hatred that killing Roger Wheeler seemed to be the only recourse.

I walked until I had only a little energy left to stumble off the beach and up the road to home. Sleep came, untroubled.

By the time I awoke, Mick and Roland were deep in discussion again. It seemed that McWilliams had set up an interview time for 2pm. He obviously had other things to do before reconvening the questions. Mick had learned that Kelly Morgan had also been interviewed yesterday. She had told a similar story to the one I had about the reasons for the comings and goings. Riley had not returned to the house. Kelly had confirmed that finally her child had been able to recall that he had been assaulted by Wheeler nine years ago.

I could see things from the police perspective. If a group of people had ascertained information about child abuse behaviour, it was unusual that we hadn't gone to the police. It was equally believable that some or all of these people had decided to kill him. Or that one person had done the deed and the others were covering up. I tried to see McWilliams as I would Phillip if he were investigating a similar situation. He wasn't my enemy, but a man who had a job to do.

With that in mind, I didn't feel quite so worried about the return to the police station. Less worried because Roland would be with me and I was sure that Mick would refuse to let me drive into town by myself. My alibi about having my husband's best friend sleeping over on the night of the crime made me uncomfortable and possibly one I wouldn't be using, but I was certain about every other detail I'd share with the investigating officers.

The morning passed quickly. Max arrived to have lunch. Archie rang to say he had contacted the police to tell them that he had to return to Mallacoota that afternoon as Henry's body would be picked up by the funeral home. He would come back after he had organised the funeral if they needed to speak to him. He would be sick of driving up and down the highway before this had all played out.

Jean rang just as I was leaving to see check on me. The police had been to the house and spoken to her and Teresa. 'She didn't hold back when she spoke to them. Teresa all but confessed to wanting to kill Wheeler for things he'd done.' I could sense Jean had a new admiration for her mother-in-law.

Surely my interview was going to be a mere formality now that McWilliams had so much information about the past and the present. Riley's story remained the one element that could make sense of things.

But I again I was wrong. Riley's story was not missing.

Mick and I met Roland outside the station. Mick was asked to wait in the reception area while they directed us through a locked door. McWilliams and another detective, who introduced himself as Shane Anthony, took us through to the interview room. We sat on one side of a long table, McWilliams and Anthony on the other.

'These folders you compiled are very thorough, Ms. O'Hara. They have helped enormously.'

Roland interjected before I could respond. 'If you are going to question my client, I'm assuming you are going to caution her.'

McWilliams shook his head. 'It won't be necessary Mr. Devine. Lily is here to simply do us a favour if she is willing to do so. She isn't a suspect in Wheeler's murder, not even an unwitting accomplice.'

The relief was enormous but again, before I could speak, Roland's hand on my back indicated that I should remain silent. A big ask given I wanted to say so much.

'Couldn't she have been informed of this before we made our way here?'

'No. Things have only just come to light. Someone presented themselves this morning admitting to shooting Roger Wheeler.'

Even if I'd been allowed to speak, there was little chance of any words coming out of my mouth. I desperately wanted to ask who but realised that McWilliams wouldn't be able to say at this time. I felt a fraud for having brought Roland all the way from Sydney and for keeping him up most of the night going over the story. He was not prepared to take any apology from me. He was only too glad to be able to do one small thing for one O'Hara, albeit the woman who would have been a cousin to his first-born daughter. He put his arm around me as perhaps he would have done with his own children. It comforted me knowing he cared enough to do so.

In the waiting area, Mick sat with a pale young man whose dark hair hung down over his eyes. He looked exhausted and nearly nodded off. Riley Morgan had endured a couple of long nights. My heart broke at the thought that this boy had been the one who had confessed to killing Wheeler, but I need not have worried. Riley had been interviewed of his own volition. He had come to tell the story of his childhood encounters with Wheeler. His evidence against the dead man began to fill in the gaps for the investigating detectives. The killer had handed himself into police at Moruya. His accomplice with him.

Chapter Thirty-one

The afternoon Henry died and Riley disappeared, other events unfolded both in Tuross and in Mallacoota. Kelly Morgan received a phone call an hour after we had left. Angelo di Michele and Fred Lewis had been to see Robert Rennison to apprise him of the truth about the night Miles died. As predicted, Rennison went crazy. He couldn't believe that the boys who had been discovered with him had been anything but guilty. No evidence had come to light to suggest that his friend, Roger Wheeler could have been responsible for anything that happened. Robert and Kelly had been protected from any of the allegations made against Wheeler and anything that might have pointed to the teacher's misdeeds had been conveniently hidden. Rennison had threatened to kill his former friends Lewis and di Michele.

The two men thought little of the threats, thinking Robert would calm down in a day and that they would try again to make him understand what had been uncovered by the people who had come to town after Benedict Jepp's death. They would help him understand.

Robert Rennison had other ideas. He drove from Mallacoota to Tuross early. He had Kelly's address because occasionally over the years they had been in contact. She had long forgiven him for his rage and violence after Miles had died. Kelly pitied him and knew the pain of his loss, but she had found happiness becoming a mother again. Her marriage to Riley's father hadn't lasted but at least she had the boy. Robert knew nothing of the assault on Kelly's son.

That afternoon he waited and watched the Morgan's home, just as I had done. He saw the women arrive recognising one immediately. Of course he knew Teresa Jepp, despite the many years since he last saw her, she had the same stature and grace as the much younger woman who lived at Gipsy Point. One unknown and the other me. He had remembered the red head who taken flight from the Karbeethong Jetty and later had fought him off in the cemetery.

A young man came out later. The women left minutes after. Kelly was alone and despite the pain of their divorce and the long years of separation only his ex-wife, Miles's mother would tell him the truth. He approached the house on foot. His car left at the same carpark I'd left mine on that first visit. Kelly embraced him at the door. She had cried in his arms. He already knew the truth without her having to utter one word. Robert thought that Kelly looked broken. The rest of the early evening the two of them waited for Riley to return, which he didn't, and they talked about Wheeler's betrayal of them. When Kelly told Robert Henry's story, he wailed like a wild animal. The truth no easier to bear years after the event. His grief in that moment, according to Kelly's account, was as profound as the moment Miles's tiny body was brought home to them from the unforgiving water that had taken him. Robert had thrown himself on the floor, clawing at the carpet, tearing his nails in the woollen loops. Kelly had to lie down beside him and hold him to stop the hysteria. They stayed on the floor until calm had been restored.

In those quiet hours between revelation and action, the two talked about Miles. They agreed to see Archie and Henry and hear their story about that night. They would see Benedict's young wife and child to commiserate his loss. The two of them would see Teresa and ask for her forgiveness. There would be a restoration. Peace would come. But not until they'd made Roger Wheeler pay.

Robert had bought his shotgun with him. He had stowed it in the boot of the car. He hadn't really known whether Kelly knew exactly where Wheeler lived, but if she couldn't tell him it had been his intention to kill her and then himself. But the enemy had been basking in the light of Kelly's friendship all these years. He must have laughed at how easily they had given Miles over to him. And then Riley. It was no use waiting for the police and the courts to do something. Wheeler had to die.

In the late evening, they went to the car and took the gun and walked to Wheeler's house. He'd been asleep for some time but had woken by Kelly's knocking on the front door and her calling his name. He had no reason to fear her. He probably imagined her as weak and simple. After he opened the door, Kelly came straight in and walked through to the kitchen. He hadn't seen the can of petrol she left at the front step. Wheeler followed her, asking what was wrong and seemed surprised that she went straight to unlock the back door. She told him she needed fresh air. She said that a terrible thing had happened and told him that Riley had asserted that Wheeler had raped him when he was nine. And that Teresa Jepp had said that he'd done the same to Miles and those other boys from St. Finbar's.

According to the police record, Wheeler just laughed at her. He said he thought the whole thing was just make believe. He said that when he saw Benedict Jepp a few months ago, that he had tried to tell the same story to Wheeler. Wheeler apparently laughed again. He went on to report his conversation with Kitty. Wheeler told him that he simply felt guilty of enjoying his time as an altar boy and that he could have saved Miles if he'd not been so gutless. 'I made you the man you are.'

Kitty could not fight off these words. Although an adult he once again had been made defenceless in the face of his abuser. The past had rushed in on him and, instead of turning on Wheeler, he turned on himself.

Kelly asked him directly if he had hurt her sons. He laughed again and said she was pathetic and a fool. He simply smiled at her and waited for her reaction.

At that moment Robert entered through the open back door. He raised the shotgun and before Wheeler spoke again, he shot him. He was four metres from him, but the blast impacted his chest and the monster fell. Blood started to ooze from the wound. It pooled around him as it soaked through his checked pyjamas. His mouth and eyes remained open, but he didn't speak. He allegedly had been alive as they left. Neither parent spoke. Robert shut and locked the back door but broke the glass in the top half. They exited the front just keeping the door slightly ajar. The two waited twenty minutes to make sure no-one was alerted to the sound of the gunshot. All was quiet. They poured the petrol through the doorway so that it spilled down the hall and splashed in on the timber window frames. The open door would give oxygen to fuel the flames. Robert lit and then threw a petrol-soaked wad of newspaper down the hallway.

The two left holding hands and walked back to Kelly's. They washed the blood and petrol off their hands and bagged their clothes. Robert would dispose of them somewhere on the highway.

They sat together on the couch until the fire brigade and police sirens could be heard. Then they slept.

They had buried their son. Separated acrimoniously and then lived in dark places since. But they had, according to Kelly, found the light when they killed Wheeler. Robert and Kelly became united again in meting out what they believed to be a suitable punishment for the crimes against children; not just their own but the others who had encountered The Rottweiler.

I was shocked by the calmness of their account. And surprised by my lack of feeling about the last moments of Wheeler's life. But mostly I was heartbroken by the loss of all those other lives. The only good thing was that Riley might be made whole, not by his mother's part in the murder of his abuser, but by the light now shining into the murky corners where perpetrators ensured children hid their awful secrets. We would no longer allow silence while lives withered.

Chapter Thirty-two

S mall towns cannot keep secrets. Within a day of Kelly Morgan and Robert Rennison confessing to the murder of Roger Wheeler, the whole area buzzed with rumour about how Kitty Jepp's death had sparked the uncovering of this evil that made its life in their community. It was the topic of conversation in hairdressers, doctors' waiting rooms and every work place up and down the south coast. People responded with pity, outrage and sadness. Not many publicly condemning the couple for their vigilantism.

With the police no longer interested in me, or the part Max, Mick and I played, Roland Devine turned his attention to helping Riley Morgan. In his opinion, his story would help his mother defend the charges now laid against her. The story of four boys from Mallacoota, three now dead, would also form the basis of Robert Rennison's defence.

All, I expect was not lost. But there seemed to be few winners.

Three days after Henry's death and Wheeler's murder, the funeral took place in Henry's hometown. Four of us set off to attend. I drove Mick, Max and Jean south to Gipsy Point where Henry's body, already cremated would be committed to his much-loved Wallagaraugh River. His ashes would flow down river with the tide and sweep around Jimmy Point, spread wide through Top Lake and wend their way between the banks of The Narrows and finally rest in somewhere in Bottom Lake. The image of him meandering on and under the water where he had spent his life, short as it was, brought some kind of peace.

The town had turned out to farewell its broken and recalcitrant son. Only one of his brothers made the journey back to the town. Archie had organised everything which included cleaning out Henry's place for the wake. He stood on the jetty with a charcoal-coloured urn that would be opened on the water to release the ashes. The cast of players all there. Teresa Jepp looked up at the house where she had tried to keep her son safe and back out of the water that Kitty loved as much as Henry. Fred and Angelo arrived together as did a dozen other business people who had known the Kellys when they ran the fishing fleet and supported Henry through the commencement of his own business. Father Burrell and Connie Harlow had both had made the long journey to farewell one of their troubled students.

We newcomers to Henry's life had only seen the worst of his thirty-six years, but Archie had seen the best too. He spoke of Henry's unbelievable and profound knowledge of the river and fishing. Henry read everything about fishing he could find. At one point he earned a second nickname. Ned Kelly was the one that stuck; the one that didn't was Funk and Wagnalls. It was a reference to an encyclopaedia that everyone had in the 1970s. "Look it up in the Funk and Wagnalls" when shouted across the school yard simply meant "ask Henry". Archie lightened the mood with a number of anecdotes about Henry being asked to determine the rightness or wrongness about some fishing exploit.

He talked about his inherit sensitivity and kindness. His love for his daughter, who also had made the trip south, brought tears. Not just for loss but for what now could never be. Jasmine Kelly looked like her father from the photos we had seen in the school magazine. She would inherit Henry's business and his house by the river. I doubted that she would ever live there, but her father's work would provide a great start for her. She had little understanding of him, knowing only that he was an alcoholic and that he was hopeless. Indeed Henry had been without hope for a long time before his death. Hope allows us to see that tomorrow has the potential to be better than the past. Without it, there is nothing to nourish the soul.

Archie, and Henry's brother Edward went alone in the small boat to release the ashes. Jasmine was asked but didn't want to go. While the men sat twenty metres up river and liberated the ashes, I sang. I played mandolin and Max guitar. *Go Rest High on that Mountain*, not an original choice for farewells, but it had poignancy for Henry's life that couldn't be denied. Maybe, somewhere, Henry would find that place where he would find rest. After the chorus had been sung once, the mourners joined in. Our voices accompanied Henry's last journey down river.

We left Gipsy Point stopping only once to put a small bunch of flowers on Miles Rennison's grave. It would be some time before his father could return to wipe the dust from the angel's wings that embraced his son. I truly believe that Miles was no longer lonely. The two boys who had suffered with him now stood beside him. The fourth, Archie, would make sure the story lived.

* * *

I was so glad to be home and that others had gone to theirs. In the two months that Phillip had been away I'd written little of my thesis, the house remained incomplete, his sister had abandoned the family, and I had witnessed misery beyond bearing.

But soon he would be home. I was twenty weeks pregnant and summer on its way. The life being nurtured in my body would not know of the monstrous things and the wretchedness that plagued other children. His mother and father would make sure of that.

The day before Phillip was due to arrive in Canberra, I made one last trip with Max. Together we went to Bingie where Kitty had ended his life. We placed a bunch of white jasmine in the crevice where he gave up. The truth had come too late to save him, but in the end set one child free. Riley Morgan's life would not wither in the way the other victims had.

Noli timere, Kitty. You are free.

www.ingramcontent.com/pod-product-compliance
Lightning Source LLC
Chambersburg PA
CBHW040223170726
48295CB00014B/785